CAMPFIRE AT THE CROSSROADS

AN ANTHOLOGY OF DARK FANTASY AND SCI-FI

ELLY CALL   KATHRYN DANETTE   BRIDGETTE DAY

MARLENA DUTCH   G.M. GRAY

CONTENTS

INTRODUCTION

There surely is a trick to telling stories around a fire, but maybe there's even more of a trick to listening to them.

Lean too close the light, and all you'll see and hear is what you already know — if you don't burn right up.

But lean too far into all that dark, and all those stories may just swallow you whole.

Here, by the fire, at the crossroads, is the threshold.

Here, reality shifts, and the whole world shrinks down to what little is illuminated and what lengths we can imagine.

The stories we tell are maps of a sort. Which is to say, they are both offerings and warnings. Because just beyond where the light flickers, something waits for you, as you rest here at the limns.

This anthology belongs to that liminal place — the crossroads of memory and myth, the past and the future, of the known world and what swims and spins in the cradling, swallowing dark.

In these stories, characters stand at the edge of something vast — something they can't yet name, and make the oldest decision in the world:

Step back, or step forward.

Some are haunted, in any and every sense of the word:

A terminally cool jacket carries an unforgettable legacy in "Memorabilia Mori." In "The Bridge at Drowning Man Creek," something hungry and ancient waits under its own crossing. A frozen mountain reveals what we bury to keep going in "The Third Man," and in "Last Flight of the Glamr," a haunted ship drifts through space and time, and takes all who board along with it.

Each story asks what we carry with us — and what carries us.

Some are on the brink of transformation:

In "The Bloody Show," a concert becomes an ecstatic, violent rite of passage into a new kind of existence; in "Forest Eyes," children's games become a survival strategy in a fairy-tale wilderness.

These are stories where the rules you know, don't hold — and the ones that do, are older than you can imagine.

The rest, they try to unravel fate. They must face what happens when we try to rewrite an unjust world that was not ever meant for us:

In "Three Algorithms," a hacker in a dystopia clings to the fantasy of escape with his violent soulmate, only to find just how many kinds of escape there are. In "You Are Falling Into the Sea," a grieving scientist reshapes the architecture of the very collective unconscious in a last attempt to undo the unforgivable things she has done. Both stories trace the thin, electric line between grief and transformation, where artificial worlds offer comfort — but never absolution.

In the end, for all of them, the only way forward is through.

This collection is also something else: a conversation across time and distance.

Every story in these pages comes from a writer who once stood around the same campfire with the others. All of us — mostly friends from our youth, mostly from Texas — were drawn together by a shared love of stories that blur the line between the uncanny and the true.

A long time has passed since then. We now live scattered across the map. But these stories have pulled us close again.

For years, we've turned to each other with tales of what lingers beyond the known — asking not just *what if?* but *what happens next?*

This book is our answer.

And we've saved you a place by the fire.

So listen close, and listen well —

You may not be by this way again.

I

MEMORABILIA MORI

BY MARLENA DUTCH

It takes Denise the better part of the morning to convince her aunt not to bury Stephen in his denim jacket. The suit will look better, she says. More formal. Aunt Margaret agrees. They take the suit to the funeral home. That afternoon, Denise helps her aunt put the rest of his clothes back in the closet.

"Shouldn't we put them in boxes?" Aunt Margaret's voice is distant. "Surely we should donate them or something? What do I do with his clothes?" She's staring at Stephen's band shirts that he'll never wear again when Denise closes the closet door.

"Aunt Margaret, don't worry about that right now, okay? Let's just get through the funeral. You don't have to clean out his room today."

"You should take his jacket." Aunt Margaret says.

Denise looks down. She'd forgotten she was holding it. "Oh. I mean—" How could she protest? She coveted that jacket. She couldn't deny it. She knew a thing or two about vintage clothing. She knew the jacket had been made in the early 1970s by a company that had long since gone out of business. That alone would have made it worth something, but the fact that it was covered in vintage patches from rock bands spanning three decades made it even more valuable. At the right auction, she could probably get a thousand dollars for it, but she had no intention of selling it.

Aunt Margaret places a hand on Denise's arm. "He'd want you to have it. I know you love rock music as much as he did. You should keep it to remember him by."

"Okay."

Denise presses the jacket to her chest, a prize won at a terrible cost. She'd loved her cousin in the distant sort of way one loves a family member they only see at family gatherings. They'd end up talking about what bands they were listening to and what shows they'd seen. It had been Christmas when she'd seen him last. That's when he'd shown up with the jacket. A gift for himself, he'd said with a laugh. Now it was April and he was dead.

Denise runs her fingers over the worn denim. Aunt Margaret was right, he'd want her to have it.

～

"Can I see it? Please?" Stacie begs. Denise is admiring herself in the mirror, but she slips the jacket off and tosses it to her best friend.

"Check out what's in the front pocket." Denise flops down on the bed.

Stacie reaches in the pocket and pulls out a patch, shiny and new. "Um, you know I can't read death metal."

"Effluvium. That's who Stephen went to see the night he wrecked his motorcycle. He never got a chance to sew it on, so I'm gonna sew it for him."

"Wait, does that mean..." The gears in Stacie's head turn. "He was wearing this when he died? This was on a dead person!? Ewww!" She drops the jacket and wipes her hands on her jeans.

Denise rolls her eyes. "Whatever." She pulls the jacket into her lap. "This thing is a treasure."

"Where did your cousin get it, anyway?"

"I'm not sure. He told me this story once about how some rock star owned it, but he overdosed and died on his tour bus and one of his roadies ended up with it. Then the roadie sold it for drug money and then like, ten other people owned it and it ended up with some guy Stephen used to know who owned a record store, but the dude died and somehow Stephen got it. It sounds like a bunch of bullshit, but all I know for sure is that this jacket is one rare piece of rock memorabilia!"

"Weird," Stacie says. "You'd think if it had really belonged to a rock star, someone would have held onto it longer."

Denise shrugs. "It's mine now, and I'm not letting it go!"

Stacie goes home before ten o'clock, complaining of an early shift at work the next day. Alone again, Denise drags out her sewing kit and grafts the Effluvium patch onto one of the few bare spots the jacket has left. She admires her handiwork, dreaming of what patch she could add to it next. It was only three days until the Algor Mortis show. She and Stacie had bought tickets months in advance. She could probably pick up a patch at the merch table.

She turns the jacket over in her hands, marveling at the fact that it had survived the crash. Stephen's jeans had been ripped to shreds, but the jacket had remained intact. She checks again for any damage she might have missed. There's a place at the side where a two inch gash has been sewn up. The front has a patch over it but the inside reveals the scar. A stain lingers deep in the fibers, tiny traces of brown.

There's a similar stain near the collar, a splash of rust hiding in the fabric. Near the inside pocket is a scrawl of black marker, faded beyond legibility, probably a name. Every patch, every mended tear, every stain is a story Denise can only guess at.

She puts on a record and imagines all the concerts that jacket must have seen. She's still fully clothed, passed out on the covers of her bed, when she feels the wind rushing through her hair. Her arms tighten around Stephen's waist and she leans with the motorcycle as it turns. It's starting to rain, and the denim jacket is already getting soaked, chilling her to the bone as the temperature drops and the wind picks up. She shivers, her teeth chattering together as she presses closer to Stephen, hoping to steal even the smallest shred of warmth, but it's futile. A corpse has no warmth to give.

Suddenly the jacket feels tight around her chest. Too tight. Her ice-cold hands clinch the grips. Denise panics as she realizes Stephen is gone and she has to steer the motorcycle on her own. The jacket constricts more and she gasps as the collar closes itself around her neck, choking her. Her vision blurs. Desperate for air, she tears at the collar with one hand, but immediately loses control of the bike. Her body hits the ground and rolls several times and the sound of her neck breaking wakes her up.

Denise sits bolt upright in bed, cold and shaking. The record had stopped some time ago and the room is silent except for her breathing. Only the eerie blue glow from her lava lamp allows her to see her surroundings. There's her paperback novels, her crates full of records, her posters and CDs. Everything is right where it should be. Then her eye catches movement at the foot of her bed.

Stephen's pale face watches her with dead eyes. He lunges, leaping onto the bed. He reaches for her, lighting fast. His finger tips brush the sleeve of her jacket.

Denise lets out a blood curdling scream and flails sideways, pushing herself off the bed. She hits the floor and wakes up.

Gasping, she shuffles backward until her back is against the bookcase. She's alone. No one is on her bed. Stephen isn't there. No one is there. It had been a dream, all of it; the motorcycle crash, the horror at the foot of her bed.

Denise breathes deeply until her heart rate slows. Maybe her cousin's death was just now hitting her. She'd heard that happens sometimes. That some people don't feel the grief right away. Grief could cause nightmares, couldn't it? Sure. That's all it was.

∾

S tephen is six feet in fresh dirt when Denise steps out of Stacie's car in the parking garage on fifth street. She'd had just enough time after the reception to go home and change clothes. Her eyes are still red from crying, but the makeup covers it pretty well. The venue would be dark anyway. No one would notice.

"Are you sure you're okay?" Stacie locks her car and drops her keys in her purse. "I mean, you don't have to feel obligated just because we have tickets. If you wanna skip out, it's totally cool."

Denise shakes her head. "I'm okay, Stacie. There's no way Stephen would want me to miss this show!"

"Well, you have to let me buy you a beer, then. We'll drink to his memory!"

Denise throws her arm around Stacie's shoulders. "You bet!"

Now that night has fallen, downtown is coming alive. Clubs open their doors, letting pop and rap music drift into the night. Everywhere, swarms of people walk to the bars and late night restaurants. The air is heavy with the smell of booze, smoke, and garbage in the alleys. The city pulses with music and life.

Denise and Stacie run up to the front of the venue. People are still filing in. From the sound of things, the opener has taken the stage. Once inside they head straight to the bar. Stacie comes back with two plastic cups of beer.

"To Stephen!" she says.

"To Stephen," Denise says, knocking her cup against Stacie's in a toast. They each take a drink and then move further into the crowd.

The opening act is a band Denise has never heard of, but they're pretty good. She makes a mental note of their name. If they ever become famous, she can say she saw them back when. She finishes her beer and gets another. The floor is crowded with bodies, pushing and pressing. The room is warm, and she almost regrets wearing Stephen's jacket — *her* jacket — but she cools down as she sweeps her hair off her neck and drinks her cold beer.

Halfway through the second band's set, Denise tosses her empty cup and locates the ladies room. The line is long and by the time she gets back they're in the lull between bands. Roadies hop around the stage, plugging in equipment and changing the banner behind the drum kit.

Stacie finds Denise in the crowd and shoves another beer into her hands. Denise hesitates. She'd barely eaten anything at the reception and the alcohol is hitting harder than usual. She isn't looking to get drunk, but she's had a rough day. She buried her cousin. Her cousin, who would never see another concert again. Didn't she owe it to him to live a little extra, for him?

She takes a drink. Just one more. For Stephen.

Algor Mortis takes the stage and cheers erupt from the fans. Denise chugs the last of her beer and moves deeper into the crowd. Bodies press around her, blocking her in. The band starts playing, each song flowing into the next. The alcohol hits Denise's blood stream, making everything feel fuzzy. Denise is lost in one of her favorite songs, drifting on the drawn out notes of a guitar solo, when someone taps on her shoulder hard enough to get her attention. She turns around.

Stephen's filmy eyes stare back at her.

Denise screams. She tries to back away, but she's trapped. There are too many people. She looks for an opening. There's a tiny space to her right. She takes a step sideways, but Stephen has a hold of her jacket. The music is loud, drowning her screams. Only the people closest to her know anything is wrong. She pushes through the crowd, looking back for Stephen's ghostly face, but she doesn't see him now.

She runs out of the venue, skidding to a stop on the sidewalk, gasping for air. It couldn't have been Stephen. That was impossible! He was dead and buried. It had to have been someone who looked like him. In the darkness, lit by the blue strobe lights from the stage, her mind had played tricks on her.

"Denise!" Stacie runs to her side. "What happened back there? What's wrong? Are you okay?"

"Yeah, I just —" Denise takes a shuddering breath. "It's nothing. It seems stupid now, but I thought I saw Stephen."

Stacie puts her hands on her hips. "I knew it. I knew you weren't okay. We're leaving now, you got it? C'mon, let's call it a night."

Denise nods. "We parked on fifth, right?"

"Right."

Denise turns to cross the street. Stacie is right, she needs to go home. She looks up and the blinding headlights are the last thing she sees before the air is knocked out of her lungs. She hears the impact of her body hitting the car. Somewhere a horn is blaring and a woman is screaming, but these things are distant and unimportant.

Her eyes flutter open. Someone offers her a hand up and she takes it.

"Goddamn it, Denise! I tried to warn you!"

Stephen is standing in front of her, but he doesn't look dead anymore. His eyes are bright and alive with anger.

Denise pats her clothing as though she's forgotten something. She looks down, confused. Her outfit is the same, except the jacket is gone. Behind her, people are starting to gather. A police car pulls up, lights flashing, blocking the road.

"What happened?" Denise asks. There are people in the street, looking at something. Stacie is there, crying.

"Stacie!" She starts to run to her, but Stephen grabs her arm.

"She can't hear you." His voice is softer now. "She can't see you. Let's go."

Denise stares at the scene in the street as Stephen pulls her away. They fade into the darkness of the city as the lights of the living world flash behind them.

Three weeks later, Denise's mother asks Stacie to come by the old apartment. Stacie stops there before work, and Denise's mom hands her a box. There are a few framed photos, a stack of notes from high school, and some other mementos. In the bottom, underneath it all, is the denim jacket.

Stacie leaves the box in the trunk of her car and tosses the jacket onto the passenger seat. She drives straight to the consignment shop she works at. If she priced the jacket for a few hundred it would sell within the week. She snatches it out of the seat and walks up to the shop. She goes right past the front door and into the alley.

She tosses it into the dumpster.

She could sell it. But she won't. She crosses herself and walks away. She doesn't look back. She doesn't see when, a few hours later, a long haired young man with torn jeans and a guitar pick necklace hops into the dumpster.

Scavenging is good in this part of town. The vintage shops toss out anything that doesn't sell.

"Dude, no way!" The young man holds up the jacket and stares at it in awe. He slides it on. It fits perfectly, like he was meant to have it. Amazing, the things people threw away. He wouldn't get rid of a find like this. He'd keep it for the rest of his life.

2

THE BRIDGE AT DROWNING MAN CREEK

BY MARLENA DUTCH

Hondo had gone out that night expecting to find werewolf tracks, but the thing staring up at him now is not a werewolf. He holds his breath as the creature in the dry creek bed raises its head, eyes flashing silver in the darkness. They hold each other's gaze for several seconds, then it looks away. It moves slowly, pale and silent, crawling over the rocks like a lazy spider. It looks like a woman. It's not a woman.

Hondo's boots scuff the worn stones of the bridge as he backs away. His footsteps crunch on the dirt trail leading up the hill, sounding louder in his imagination than in reality. He prays that the thing isn't following him.

He gets in his jeep, closing the door as quietly as he can. It's too warm to have the top up, but the forecast had predicted rain, and the distant rumbling of thunder tells him that the weather man was right for once.

Orange light flares and then fades to a red ember as he lights his cigarette. He takes a drag before pulling out his phone. The reception is terrible out here, but he needs backup. That's the protocol when facing the unknown. Call for backup. Some guys in Hondo's profession didn't like to do that, didn't like to ask for help. Those guys didn't live long.

Gemini picks up on the third ring.

"What's up?" She's awake. Blood Hounds rarely slept at night.

"I'm not sure," Hondo says. "I need a second opinion."

"Oh." Gemini's tone changes. This is a business call. "Where you at?"

"Drowning Man Creek. Couple of teenagers are missing, last seen near the old bridge. Thought I'd check it out. There was a pack out this way not too long ago, thought I might have missed one. Found something else."

"Vampire?" There's interest in her voice. A vampire would be her territory.

"Nah..." Hondo keeps his eyes on the bridge ahead, scanning the area for any signs of movement. "I dunno what the hell it is. We need a Gabriel Hound."

"Juliet's still in New Mexico. I'll give Fred a call. I'm getting in my truck now. Be there soon."

The call disconnects. Thunder growls in the dark sky above. Hondo takes another drag off his cigarette and waits.

F redrick Jonathan Billingsworth is too long a name for the young man it belongs to. As a child, he had shortened it to Fred John Bill. Now in his twenties, he's simply Fred.

His brown coat hangs off of him, a size too large, making him seem smaller than he is. Most of the year it's too warm to wear the coat, summer being the longest season in Texas, but the material is thin. He doesn't wear it for warmth. The occult symbols drawn inside and the charms sewn into the lining give him some measure of protection from the dangers of his job.

He sees Gemini's old pickup parked off the road and follows the dirt path toward the bridge. He picks the shape of Hondo's jeep out of the darkness on the hilltop and quietly makes his way toward the vehicle. He taps on the window before sliding into the passenger seat.

"That was fast," Gemini says. She sweeps her blond hair out of her face, the same blond hair as her cousin. Next to each other like this, Fred can see the resemblance between the two.

"I was awake." Fred takes his glasses off and cleans them. "So, what do we have?"

"Damned if I know," Hondo says. "Couple of teens have gone missing around here, 'bout six months apart. Not a trace. There's something under the bridge. Looks like a ghost. Like a woman. Pale, white gown. Hell of a weird vibe, made the hair on my arms stand up. Something's off. I don't like it."

"Hmm." Fred pushes his glasses back into place. "Ghost of one of the missing teens?"

"Nah, they were boys."

"A demon, then. How's the water down there?"

"Dry. Hasn't rained in two months. Sounds like it's gonna tonight, though, and this place floods."

"Then I'd better get down there and check it out."

Fred closes the jeep door softly and walks with the practiced silence of a Hound to the bank of the creek. The bank slopes downward, dusty and rocky beneath his boots. The creek bed is parched from the drought. The old bridge looms straight ahead. It's an ancient thing with arched stone pillars. No cars cross here, only foot traffic.

The night is eerily silent, as though even the insects sense something unnatural in the air. Fred looks around, but sees no sign of the woman Hondo had mentioned. He reaches into his pocket. A chain drops down from his hand, a point of smoky quartz dangling from the end. He stands motionless, scarcely breathing, watching the pendulum. The point of crystal swings in small circles, clockwise, then reverses.

Then something shifts.

The air changes. A sudden rush of cold wind blows, tousling Fred's wavy brown hair. The pendulum jerks straight ahead, defying gravity, pointing toward the direction of the cold air. Fred steps forward slowly, letting the pendulum lead him to the spot under the bridge where the shift has occurred.

The air ripples like water, shining so faint that few would notice it. Fred stops in his tracks. He slips the pendulum back into his pocket.

There's a portal here, a large one. Fred raises his hand, feeling the invisible tendrils of energy that quiver in the air before him. It's not a ghost portal. It's something else. Fred looks up; the light of the full moon is blocked by the gathering rain clouds, and it's darker still beneath the deep arches of the bridge. His hand goes to his necklace, feeling for the medals of Saint Michael and Saint Benedict, as he silently mouths a prayer. He's about to do something incredibly brave. Or incredibly stupid, depending on who you ask.

Fred steps forward and the world around him warps. He's no longer in the creek, surrounded by dry dirt and rocks. The bridge overhead is gone. This is a cave of some sort, rocky and damp, lit with its own mysterious red glow. The air is stale, like an attic that hasn't been opened in years, with a hint of something putrid. He takes a cautious step forward and nearly trips over a stone. He looks down to get his footing and stops in his tracks.

Anyone who wasn't a Hound would scream.

Skeletons litter the floor, dozens of them, in pieces. Femurs, collarbones, broken rib cages, all of them unmistakably human. Jawless skulls watch him in the darkness. Fred takes a deep breath and exhales quietly. His ears strain to detect any sound. Carefully, he takes a step forward, nudging a pile of bones aside with the toe of his boot. Step after step, slowly, quietly, he walks twenty feet around a curve in the cavern when he hears it: a scratching sound, sharp and hard, reverberating in his eardrums and shivering down his spine.

He peeks around the corner and he sees it. The woman. The thing. Its white gown glows pale as moonlight. Its head is down, dark hair obscuring its face, gnawing the remaining flesh off the bone in its hands.

Fred's heart races. This isn't normal demon behavior, but the woman isn't a ghost. Werewolves and vampires don't use portals. It must be a demon. Fred glances around the corner again and the scratching sound stops abruptly. The demon lifts its head, and Fred pulls back just in time to avoid being seen. He remains perfectly still, pressed against the wall, listening for even the smallest sound of movement. Then the scratching resumes. Fred breathes a quiet sigh of relief. He goes back the way he came. As soon as he's around the bend, he moves quickly through the scattered human remains, careful not to make any unnecessary noises, back through the open portal.

He stumbles out onto the creek bed, tripping over a rock in the dark. He hits the ground, scrambling backward, eyes on the portal, but the creature hasn't followed him. He gets up, wiping his hands on his pants and climbing up the bank toward the jeep.

"So, what is it?" Hondo asks.

Fred takes a shaky breath. "You said two teens went missing here?"

"Yeah."

Fred shakes his head. "It's more than that. A lot more. This thing has been here for years, maybe decades."

Hondo and Gemini exchange a look.

"How can you tell?" Gemini asks.

"There's a portal," Fred says. "It's full of skeletons, just take my word for it. The two of you grew up around here, didn't you?"

"Yeah," Hondo says. "Why?"

"Have there been any other occurrences at this bridge? Anything unusual?"

"Eh, I dunno..." He shrugs. "It's mostly just a place teens go to drink and makeout."

"Some people call it Cry Baby Bridge," Gemini offers. "One of several, I guess, cause it's a story I've heard before."

"Cry Baby Bridge?" Fred says.

"Yeah, some urban legend about a woman getting caught in a flood and her baby getting swept away and you can hear crying at night. That sort of thing. I swear there's a hundred bridges with the same story. I don't think there's any truth to it. Pretty sure it's just a campfire tale."

"Hmm. There's no way to know whether or not it's true, but if this place is prone to flooding, people could have died here. I'm sure that's how the creek got its name. As for the crying, it's possible that people have been hearing demon noises and mistook them for something else." Fred rummages in his coat pockets. He pulls out a pen light and a small leather journal. He flips through the pages, reading the cursive scrawl. He mutters softly to himself as he consults his book.

Hondo taps his fingers on the steering wheel impatiently. "Well, are you gonna tell us what it is?"

Fred looks up from his book. "It's a type of composite demon. I'm sure of it."

"The hell is that?"

"A fusion of a demon and a ghost. They're very rare. Capricorn wrote about one in his journal."

"Cap tangled with one, huh?" Hondo says. "How'd he kill it?"

"It doesn't work that way. You can't kill it. The best we can do is trap it. I need a Solomon Jar."

"A what?" Hondo says.

"A Solomon Jar. A Vessel of Brass. They've been used to trap demons since ancient times. A brass jar or bottle is best, though other materials can be used in a pinch. I just need something with a stopper."

"Uh, I don't think I have anything like that," Hondo says.

"Would copper work?" Gemini pulls a flask out of her back pocket.

"Yes! Is it empty?"

"It can be," Gemini says, screwing off the top. She downs the last of the whiskey and hands the empty container to Fred. "What else do you need?"

"Some things from my bag, some rope, and some muscle. How many Hounds are available right now?"

"Wolf Hounds or Blood Hounds?" Gemini asks.

"Either, and as many as possible."

Gemini and Hondo pull out their phones and start texting. Within moments, the replies come in.

"Alright," Hondo says. "Cavalry's coming. Get your bag."

Fred walks briskly back to his car and pulls his bag out of the back seat. The large brown camera case is a relic from the 1970s, outdated, but otherwise nondescript. Instead of the camera and film one might expect, the inside is filled with candles, charms, crystals, talismans, a crucifix, and all manner of occult paraphernalia. Fred shoulders the bag and heads back to Hondo's jeep.

In some ways, it would be better to come back tomorrow, but it was Hound policy to take care of threats immediately. A threat left unchecked could mean more lives lost. The thing under the bridge was hungry, and more victims would follow.

Hondo is waiting outside of his jeep, flicking ash from his cigarette. "You've done this before, right?"

"No," Fred says.

"What do you mean 'no'?"

Fred flips his book open to a page full of arcane symbols. "I told you, this type of demon is very rare. Capricorn successfully bound the only one he ever encountered. He left instructions, which I'm following. I'm the best and most qualified person for this job. What more do you want?"

Hondo shakes his head. "I dunno. I was kinda hoping you'd say this was gonna be a piece of cake."

"It won't be," Fred assures him. "Demons fight tooth and nail. If this thing is strong enough to kill humans, and it is, we're going to need half a dozen Hounds to hold it."

"I don't get it," Gemini says. "I thought demons were usually intangible, like ghosts?"

"Mostly," Fred says, rummaging through his bag. "This one isn't. Like I said, it's not your standard demon."

"You sure you're right about this?" Hondo says.

Fred pauses. There could be no room for error. Mistakes get Hounds killed. "Capricorn described it as having traits of both ghosts and demons. It makes sense. I just need you to hold it while I perform the ceremony."

Fred pulls a black pillar candle out of his bag and lights it. When the hot wax has pooled on top, he pours it onto the copper flask. Immediately he presses a metal seal into the wax, leaving behind a complex sigil.

Headlights shine in the distance. Tires crunch on gravel as an old truck pulls up next to them. The driver kills the engine and two men get out.

"Gem. Hondo." The older of the two men nods in greeting. "Howdy, Fred."

"Hello, Hawk." Fred doesn't look up from his work. He opens a small bottle of oil and pours a few drops into the flask. He closes the lid and shakes it.

"Has Grackle got his demon hunting badge yet?" Hondo says, laughing at his own joke. Hawk and Gemini chuckle.

"What?" Grackle says, confused. He's tall and lean, with black hair that falls to his shoulders in curls. His large eyes look worried. A few years younger than Fred, he's still a Hound in training, and subjected to constant teasing by the older Hounds.

"Relax," Fred says, taking pity on him. "I just need you to hold a rope."

"Oh. I can do that!" Grackle says with some relief. "I do calf roping at the rodeo!"

Within half an hour, three more Hounds show up. Thunder rumbles angrily over their heads. The wind picks up, stirring the tree branches. The air is thick with the scent of rain.

"Fred, we better light a fire under this," Gemini says. "Storm's a brewin'."

"I know," Fred says. "Bring me the ropes."

Seven ropes with lassos are handed to him. He opens a small bottle and begins to pour something on them.

"What's that?" Grackle asks. "Smells like cinnamon."

"That's one of the ingredients," Fred says. He mutters some words over the ropes, tracing a sign in the air with his finger. "There. That should do it. Alright, everyone. Let's get this over with."

They make their way down into the creek, spreading out in a semi-circle around one side of the bridge. The clouds open up above them, and fat raindrops splatter down, ice cold in the hot summer night.

"The portal is right there." Fred points into the darkness. "I'll lure the demon out. The rest of you get ready. As soon as you see it, lasso it. It'll fight, but hold steady. I'll do the rest."

Fred takes a shuddering breath. No fear. That was rule number one when dealing with demons. They'd smell fear a mile away and feed on it, worming their way into your head, turning the smallest grain of doubt into full blown insecurity. They'd weaken your hold on them and slip out of your grasp. He couldn't allow that.

The storm crashes, sending rain down in sheets. Fred touches the medals on his necklace and marches forward. The weather wouldn't stop him. Nothing would. He parts the veil between worlds with the wave of his hand, stepping through the portal. He's prepared this time, kicking aside the bones at his feet.

"Alright, demon!" Fred yells into the eerie red cavern. "Show yourself! Come on!"

An ear-piercing shriek echoes through the cavern. A blur of glowing white emerges from the darkness, running straight for him. It slams into him quicker than he can dodge it. He hits the floor hard.

Either a rock or a bone digs into his left side, sending pain through his torso. The demon is on him in an instant.

Clawed hands reach for him and he grabs the thing's wrists to keep it away. It opens its mouth, revealing sharp, pointed teeth. Fred nearly gags on the smell of rancid blood as it pushes its face closer, trying to bite him.

He kicks out, getting the upper hand on the demon, and twisting its arm behind its back. He pushes the creature forward, though he loses his grip on it as they stagger out of the portal and onto the creek bed.

The rain is coming down in waves now, making it almost impossible to see. Fred's hair is soaked in an instant. His glasses are useless. He takes them off and crams them into his coat pocket. The water in the creek is up to his ankles already, and getting deeper by the moment.

"I got it!" Grackle yells. He's the first to get a lasso around the demon. He pulls the rope tight just as a second rope loops around it from the other side. Soon its held on all sides by the ropes, hissing and shrieking, attempting to writhe free.

Fred sweeps his wet hair out of his eyes. Now comes the hard part. From his coat he pulls a crucifix. He begins with a prayer to Saint Michael the Archangel, to begin the process of exhausting the demon. Capricorn had been vague about this part, saying only that the sealing ritual couldn't begin until the demon was weakened.

The storm rages on and on. The demon shrieks, splashing frantically, attempting to free itself. Fred recites prayer after prayer. The rising water rushes at his shins. He struggles to stand still in the strong current, taking a wider stance to keep his balance.

Near the far bank, Jax, a Wolf Hound, loses his footing in the mud. His rope goes slack while he gets to his feet, fighting against the storm and the rapidly rising creek.

"Fred!" Hawk yells. "Work faster!"

Fred rests his hands on his knees. He licks his lips, tasting rain. The demon should be worn down by now, but it isn't. It rises to its feet. It shouldn't be able to do that. It shouldn't be pulling against the ropes this hard. Something isn't right.

Between the horrible wails, a string of syllables drift on the wind, barely heard above the roar of the storm. Fred strains to make them out. He's fluent in Latin, and it takes him several confused moments to realize why he can't translate the demon's words.

Fred strides forward, standing dangerously close to the demon. Its arms are bound by its sides, lassoed close against its torso. It looks up at him through strands of dark, wet hair, eyes gleaming. Words are still falling from its lips, words that Fred doesn't understand. He lifts the crucifix and presses it to the demon's forehead. It doesn't scream. It doesn't recoil. Its flesh doesn't burn. Nothing happens, nothing at all. Fred's blood turns to ice.

It isn't a demon.

An earth-rattling boom shakes the night and lightning splits the sky in half. The sound of rushing water grows louder. The Hounds edge closer to the banks of the creek, grasping desperately at the ends of their ropes.

"Damn it, Fred!" Hawk yells. "Trap the damn thing already! We can't stand here all night, we're gonna drown!"

How can he trap it if he doesn't know what it is? If it's not a demon, then the ritual is useless. The creature is too dangerous to let go and time is running out.

"What the fuck are you?" Fred whispers.

The thing is standing motionless, staring into Fred's eyes, growling and muttering, muttering words that sound like — Gaelic? Is it some form of Gaelic? Other voices are yelling at him now, telling him to hurry, that the creek is filling up. He has to think of something.

Fred sloshes his way over to Grackle, ignoring the shouts of the other Hounds.

"Do you have any horseshoes?" Fred asks.

"What?" Grackle looks at him as though he's lost his mind.

"Horseshoes!" Fred throws his hands in the air. "You ride horses! Do you have a horseshoe?"

"Yeah! There's a few old horseshoes in the back of the truck! Why, what do you — Hey! Where are you going?"

Fred scrambles up the muddy banks of the creek on all fours, clawing for traction. He runs to Hawk's truck, leaping into the back. It's dark. He isn't wearing his glasses. He rummages around, tossing aside empty beer cans and other trash, until his hand rests upon something curved and metal. He grabs it, along with a length of twine, and runs.

"Let it go!" Fred yells, splashing back into the creek. "Release it!"

"Are you crazy!?" Hondo says.

"Don't argue, just do it!"

One by one, the Hounds let go of the ropes. Immediately, the thing begins to wriggle free. Fred grabs it by its hair. He's been wrong once tonight. If he's wrong again, he's dead.

He presses the horseshoe to the thing's forehead. The sound the creature makes will haunt Fred's dreams for years. It falls to its knees in the rushing water, but Fred drags it, following the current of the water, back to the portal.

"I don't know how to kill you," Fred gasps between ragged breaths. "But I can get rid of you."

He wraps the twine around the thing's neck, securing the horseshoe along with it. The creature twists and turns like a dying spider. It claws at its own neck, nails tearing flesh as it tries to sever the rope. Fred drags it back into the portal. He leaves it on the floor of the cavern, writhing in agony in a pile of dry and broken bones.

Fred turns around and jumps back into his own world. Something is happening to the portal. Waves of energy fluctuate around him, sending iridescent ripples through the air. Fred holds his hands flat in front of him, palms facing out, and feels the threads of energy there. He moves his hands slowly, concentrating, guiding the energy into a smaller and smaller circle.

"Close...close, and never open again."

There's a crackle of electricity underneath the bridge, like a tiny spark of lightning, and the portal disappears. The energy is gone. Fred doesn't have time to feel relieved before he's swept off his feet by the flooding creek. His ears roar with the rush of water. Disoriented, he's carried off by the current. By the time he's able to get his head above the water, he's further down the creek on the other side of the bridge.

"Fred!" a voice calls.

Something hits him in the face. It's a rope. Fred grabs it and Grackle pulls him to shore. The Hounds gather around him.

"Is it gone?" Hondo asks.

Fred nods, coughing up creek water. The storm is still raging.

"Reconvene at the shack!" Hawk says.

The group splits up, each going to their respective vehicle. Fred sits in his car for several minutes, enjoying the feel of air in his lungs. When his hands finally stop shaking, he turns the ignition and follows the caravan of trucks to the shack.

Fifteen minutes later, down miles of dark country roads, the caravan pulls into the yard of the shack. The motion sensor lights kick on as soon as they pull up. The old barn, affectionately called "the shack", serves as a headquarters for the Hounds. The shack contains everything the Hounds need in their line of work: medical kits, weapons, a full length bar with a well-stocked supply of alcohol.

For the first half hour, nobody speaks. Soggy boots are left by the door. Towels and blankets are issued. When everyone is a little warmer and drier, Hawk asks the question on everyone's mind.

"So what the hell happened out there? I thought you were gonna trap that thing in the flask?"

Fred clutches the blanket around his shoulders. How can he tell them? How can he admit that he'd been wrong? They'd lose faith in him, in his abilities as leader of his division. But there's no avoiding the truth.

"I may have miscalculated," he says quietly. He wants them to leave it at that, but they don't.

"Miscalculated?" Hawk says. "What do you mean, *miscalculated?*"

"In what way did you miscalculate?" Jax chimes in.

"The creature fit the description of a demon Capricorn wrote about, but it wasn't that. It was something else."

"So you didn't identify it correctly," Hondo says. "You said you were sure —"

"I was wrong!" Fred snaps. "I was wrong, but I figured it out, okay? The thing is gone, the portal is closed, it's over."

There is a moment of quiet in which only sound is the rain pattering on the rooftop.

"So...what was it, then?" Grackle asks.

Fred pulls the blanket tighter. "It was a type of fae."

"Fae?" Hawk gives him a skeptical look. "You're not talking about —"

"*Don't.*" Fred cuts him off. "Don't think for one solitary moment that I am talking about Tinkerbell. Their lore is older than were-wolves or vampires, and they can be just as nasty."

"What did you need the horseshoe for?" Grackle asks.

"Iron," Fred says. "It's like poison to them."

"Why didn't you realize what it was in the first place?" Gemini is perched at the bar with a glass of whiskey in her hand and towel around her shoulders. Fred's coat is on the back of a chair, dripping water onto the floor. He pulls Gemini's empty flask out of his pocket and returns it to her.

"I didn't realize what it was at first because it isn't supposed to be here. Don't ask me how it got here, either, because I don't know."

Satisfied with what answers Fred has to give, the Hounds turn the conversation toward food. Jax offers to cook something. Hondo turns on the radio. The mood lightens. The storm passes over them, leaving behind the clean smell of rain. Frogs sing joyously in the night, thankful for the end of the drought.

Fred is lost in thought when he feels a hand on his shoulder.

"You did good out there," Grackle says. "That was quick thinking with the horseshoe. None of us would have figured that out on our own. I dunno what we'd do without you Gabriel Hounds."

"Thanks." Fred offers him a weak smile. Grackle's words give him little comfort when he still has a mystery to solve. Fred grabs a pad of paper and an ink pen from the bar and starts making notes. The discovery of a bloodthirsty fae in Hound Hollow, Texas is not the sort of thing he can ignore. The night is almost over, but his work is only beginning.

3

FOREST EYES
BY G.M. GRAY

Humans were rare guests in the old, dappled forest, but the woods were far from quiet even without their presence. Every day, the forest sang, raising its voice to the bright sun and rolling clouds above. Here was the low murmur of the bubbling creek, and there were the crinkling whispers of wind through the leaves. The birds sang songs about their lovers and their wars, songs of cold nights and the delight of dawn, accompanied by a raucous chorus of insects. As they sang, the birds flitted between the trees, warbling in joy at the sun's summer beams.

Leaves rustled with the cautious cunning of a hare, but the branches did not part. When the creature spoke, it was in the strange and unfamiliar tongue of Man.

"Гуси, гуси!" Katya cried out.

Goosey, goosey!

She spoke in a sing-song tone, her mouth cupped by a nut-brown hand to help her voice pierce the thicket of birch trees before her.

No child of the Forest was she, but a daughter of Man, and all the wood's denizens knew it. Yet this wood was so deep and so ancient, none of its people feared Man. Neither the creek, nor the leaves, nor the birds, nor crickets ceased their singing.

Katya was as still as a seasoned hunter as she knelt in the dirt.

At last, the voice of another child, distant and laughing, answered. "Га-га-га!"

Katya held back her own giggle. "Есть хотите?"

"Да-да-да!" The other voice replied as it drew closer.

Goosey, goosey!

Ga-ga-ga!

Are you hungry?

Yes-yes-yes!

Katya took care to remain still. No part of her moved except for her eyes, which darted to-and-fro in search of her quarry.

"Ну летите!" She called, and this time, she rose enough that the leaves around her dress fluttered in disapproval.

Then fly this way!

"Нам нельзя! Серый волк под горой не пускает нас домой!"

We cannot! The gray wolf under the hill won't let us go home!

Katya burst from the underbrush.

Oleg stood before her, but just as she caught a glimpse of her brother, he noticed her presence and zipped between the trees. As Oleg ran, he flapped his arms as if they were wings, laughing and honking like a goose. With nimble grace, he leapt atop a fallen log before racing through the sun-dappled birch trees toward the dark and sleepy cedars.

"I'm gonna get you," Katya growled between fits of laughter.

She howled like a wolf, which only made Oleg giggle harder. As fast as he was, Katya was faster. She was older by two summers and her legs were longer, her arms stronger. She cut along a narrow path that followed the raised bank of a stream and leapt to the other side, cutting off Oleg. He had no time to react before she grabbed his arm, but the path was narrow and the terrain rocky. Her foot caught on a stray root. She tumbled over, bringing Oleg to the ground with her.

"Olezhka!" she cried in dismay.

Katya watched as her brother rolled along the forest floor, but only after she raced to his side did she realize the tears streaming down his cheeks were from laughter rather than pain.

"You're far too clumsy to be a wolf. You're still just a bear, Katushka," he giggled.

"Hmph." Katya's long braid had spilled over her shoulder and she tossed it out of her way, the tip flicking in annoyance. "Better a bear than a silly goose."

She pounced on Oleg, tickling him until he could do nothing but beg for mercy between wheezing laughs.

Though they were sister and brother, they shared little in mien. Like her father, Katya had warm, brown skin flecked with pale freckles, while Oleg, like his mother, resembled a china doll — white skin so thin that the blue from his veins shone through. Katya's blonde hair and green eyes came from their mother, while Oleg's hair and eyes were as black as a still lake.

They looked nothing alike — Katya with her sturdy frame and stout hands, and Oleg with his willowy build and birdlike bones. Katya had been born of the sun, a bright summer day, while Oleg was born of the moon, all pale whites and deep blacks of a winter's night. Yet despite their differences, they'd grown up far from any town or village, and they knew each other's deepest thoughts almost as soon as the other could think it.

"Hey," Oleg said, pointing past Katya toward something deeper in the wood. "Is that a house? Does someone live all the way out here?"

Katya leaned back onto her haunches to gaze in the direction he was pointing. Oleg rose from the ground, dusting off his pants and shirt before offering Katya a hand.

"There's no one out here," Katya said, still staring at the beams of wood with suspicion. "That's what Granny says."

Primitive as it was with its rough-hewn logs and mossy roof, it was most definitely a house — an izba with a crooked fence. Katya flashed a mischievous smile. "What do you think, Olezhka? Does a devil live inside?"

Oleg's already pale face grew whiter and he took a step back as if afraid. "We should go, Katushka. We shouldn't be here."

But Katya did not listen, because she was two summers older and feared nothing. "Come, Lyoshka, we'll just take a peek."

Oleg shook his head, but when Katya started toward the house, he hesitantly followed. The fence was broken, little more than crooked branches pressed into the ground, and where the gate should have stood was an empty space. Katya slipped inside.

The house was quiet, seemingly abandoned, and as Katya drew closer, she felt herself grow bolder.

There stands a forest, she thought to herself. As she peeked through the faded slats along the windows, she continued to hum the nursery rhyme under her breath. *In the forest, a house. In the house, a stove. In the stove, a pot. In the pot, dough.*

The door was cracked open, and she couldn't resist peering inside.

"Katya!" Oleg's voice was a harsh, fearful whisper, but she shrugged off his concerns, gesturing for him to follow.

"No one is home, Olezhka. Come, come. Let's look inside. We'll go home for supper right after."

There stands a forest. In the forest, a house. In the house, a stove. In the stove, a pot. In the pot, dough.

The wooden floor was old, and it creaked beneath the children's feet as they entered. Everything was covered in dust and cobwebs, and the room was small enough that they could see the whole space from the entrance. The stove was coated in soot, and a single, dented pot occupied its chamber. Beside it, a rusted samovar rested on a table draped with a moth-eaten cloth. On the ground was a broken spinning wheel and a heavy wooden chest, but there was little else. Not a single icon decorated the room's corners.

"See? It's empty. No one has lived here in a long time."

There stands a forest. In the forest, a house. In the house, a stove. In the stove, a pot. In the pot...

Katya sniffed the air. The air of the hut was moldy and stale, but it smelled like something was cooking.

In the pot...

She moved toward the stove, and as she did, a sound came from the yard.

Both Katya and Oleg froze. They heard a shuffling *clunk clunk*, as though someone with a wooden limp were approaching the hut. Their eyes met, and at once they dashed to hide. Despite the darkness, there were few places to conceal themselves. Oleg ducked under the table, while Katya squeezed into the stove behind the blackened pot. Covered in soot, she held her breath. Tears watered the back of her eyes, but she let out neither a breath nor a sneeze.

The shuffling stopped before it reached the porch. It was replaced by soft, waddling footsteps. Hoarse rasps reached Katya's ears. The door opened, and from the quiet grunts and murmurs, Katya guessed it was an old woman. An old woman was nothing to fear, but a cold sense of dread held Katya in place.

There stands a forest. In the forest, a house. In the house, a stove. In the stove, a pot. In the pot...

The woman sniffed the air.

"What's that smell?" She sniffed again, this time so deeply Katya covered her mouth to hold back a gasp of fear. "It smells like...a human."

The old woman began to pace the room, and when she passed the stove, Katya glimpsed her monstrous figure. Old and shriveled like cracked leather. What few wisps of hair remained on her head curled around her, trailing and writhing as they moved on their own. Her eyes were clouded glass, as if she were blind, but her teeth...her teeth were sharp and clean, shining brightly even in the dim light.

"So young and tender," she said, as she sniffed the air again. "How delicious."

From her place behind the pot, Katya could see the old woman shuffling toward Oleg. He'd yet to make a sound, and he'd concealed himself well — better even than when he hid from Katya during their games, when even Katya, who knew his every thought, could not find him. But the old woman circled like a great, black crow. She drew closer. Closer.

In the stove, there is a pot.

Katya picked up a piece of charcoal and lobbed it into the room. It clacked against the wooden chest, and at once, the woman rushed toward the sound, clucking her tongue in annoyance.

"Fa! You won't get my treasures," she hissed. "They are mine — offered freely and earned fairly. Isn't that right, my pretties?"

She crooned at the chest, and Katya heard the lid creak open.

"An egg from a hare, tears from the moon, faded eyes of the forest, and memories of a sunlit childhood..." The old woman continued to babble, lulling away her agitation and seemingly forgetting the smell of the humans. Katya squeezed her eyes shut.

Fly away, Lyoshka. Fly away home.

They knew each other's thoughts almost before the other could think them, and Oleg darted from his hiding place, as if Katya's prayers were his own. As fast as a shadow, he shot from the house, and nimble as he was, Oleg cleared the hut's porch in a single bound.

The old women let out a screech so piercing, Katya's blood ran cold. She shuffled after Oleg, and though her walk was slow, little more than a limp, once she exited the house, there was a dull earthen roar, and the winds themselves seemed to pick up.

Fly home, Lyoshka, please fly home.

Tears streamed down Katya's dirty cheeks, and she squeezed her fists so tightly she felt her nails draw blood.

When the wind died down, Katya at last dared to squeeze past the dented pot (and it did smell of bread, why did it suddenly smell of bread?), before running out the door and through the gate. She raced home as fast as her legs could carry her.

∼

B y the time Katya reached their home, an ail built of wood and bark, Oleg was waiting in the yard. Both of them were panting, out of breath, but neither spoke a word to their parents or grandmother. They prayed to all the icons and ongod upon entering the house, and then again before dinner, showing unusual diligence and respect.

When they ate, it was in silence. The food tasted bitter and cold despite how skillfully their grandmother had prepared it. No matter how much their mother pried, they kept their mouths sealed as tightly as pickling jars. But when the night came, and no shadows emerged from the forest, and no howls came on the winds, Katya and Oleg at last felt safe enough to breathe. They both fell into a deep sleep, side by side, exhausted from the day's events.

At dawn, Katya woke to find Oleg pale and hot with fever. He did not stir from his slumber no matter how much Katya shook him.

"Mama, Papa, come quick!" she cried.

At once their papa set off on horseback, accompanied by his hunting dog, to seek help from the nearest village. It was a day's ride, going as hard as he could on the family's only horse, so Mama and Granny busied themselves in the kitchen. They prepared herbs and tea to lower Oleg's fever as best they could while they waited for the doctor. Katya was all but forgotten in their urgency, so she slipped outside to sit by the fence and cry.

"Why do you cry, Daughter of Man?" a raven asked, alighting on the wooden post beside her.

"Because my brother is sick, and he won't wake from his fever," Katya sobbed. "And I think maybe...maybe it's because we went into that hut in the woods."

"Oh dear, oh dear," the raven croaked. "You went into a hut without asking permission?" It wiped its beak along the coarse wooden railing then stamped its clawed feet in dismay. "That was foolish, Daughter. That was very foolish."

Katya choked back another round of sobs. She knew the raven's words to be true, and she was ashamed of her foolishness.

"W-what should I do?"

"It is too late, Daughter. Even if the shaman or priest comes, it is too late to bring back your brother's soul. It belongs to the forest now. You are lucky the forest didn't take yours as well."

Katya shook her head. "It should have been my soul," she insisted. "I was the one who went into the house first. It's all my fault. Please. If there's any hope at all, even hope that's smaller than a thimble, I want to know what can be done."

The raven paused as if unwilling to speak, and it hopped once, then twice, then thrice along the fence in uncertainty. When it turned to face Katya, it cocked its head to peer at her with one golden-black eye.

"There is a way, Daughter, but it is dangerous. Your chances of succeeding are slim, and you may not live should you try."

Katya leaned forward on her hands and knees. "Tell me! I am not afraid!"

She spoke the truth, because to lose Oleg would mean losing a part of herself. Their hearts had been connected since his birth, and she feared the forest taking him more than she feared for her own life.

"If that is the case, Little Sun," the raven cawed with reluctance, "then you must again find the hut in the forest. You must go to the door and knock three times. If the old woman deigns to answer, you must beg for her forgiveness. You must obey every command she gives — even if it is to hop into a pot so she can eat you for dinner. If you pass all of her tests and if you survive, then the debt will be repaid. She will free your Little Moon."

Katya bowed graciously to the raven and thanked him for his words, but he did not seem happy as he took flight. It was true Katya felt a flutter of fear. She did not want to be eaten, but neither could she let the old woman to claim Oleg's soul if there was any chance of saving him.

It was Katya's debt to repay, and she would see it done.

The next morning, Katya woke before dawn and packed a bag. She took a hunk of bread and an apple to eat along the way, as well as several good luck charms to aid her on her mission — a handful of translucent pebbles she'd found in a stream, a pressed flower her grandmother had made for her, and a shining blue feather gifted from Oleg. Lastly she took her mother's ongon from its house of ribbons. It was her ancestors' protector, and Katya took it because her mother warned her never to enter the forest alone.

The ongon was shaped like a doll, with a body and two arms made from leather, and it was wrapped in cloth to keep it warm. The ongon had a face made of antler, smoothed with age 'till it glowed with a soft light, but three pits in the antler gave it the appearance of having eyes and a mouth.

I am sorry, but please accompany me and keep me safe, Katya prayed to the ongon. She knew it was wrong to snatch the spirit from its home, but Katya hoped the ongon would take pity on her and protect her.

Neither her mother nor her grandmother noticed Katya's leaving, so sick was Oleg. Katya retraced her steps through the woods. She walked past the fence, down the meadow's grassy path, and between the whispering birch trees.

She ate a bite of her bread to break her fast and drank from the stream, and before the morning ended, she reached a clearing in the forest. In the clearing sat a tidy hut surrounded by a well-tended yard and lined with neat fence posts. Katya opened the gate and stepped through, careful not to let the chickens that were pecking in the dust escape. She walked to the door, and with a trembling hand, Katya knocked three times.

"Who's there?" an old woman called in a sing-song voice.

"I am your neighbor, and I wish to visit you if you would care for my company, Granny."

"Oh, very much so, very much so, Daughter!"

The door opened, and an old woman with wrinkled skin and gray hair beamed at Katya with a nearly toothless smile. So bent over with age was she that her sharp gaze stared right into Katya's own eyes.

"How wonderful to have human company so far from the world of Man." The old woman gestured for Katya to enter. "Please come in. I will make tea and blini."

Katya was careful to offer her respects to the icons and ongod before accepting a seat at the table. The old woman busied herself in front of the stove. The aroma of butter and yeast filled the room as the woman presented Katya with a delicately painted teacup.

"There is jam here, if you'd like."

Though Katya's heart was weighted with trepidation, the smell of tea and blini awoke her appetite, and she gladly took a spoonful of jam before sipping the tea.

"Please, Granny," Katya said as the old woman placed an enormous stack of delicate blini before her. "I wronged you by coming into your home without asking. If there is anything you want from me, it is yours. I will pay any debt you wish to collect."

"Oh, dearest Daughter," the old woman crooned. "It was not me that you wronged, but my sister, who lives deeper in the woods. It was unwise of you to enter her house, but what's done is done. The road there is treacherous, and she has a temper when visitors come. You shall stay here for a night, and leave in the morning to find her."

Katya opened her mouth to protest the delay, but then she remembered the raven's words and held her tongue. With a meek bow, she accepted the old woman's hospitality.

"If you have any chores in need of doing, I am happy to complete them," Katya said.

The old woman patted her on the head with gnarled fingers,

gentle as a songbird. "Then scrape this pan clean. The last blin got burnt."

It took all of Katya's strength to carry the giant pan to the river, where she scrubbed at the burnt blin. She scrubbed and scrubbed till her fingers were raw, but the blin did not come off. She scrubbed until it was nearly dusk, but she made not even a little progress.

When she started to cry, a small voice from her bag spoke. "Dearest child, there is no need to cry."

Katya reached into her bag to pull out the ongon.

"Leave the pan here with me, and go back to the house to eat your supper. In the morning, all will be well."

Katya dried her tears and did as she was told. After supper, she went to bed and fell into a deep sleep. In the morning, she awoke to see the pan, clean and shining with oil, hooked on the wall as the old woman bustled, making tea and porridge for breakfast.

"You did well, Daughter," the woman crooned in approval as she regarded her pan. "But will it be enough, I wonder?" She turned to stare at Katya. "You have cursed eyes, Daughter. Forest eyes. The debt you bear is from long ago, but my sister has not forgotten. You must take care lest you bring ruin on those you love."

Katya shivered but said nothing. When she took her leave, Katya offered the old woman a gift — the pressed flower made by her grandmother.

"What a delight to receive a gift of Man," the old woman said, nodding her approval. "Dead though the flower may be, it still remembers the gentle rains of springtime."

Katya bowed once more, careful to remember all the manners her mother and father had taught her, and she continued deeper into the forest.

Once Katya was deeper in the forest, the hut lost from sight, she asked the ongon, "Why did she say I have cursed eyes?"

A voice barely more than a whisper floated from her bag. "You have your mother's eyes, dearest child. Eyes gifted from the forest."

Katya pondered this. "But if they are a gift, why did she call them a curse?"

"Curses and gifts are the same thing seen from different angles," the ongon replied. "Your eyes are fresh — the color of new foliage. They are sharp — able to pierce the deepest forest's gloom. But they can also see what was not meant for Man to see."

Katya took a bite of her apple, and well after midday, she reached another clearing in the forest. In the clearing sat a tidy hut surrounded by a well-tended yard and lined with neat fence posts. Katya opened the gate and stepped through, careful not to let the goats that were chewing on the grass escape. She walked to the door, and with a trembling hand, knocked three times.

"Who's there?" an old woman called in a sing-song voice.

"I am your neighbor, and I wish to visit you if you would care for my company, Granny."

"Ooh, how brave to venture so far into the forest!"

The door opened, and an old woman with wrinkled skin and white hair beamed at Katya with a toothless smile. So bent over with age was she that her glassy eyes peered right into Katya's face.

She gestured for Katya to enter. "Come in, come in! I have kvass and pelmeni ready to eat."

Katya offered her respects to the icons and ongod before accepting a seat at the table. The old woman presented Katya with a mug of kvass and a bowl full of pelmeni.

"There is plenty of butter too."

Though Katya's heart was weighted with fear, she dug into the pelmeni and drank deeply of the kvass.

"Please, Granny," Katya said as the old woman refilled her mug. "I wronged you by coming into your home without asking. If there is anything you want from me, it is yours. I will pay any debt you wish to collect."

"Oh, dearest Daughter," the old woman murmured. "It was not me that you wronged, but my sister, who lives deeper in the woods. It was unwise of you to enter her house, but what's done is done. The road there is treacherous, and she has a temper when visitors come. You shall stay here for a night, and leave in the morning to find her."

Katya remembered the raven's words and accepted the old woman's hospitality.

"If you have any chores in need of doing, I am happy to complete them," she said.

The old woman patted her on the head with gnarled fingers, dry as a summer's branch. "Then clean the stove. I am too old to reach inside and it is covered in soot."

Katya filled a pail of water from the river and dragged it back to the house. She scrubbed and scrubbed at the stove 'till her fingers were raw, but the soot did not come off. She scrubbed until it was well past dusk, but she made not even a little progress.

When Katya started to cry, a small voice from her bag spoke. "Dearest child, there is no need to cry."

She reached into her bag to pull out the ongon.

"Leave the pail with me, and go back to your bed. In the morning, all will be well."

Katya dried her tears and did as she was told. She went to bed in the corner and fell into a deep sleep. In the morning, she awoke to see the stove cleaned and shining as if brand new. The old woman bustled, making tea and porridge for breakfast.

"You did well, Daughter," the woman crooned as she regarded her stove. "But will it be enough, I wonder?" She turned to regard Katya. "You have cursed eyes, Daughter. Forest eyes. Were they given as a gift or stolen from the forest through Man's cunning? Who can say anymore? Yet the forest will always claim what belongs to it. You must take care what you promise to my sister."

Katya shivered but said nothing. When she took her leave, Katya offered the old woman the clearest, most beautiful pebble from her collection as a gift.

"What a delight to receive a gift of Man," the old woman crowed in approval. "Although a pebble now, this was once a mighty boulder, witness to war, and famine, and plague. But see how gently it sleeps."

Katya bowed once more, careful to remember all the manners her mother and father had taught her, before continuing deeper into the forest.

Soon after the hut disappeared from view, the forest became darker and thicker, and the path more treacherous. Katya walked all day. She finished her apple and her bread before dusk, but there was no sign of another hut. The sun had almost set when she at last reached a clearing in the forest.

In this clearing sat a darkened hut surrounded by a haphazard yard and lined with fence posts made of human skulls. Katya mustered all of her courage to open the gate, and as she stepped through, fire flared to life in the skulls, lighting her way as she walked to the door. Katya's heart pounded as she knocked three times.

"Who's there?" an old woman called in a suspicious voice.

"I am your neighbor, and I wish to visit you if you would care for my company, Granny."

"Fa! Humans for company? More like for dinner!"

The door opened, and the wrinkled old woman with writhing hair glared at Katya in a toothless grimace.

She gestured for Katya to enter. "Fa! It took you long enough, but you will find no bread or salt here."

Inside the house, here were no icons or ongod to offer respects, and Katya nervously entered. It was the same as the izba she and Oleg found in the woods — covered in dust and cobwebs, and dark except for where the light of the skulls peeked through the cracks in the wood.

"Please, Granny," Katya said as the old woman sized her up as if to determine whether Katya might fit in her pot. "I wronged you by coming into your home without asking. If there is anything you want from me, it is yours. I will pay any debt you wish to collect."

"Cursed child with stolen eyes, what could you possibly give me that I cannot take?"

Katya gazed across the dirty room. "If you have chores in need of doing, I am happy to complete them."

"Fe! What can a scrawny mortal like you hope to accomplish? You wish to pay your debt so I forgo collecting your brother? Fine then. Clean this house! Top to bottom, inside to outside. The whole place must shine, not a cobweb or speck of dust remaining."

Katya accepted this command with a bow before walking past the flaming skulls to fill a pail of water in the black river that flowed behind the house. As she dragged it back into the hut, the skulls murmured and jeered and wept for her. She scrubbed and scrubbed till her fingers were raw, but not a cobweb could she brush away, nor a speck of dust wipe down. She scrubbed long into the night, but the house was still dusty, and the stove still full of soot.

When she started to cry, a small voice from her bag spoke to her. "Dearest child, there is no need to cry."

Katya reached into her bag to pull out the ongon.

"Leave everything to me and sleep, dearest one. In the morning, all will be well."

Katya dried her tears and did as she was told. She went to a pile of moth-eaten blankets in the corner and fell into a deep sleep. In the morning, she awoke to see the house cleaned both inside and out, and bottom to top. The old woman peered at every corner and every nook, searching for even a speck of dust, but she could not find one.

"You did well, Daughter," the woman begrudgingly admitted. "As promised, I will lift the curse. Your brother's fever will break, and his soul will return to the Land of the Living. Now leave me and never return."

Katya shivered, but said nothing. She hurried to the door lest the old woman decided to eat her.

"Wait."

Katya froze in her tracks, but she forced her voice to remain even as she asked, "Yes, Granny?"

"What about my gift? Give me a feather, and you may leave. I want a feather as blue as a sky before a summer storm, shining with memories of flight. A feather lost then gained then given freely. That is the gift I require."

"It's a trap," the ongon warned. "If you give her Oleg's feather, his soul will be lost to her."

Katya offered the old woman another humble bow, but though her mother and father taught her all sorts of manners, she also knew how to be clever and refuse hospitality without breaking custom.

"Granny, such a feather is not mine to give, but I will find one just as good for you in the woods."

"Fa! If I cannot have that exact feather..." the old woman paused as if considering, and her dead fish gaze shone with an eerie gleam. "I will take your eyes."

"She has wanted her eyes back for so very long," the ongon murmured, its words a mirror of Katya's own thoughts. "Was this her plan from the beginning?"

Katya always listened to her father and mother, but she knew how to lie and play tricks when needed. She agreed with another, deeper bow. "Very well, Granny. I will give them to you."

Katya pretended to pull out her eyes, but instead she reached into her pocket. She removed two of her remaining pebbles — the roundest ones she could pinch between her fingers.

The old woman chortled with delight as she took the pebbles. She felt them in her hand for a moment before popping out her glassy white eyes. The old woman laughed and crooned as she placed the pebbles into her empty eye sockets, but as soon as she did, she realized the trick.

"Fie! Wicked child! You tricked me!"

Katya smacked the old woman's hand with her own. The woman's eyes went spinning to the floor, and they rolled into the darkest corner of the room. Without wasting a moment, Katya dashed out through the door, running as fast as her legs could carry her. As she passed the flaming skulls, they cheered, sneered, and wailed in agony. Katya turned long enough to see the hut rise up onto chicken legs, roaring and stamping its disapproval. A black shape, like a great mortar and pestle, darted out through the window in pursuit.

"Quick now, dearest!" the ongon urged. "Quick as the hare fleeing the wolf. Quick as the wolf chasing the hare. We must leave the forest before she catches you!"

Katya ran faster than she'd ever run before. Though it was early in the day, the forest grew dark around her. She could feel slavering breath on the back of her neck and claws pricking at her clothes, but she ran, her feet guiding her true between the vines and tangled roots. Ahead was a clearing bathed in light, and Katya knew she was close to home.

If you flee now, a hateful voice whispered, *I will take everything. Keep your precious eyes, Daughter. I will take all the rest.*

For a moment, Katya's resolve wavered, but the clearing was so close, and she was too breathless to ask the ongon, so she ran without stopping.

Only after she was clear of the forest did she slow her pace, but only after she was clear of the forest did she realize what had happened.

Her house, the ail built of wood and bark, was ablaze.

"Too late!" the ongon cried. "We're too late! If only I'd made it back in time...if only I'd been here to protect them!"

Katya stumbled toward the well to fill a bucket of water, but with the ongon's wails, the sky opened up, and raindrops, like tears, fell from the sky, extinguishing the flames. In the wake of the fire, Katya could see nothing but smoke and the burning rubble of the house and barn.

Tears of anguish streamed down Katya's face as she choked on the smoke. The raven alighted beside her on the ground to join in her sorrow.

"They are gone, Daughter," the raven said. "Your momma, and papa, and your gran. Even the old horse who shared her apples with me and the dog who told me tales of his hunts. All gone. All lost."

Katya could do nothing but weep. Through her actions, she'd cursed them, just as the grannies in the forest warned she would. She'd brought nothing but ruin with her cursed eyes and petty tricks.

"If only I'd given her my eyes," Katya wept, feeling a deep bitterness flow into her heart.

"What's done is done, dearest," the ongon replied. "The forest will take what the forest is owed, but look: all is not lost."

Katya produced the shining blue feather from her bag, and saw that it still glowed bright in the smoky air.

"Your brother yet lives," the ongon said. "The Lady has taken him into the wood, where she waits to see what you will do — to see what you will become. You with your Forest Eyes that can navigate the deepest shadows, that can reach places no Man was meant to step."

"What will you do, Daughter?" the raven asked, cocking his head.

Katya thought for a long moment before securing the feather to the ongon. She scrubbed the dirt and soot and tears from her face, then rose to her feet. She stared into the forest.

"I will show her that debts must be paid," Katya murmured, and her green eyes glinted with a ruthless gleam. "If it takes a monster to hunt a monster, then so be it. These cursed eyes of mine will find her. Then she will understand that sometimes a gift is a curse, but sometimes a curse is a gift."

4

THE THIRD MAN
BY KATHRYN DANETTE

On a clear day, you could see for miles up the mountain, and today was clear enough that Sangye could watch the seven bright parkas moving up the slope and away. They had a lead of more than an hour, which would only grow if Sangye didn't find a way to pick up the pace.

No one would wait for them. They never did.

Sangye darted a glance through the slat created by the low brim of her hat and the high collar of her coat. It was like peeping through a chink in the wall of a house and into the street outside.

Mackenzee had stopped climbing again. She held herself ramrod straight, but she was panting for breath. In a moment, Mackenzee would start to walk again. She would take a few steps before stopping once more, her narrow chest and slight shoulders working like frantic bellows as she gasped for air.

Sangye looked away again so as not to embarrass her. She wondered, not for the first time, if she should suggest going back down. Perhaps she could insist — there were times when she imagined herself as a forthright and insistent person rather than just a quiet and enduring one. Mackenzee might even be grateful.

However, Sangye knew what was in Mackenzee's pack, and so she said nothing. Over the course of the interminable day on the slope, Mackenzee had gradually shed her gear, passing items over to Sangye to carry, until she was down to just her oxygen cylinder and the small zip-up bag that was slung across her chest. Sangye couldn't take one, and she didn't want to ask for the other. The thought of what was in there sent little shivers over her skin, like electric currents.

Presently, Mackenzee nodded and started to ascend again. Sangye fell into step behind her. They hadn't tried to speak for a long time. They were both soft spoken women, and half of what they tried to say to each other was caught by the wind and swept away, or else suffocated into silence by the layers of cold weather gear wrapped over and around their faces.

At least they had that in common. Sangye had begun to suspect that they shared other traits as well, most notably the tendency toward quiet endurance. When Sangye had realized that, she had begun to dislike Mackenzee immensely, with a specific dislike that was different from the throbbing unease she usually felt around the climbers. Throughout the season, a parade of strange faces swarmed over the mountain, trampling it flat, picking it clean, and sometimes marking it with the indelible litter of their frozen corpses. Sangye could not tell one from the next. They were an undifferentiated mass, yelping too loudly into their phones, distributing too little money too begrudgingly, leaving too slowly with no intention of ever returning in order to try to keep held together what was left of the mountain.

From out of all that, Mackenzee had distinguished herself as singularly detestable. That was quite the feat, Sangye had to admit.

When Mackenzee stopped again, huffing and panting and scrubbing at her runny nose, Sangye took a moment to adjust her pack. She did it discreetly, lifting the bulk of it away from the small of her back, tugging her parka so it lay flat, scratching through the layers at the line of irritated skin.

The pack had never bothered her father like this. In his day, Dawa Sherpa had fairly flown up the mountain. They said he never even left tracks in the snow, floating effortlessly over the top without breaking the frozen crust. They used to say a lot of things about him. Dawa had a lot of things to say about himself. He used to sail down from the mountain and sweep into the house, bursting with stories about how he had slipped down a crevasse but had caught an updraft of wind that had gusted him back up to the rim. How he had mounted one of the countless yeti that swarmed over the mountain and had rode it to the peak and back three times in just one day, until the yeti was so tired that Dawa had to carry it back down.

Sangye and her brothers had howled with laughter at his stories. Then the avalanche had come, and they hadn't laughed much at all since.

Further up the slope, the seven bright parkas had dipped into a couloir and disappeared. Sangye watched, waiting for a particular sky blue one to re-emerge. That would be Tashi. He would be out in the front of the pack. Her little brother never waited for anyone. He had scarcely stood still long enough to bark an order at Sangye to stay back with the stragglers before vaulting up the slope. Sangye had been following in his tracks ever since. On a mild clear day like this, tracks remained behind for a long time. At least it could never be said that Tashi glided over the top of the snow without breaking through.

Beside her, some distance away, doing her best to pretend that she could not see Sangye or be seen by her, Mackenzee had fished out her phone. Sangye could see that the ends of her fingers were red and chapped with cold. She would have to keep an eye on that. Even the most sensible and pragmatic climbers generally considered a couple of fingers or toes a small price to pay - in the most literal sense of the word. Sanye knew how much it cost them to be here — for summiting, and Mackenzee was far from sensible or pragmatic.

By now, she had unzipped her parka enough to free her mouth

and she had pushed her knit hat back to show her brow, still bearing the smoothness of a Botoxing that was none-too-fresh.

Her smile was practiced as she gazed into the lens of the camera and said, "Ben always used to say to me, 'Believe you can, or believe you can't. Either way, you're right.' That's why I know that I can do this for him."

Mackenzee's hand was resting on the bag slung over her shoulder, fingers curled, feeling the shape of the metal cylinder inside. Sangye wished she had not looked just then, had not been forced to see the unconscious gesture. It caused a crevasse to open up in her chest, a deep pit with seemingly no bottom.

She'd found many such cracks within since Dawa had not come down from the mountain. They cleaved apart and then closed again with little warning. Some of them were covered with snow and could not be recognized until she stumbled upon them unwary. That was what had happened now.

At basecamp, Mackenzee hadn't talked much with the other climbers. She had looked her up, and then burst out into raucous laughter, so loud Sangye had glanced over. Those people might move in and out of her life like spirits, and blow over the mountain like destructive and temperamental storms; there was no sense getting attached to any one of them. Still, Sangye had come to recognize when something *spicy* was about to happen.

"Fucking *Benkenzee*," India, the Australian yoga instructor, had laughed. "I would have known that Children of the Corn potato face anywhere."

Benkenzee and the Crew: Mackenzee, her husband Ben, and five blond children of graduating sizes, like a set of Russian nesting dolls. 'Goddamn Mormon mommy blogger' was how the Australian had put it. They'd gotten big for their homeschooling crafts. They scandalized their followers by letting their youngest son walk to school alone, and then had been redeemed through a series of tearful and candid videos. They immediately lost it all again when Mackenzee proudly said that, while they followed a mindful vegan diet at home, it was quite all right with her if the kids had no more than a quarter of a cup of ice cream at a friend's birthday party.

"But then," India had said, "Ben got ass cancer. He got cancer of the ass."

"I assume you mean his prostate?" asked Dr. Lacks. He was a plastic surgeon, not a real doctor, but he was taking this opportunity to reinvent himself as so many tried to do on the mountain. "It's the fourth most common cancer in the world. Very difficult to catch in time."

In Ben's case, it seemed, it had been no different. Within the month, Beckenzee's blogs were almost entirely about hospital visits. Within the year, Ben was dead.

And so, Mackenzee was here, with that pathetic little metal canister strapped to her chest. Ben had always wanted to do something big, make a name for himself. In the end, it fell to her to do that for him. The plan was to carry him to the summit and then release his ashes to the wind. To be lost on this mountain forever — it seemed that was what he had wanted.

Mackenzee had noticed Sangye looking at her. Though Sangye had taken great pains to keep her expression neutral, Mackenzee read some of her impatience there all the same. Perhaps one did not get to be the internet's perfect wife without at least some of that particular sixth sense.

"Sorry," she said, "I'm fine to keep going. I feel a lot better."

Indeed, Mackenzee did seem somewhat lighter on her feet now. Perhaps speaking into the camera had helped to unburden her of the things weighing that had been her down. Maybe it helped to talk to someone sometimes, even if that person was only waiting for you to make another mistake.

Sangye banished the thought. It was absurd, and she had no business thinking it. You didn't get up mountains on the strength of a good feeling, especially if you were an only daughter. The only thing that weighed you down was too much weight.

"It's all right," Sangye said. "They're not as far away as they look."

She motioned with her head up the slope. With Tashi setting the pace, the group would have come out of the couloir by now. She would once again be able to pick out the seven bright parkas against the blank canvass of snow.

But when Sangye looked, there was nothing there.

She felt her expression dragged down by a furious gravity. Beside her, Mackenzee became animated, "What's wrong? What is it?"

"Nothing," Sangye assured her. The last thing she needed was for Tashi to think she had worried. Every climb, he told her that this one was to be her last. Every climb, he had been wrong. So far, at least.

They began to ascend once more. Though Mackenzee huffed and sputtered with every step, they still made progress. As long as they were moving forward, things were manageable. She kept her focus on the upward slope, waiting for the appearance of Tashi's sky blue parka. It never came.

Likely, they had decided to hike along the bottom of the couloir. There was a route down there, winding around the face but continuing the inevitable upward momentum. Tashi had decided to take it, for whatever reason.

They climbed into the mid-afternoon. There was still daylight left, but it was burning. The plan had been to cross the couloir and set up camp on the opposite side. They were still on schedule, in spite of the delays, but Sangye had no idea what she would encounter when she reached the couloir. If it had given Tashi problems, it might be bad.

She banished the thought. Tashi had not encountered any problems. He had simply decided to take an alternate route for inscrutable reasons that were all his own. That he had not informed Sangye of his plans was the most believable explanation of all.

"Have you noticed everyone wants to be the first of something?" Mackenzee asked abruptly. She had to pause in the middle of the sentence to catch her breath, but she got everything out all right.

"Like that Australian girl wants to be the first Australian under 23 to summit three peaks in one season. And Dr. Lacks wants to be the oldest American from the Midwest. They're pretty tenuous firsts, if you ask me."

Mackenzee did not have a first of her own. Her motives were the opposite of that inscrutable drive that compelled people to attempt the mountain just to see if they could. To reassure themselves that they had some inner core of strength that had not been entirely corroded away by soft modernity. Mackenzee was not so opaque in her reasons; the only confusing thing about her was that she had chosen now, of all times, to suddenly become talkative with her otherwise invisible guide.

Sangye gave her a wary look, wondering why Mackenzee had chosen to share this particular gem of wisdom with her instead of with her phone. She was using Sangye as a sounding board, she suspected. Getting the idea out to see how it landed so she might spare herself another debacle like the time she had taken little Jaydee to a Western doctor when he had stepped on a piece of broken glass. This had been 'literally child abuse' according to India.

"You're a first too, though," Mackenzee went on. She seemed cautious now, but she forged ahead. "I mean, aren't you? It doesn't say it anywhere, but I was looking at the wall where they hang up the photos of all the porters. I can do the math. You beat the Laksmi girl by like two years."

"To the summit, you mean?" Sangye replied. "I wasn't the first person to the summit."

"No, but you were the first... you know. I mean, I don't know how things are where you're from. But when I was getting ready to come here, I read about Junko Tabei. She was the first woman to climb Everest. Men had been climbing it for like, forty years. It must have been amazing for her, but it's weird, right? That it was someone from Japan and not someone who actually lived there."

Sangye didn't answer. She looked up at the sky and pretended she was making some advanced calculation based on the angle of the sun. The sun didn't interest her, but the bank of clouds that had formed on the distant horizon did. They were still a long way off, hanging harmlessly in the colorless sky. Sangye glared at them, willing them to blow in a different direction.

"Oh, no!" Mackenzee exclaimed suddenly. "Dr. Lack's little hat!"

Sangye's eyes snapped back, keeping close watch on Mackenzee as she veered off the path established by Tashi's bootprints, and then blundered into a snowbank. She waded in up to her waist, but emerged carrying a small knit bundle.

Sangye frowned. The hat was crusted in dry, icy snow, as if it had lain there for a long time, however, the ring of knit reindeer chasing each other around its circumference was unmistakable. The balding Dr. Lack would be feeling the cold without it. Sangye studied the tracks in the snow, but found they continued on straight, without a single deviation from the path. No one had circled back to look for the lost hat, or had even wavered in confusion at its disappearance.

It was only because Sangye was looking at the tracks so intently that she saw what happened next. The glittering crystals that made up the top layer of snow began to levitate, until they were a few inches above the ground. They hovered there, a shimmering translucent cloud at the height of Sangye's knees.

She blinked furiously in an attempt to will the crystalized snow back into its proper place. Hallucinations were one of the signs of hypoxia, she had time to think. Then, the entire world overturned.

A tremendous gust of wind swept in a perpendicular direction across the peak. It lifted Sangye's boots clear of the earth and deposited her in a writhing heap in the snowbank that Mackenzee had just slogged out of. Her limbs felt impossibly tangled, as if they had been disassembled at the joints and rearranged haphazardly. The wind was howling, and it sounded like screaming.

Mackenzee was screaming, coughing out little "Oh! Oh!" syllables right next to Sangye's ear. She had landed on top of her when the wind had bowled her over, Sangye realized, which accounted for the tangle of limbs that did not feel entirely like her own.

Once she realized that, she was able to extract herself from the snow bank, and climb to her feet.

The wind nearly knocked her back. It battered against her, and she had to brace, leaning her head into the gusts like a charging animal. The wind did not ebb and flow, did not abate, and the sound of it was horrible and deafening, like a howl from bottomless lungs. Sangye caught a glimpse of something dark, out beyond the high white wall of blowing snow. It was the far-off bank of clouds she had seen earlier, only now it was almost on top of them.

Lightning slashed the sky, parallel lines that moved toward the ground as if dragged by abnormal gravity.

Sangye moved before conscious thoughts had a chance to trip her up, before she could think that this must be impossible, a night-mare. When she moved, it was not with a nightmare's dreadful slowness and lack of coordination, but rather with a steadiness she did not feel.

She thrust a hand in Mackenzee's direction, and Mackenzee caught hold of it, allowing herself to be dragged to her feet. Her other hand was fisted around the bag across her chest, curled around the canister of ashes within. She clung to it furiously. It was her respon-sibility, hers in trust, just like she was Sangye's. This foolish and sentimental woman, not prepared in the slightest for the mountain. It was Sangye's job to get her out alive.

Sangye cupped her hands around her mouth and pressed the funnel it made to Mackenzee's ear so she could shout, "Head for the couloir. It will block the wind."

Mackenzee nodded. Sangye guided her hand to the back of her belt and forced Mackenzee's fingers to curl around it. That would keep them together, even if visibility dropped to nothing. Then, she started to ascend. She could feel which way was up, and she knew the couloir was up there. Tashi was up there, too, she hoped.

The storm was right on top of them, a swirling vortex that seemed to spiral up into an endless black sky. The wind was constant and without respite, but the storm had not brought fresh snow. It gusted up what was already on the mountain, but the air remained dry. Somehow charged, as if perpetually poised in the moment after a lightning strike.

Fog closed in, soupy and gray. Unmoving. It boxed them in as they climbed. The opaque wall of it seemed to be always about twenty meters ahead, never drawing any closer, never further away. Never yielding a single break through which the rest of the mountain could be glimpsed.

It was as if they had been plucked out of their world and deposited in another. One that was not quite finished, that had to be sectioned off by this impenetrable fog to spare them from seeing the horrors that lay beyond.

Sangye could see more than enough already. Climbing gear, half-buried in the snow. First, there was only the occasional glove or scarf, but then she began to see lost packs. New ones made of state-of-the-art Gore-Tex, but also ones that seemed older. Canvas packs with tarnished brass fittings, the kind you saw on photographs of bearded and weathered men who had attempted the mountain even before Dawa's time.

A row of ski poles thrust out of the snow, like a jaw full of broken teeth. An oxygen cylinder blew past, whipped into a deadly projectile by the wind.

Sangye did not turn her head to follow it. She did not acknowledge its passing in the slightest. Her jaw was set and her eyes were fixed straight ahead. She could feel Mackenzee's hand fisted around her belt. The rest may well have not been happening.

She nearly walked right off the edge of the couloir.

She was able to pull up just short of it. Mackenzee kept moving, colliding with her back, but somehow not sending them both flying over the lip of rock and into the void.

The fog was below them, too. Filling the couloir. Sangye couldn't make out the bottom, but it was down there; she knew that. If she stopped now, the dread that had taken root in the pit of her stomach would overwhelm her. She could feel it there, slowly ballooning. It was not the terror of the storm. She had seen storms before and she felt she understood their sudden fury. They did not frighten her. The only thing that scared Sangye was that she would fail.

Without hesitation now that her course had been decided, Sangye slipped over the lip of the couloir and began to descend. She had to work her way down slowly, sliding on her butt, feeling her way with her feet, and bracing herself with her hands. Her entire body was engaged in the task in a way that left no part open for doubt.

After a moment, Mackenzee followed her. She kicked an accumulation of snow loose as she settled onto the slope and it showered down over Sangye's head. For a moment, the world went white.

When her vision cleared, she realized she could see the bottom of the couloir. The fog had retreated before her and she could make out the ground. Incredibly, the sound of the wind had retreated as well. It had gone from a deafening roar to a distant rumble, as if the storm had not followed them down the slope, but rather contented itself with forming a dome over them.

In the bottom of the couloir, it was almost peaceful.

Sangye found her footing, then turned around to help Mackenzee down. Mackenzee's face was streaked with icy tears, but she wasn't crying now.

"Is it over?" she asked, desperately hopeful.

Sangye scowled. They were scarcely safer here than they had been on the bare slope. Couloirs were notorious avalanche hazards, but she felt that she had chosen this course of action and she couldn't second guess it now. Besides, it was the last place where she had seen Tashi.

"We'll climb a bit further. Find a place where it evens out into a ridge. Then we'll set up camp and dig in."

Mackenzee nodded. It seemed she found the plan a sound one. Sangye was, barely, cheered by that. She drove her boot into the snow and felt her crampons make purchase with the ice underneath.

It made a satisfying click, like a completed circuit, reconnecting her to the mountain.

She could get them out of here, as long as she kept her head.

Slowly, she began to ascend the couloir. Though visibility was still poor, she knew that there were spots where the steep ascent leveled out, where the debris from old avalanches and glacial slides would provide enough shelter to set up the tent. They would settle in, ride it out. The most ominous thing about it was that she might have to be snowed in with Mackenzee for a while.

The detritus of former expeditions still littered the ground around them. A pair of snowshoes lay over a rock, snapped cleanly in two like a broken spine. Leather cords, stiff and brittle from the cold, dangled off of them. It was the kind of leather that hadn't been used on gear in 50 years. Slashes of vivid red peeped up at them through the snow, as if the ground had been rent open by massive claws. Then, as Sangye came closer, she saw that it was the nylon fabric of a tent, mostly buried in the snow.

Tashi's group had been carrying red tents, she remembered, but then immediately dismissed the thought. It would do no good to think about that.

The walls of the couloir narrowed ahead of them. That was a good sign. In places like this, the glacial flow backed up and sometimes created areas of relative flatness. She looked back to make sure that Mackenzee was still behind her, and then went toward it.

The boot laying on its side in the middle of the trail brought her up short.

It was a high-end and modern hiking boot, piped with brown and with bands of fluorescent green and orange. There were no crampons on it; the laces were still tied.

Sangye paused, staring at it, as if she had come upon an illusion. Like a picture of endless flights of stairs she had seen in a book once, the boot seemed mundane at a glance, but the longer you stared...

On top of that, it was familiar, in the way that Dr. Lack's lost knit hat was familiar. She had seen this particular boot before.

Mackenzee came up beside her. They had to stand very close in the narrowing confines of the couloir. Sangye thought she could hear Mackenzee's breath wheezing wetly in her chest. It didn't sound so good.

Mackenzee was luminously pale, with her blond hair lank as wet fabric around her face and her blue eyes big as plates and rolling wildly. She crouched down over the boot, as if in a trance. With one hand clutched around her pack, she reached out with the other to turn the boot upright.

A gout of red spilled out onto the snow. Sangye saw a glimmer of white peeping out from the red soup that filled the boot. Then she was reeling back, fighting back vomit, her head filled with Mackenzee's cries of "Oh! Ew! Yuck! Oh!"

It had just been a glimpse, but she knew what she had seen. The foot was still inside.

Mackenzee reeled back, pushing to her feet and not quite making it. Her legs wouldn't hold her; her knees unhinged. Sangye made a grab for her, and miraculously her hand hooked into the strap of Mackenzee's pack. She felt the cylinder inside shifting like a counterweight as she anchored herself and pulled Mackenzee upright.

"Sorry!" Mackenzee was saying, before she'd even found her footing again. "I'm sorry. What a klutz! Sorry, sorry!"

She coughed, a wet and rattling noise. Then she jerked forward and started to ascend again, pushing herself up against the rock wall to give the boot that lay facing upright, the shards of ankle bone glittering in the open upper like a grinning mouth full of broken teeth.

Mackenzee scrambled past it as if it were a big spider crouched in the middle of the bathroom floor, and Sangye followed her.. Beyond the narrow point in the couloir. They could stop there and catch their breath.

There was sobbing in the wind. Great, wrenching cries that could not be mistaken for anything else. They were wound around, tangled up with the storm, so that one could not be extracted from the other.

Sangye still knew, though, what she heard. She braced herself as she came up on the ridge of flat ground.

A figure was crouched over with her back against the wall of the couloir. She wore a purple parka, and a pair of ski goggles were perched on her head. When Sangye tried to approach, she sprung to her feet and spun around to face her. There was a glint of metal in her hand, which she brought to bear.

"Is that a gun?" Mackenzee exclaimed. "What the fudge, India?"

India turned on her, eyes wide, making wild gesticulations with the weapon. Mackenzee didn't flinch. "You don't know what the heck you're doing. Let me have it."

She put out a hand, no-nonsense, like a mother. That worked on India, - - because she dropped the weapon to her side and said, "No one's impressed by the Mormon baby swears. Just say what you want to say."

Mackenzee stepped forward and made a grab for the gun, but India snatched it back, out of her reach. "Don't touch me! You didn't see it!"

"See what?" Sangye realized that she sounded calm. She did not feel it, but sounding that way helped. "Where is everyone?"

India laughed, with a high and cracked edge to it. Then she stopped abruptly, and looked around as if seeing her surroundings for the first time. "Give me something to eat. I'm fucking starving."

The mention of food made Sangye's stomach clench. Her mind was not done with the sight of the abandoned boot and its contents, it seemed, though she nodded. "We will make camp. Rest. Nothing is going to happen until the storm passes."

India looked at her darkly. She wanted to protest. For the moment, however, she relented.

The tent Sangye was carrying was only made for two, but with a little clever maneuvering, all three of them fit. Their legs were tangled and none of them could lay down, but the body heat felt good.

India had not relinquished the gun. She also had not said where she had gotten it. What she had said was more concerning:

"The storm dropped down right on top of us, and that awful wind, too. We could barely walk in it. Like every step we took it just pushed us right back to where we had been. I lost sight of the guide in the fog, and I lost sight of the people coming up behind me, too. Only Dr. Lack was keeping pace. He kept shouting, "We'll find someone eventually. We'll come out eventually." I think he lost his voice at some point, though."

Her eyes slid over them, around the confines of the tent. It was dark inside, and Sangye could not make out the contours of her face.

"Then, the screaming started. It sounded like it came from every-where, all around us, but that was just the way it echoed off the rocks, right?"

She looked to Sangye for confirmation, but Sangye kept her reaction carefully blank. After a moment, India looked down. She took care with that movement as well, though. Framing it so it was only a flash, only the briefest window opened onto what she was thinking.

"I know about climbing, okay?" she said. "This is my fourth 8000-er. I know what it sounds like when people get hurt, even hurt bad. I've never heard anything that sounded like that before."

Mackenzee shifted in her seat, bringing up both hands to grip the canister in her pack, kneading it through the fabric. Except for that, her manner was flat, her expression unreadable. All three of them preparing for the inevitable catastrophe, like sisters, all the same.

"Dr. Lack froze up. I looked over at him, and his mouth was hanging open like an idiot. You could practically see the seams on that cut-rate jaw contouring of his. Anyway, I told him we needed to move. That came from right behind us. And he was like, no, no, that came from in front of us. And I was like, do you have some kind of age-related hearing loss? And then he didn't answer. Because then something started happening with the fog."

She stopped talking then, so abruptly that her teeth made a clicking noise when they came back together. Then she was quiet for a while. She had come up against something she didn't want to talk about, and it was like she had conjured a rock wall out of thin air. Sangye waited. She would either get past it in time, or she wouldn't. Either way, the immediate situation would not change.

"Something happened with the fog," India tried again. "It parted. Not like it was burning off, but like it split open. Like a door was opening in it. The two sides peeled back like the curtain on a play. I could kind of see what was back there, and it didn't look like the mountain. It looked like a big cave. It went back as far as you could see, and there were massive crystals that hung down from the ceiling and shot up from the floor. They were as big as houses."

She remembered herself. Pulled herself up so she was sitting straight, and arranged her chin and her gaze so that she was staring into an imaginary lens. That composed her.

"Something came out of there. It moved fast. I couldn't get a good look. But it was big, like a lot taller than me, and it was white. The exact white of the snow. Not just like they're both white, but like this thing had camouflaged itself to blend in perfectly. I could only tell it was there because of the movement it made. It got its claws in Dr. Lack, its teeth. I heard him screaming. Then I ran. I didn't see what happened to him. I didn't see what that thing did. I practiced some radical self-care and I got my ass out of there."

India was glaring at them now, as if she expected them to find some fault in that. Whatever fate might have befallen Dr. Lack, Sangye could not bring herself to pass judgment.

"The doctor was wearing gray boots," Mackenzee murmured, as if just recalling the information. "Wasn't he?"

India nodded. "Salomon Quest GTX. Did you see him out there?"

Mackenzee laughed all at once, a single shrill giggle, then

clapped her bag over her mouth and clutched it there with both hands to stifle the sound.

India's eyes slowly focused on Sangye, drawing her into view, as if seeing her there for the first time. "What the hell did I see?" she asked.

Sangye would have preferred to stay agnostic on that account, but she didn't think she could. "The mountain has many guardians. Nyalmo is the fiercest and most territorial. He comes when people trespass where they should not. He takes revenge for the land that has been violated."

"Are you talking about some kind of yeti?" India said.

"That is exactly what I am talking about."

It was of little surprise to her that India rolled her eyes. "I'm talking about something real here. Not some dumb superstition. What was it actually? A bear?"

"You asked her what she thought," Mackenzee said quietly. "Don't get angry when she tells you."

"Because I assumed she'd give me something we could work with," India snapped back. "Not surprised you buy it, though."

"At least I'm not saying it's not a dang bear! Bears don't live at this altitude."

"I *know* that! I'm not stupid, babe!"

"You're the one with the gun!"

That brought India up short. She hunted around the tangle of their legs until she found the weapon again. "It's not for bears."

"Then what's it for?"

India hesitated. She looked guilty, but that didn't stop her from biting out, "I've heard dodgy things about some of the locals, okay? We can't all hide behind a man for protection. Some of us need to take care of ourselves."

"A local is sitting right there," Mackenzee hissed.

"I'm not offended," Sangye put in quickly, before the argument could escalate. "You saw an animal. That's what we do know. An animal that has now fed and won't come back to trouble us."

The other two women exchanged a dubious glance. It seemed they were speaking to each other without words, but Sangye could not bring herself to care what was exchanged.

"Don't fire the gun," she added. "We are in an avalanche zone. You will bring the mountain down on us."

"I thought that was only in cartoons," Mackenzee said, and India rolled her eyes.

~

They spent the night in the tent. There was nothing they could do until the storm let up. If luck was on their side, it would do that soon. Such fury was unsustainable.

No one slept. Sangye knew she ought to at least try. It would be the responsible thing, the smart thing, and yet she did not move. Not even to close her eyes. She was listening both to the wind, and for things that were not the wind.

It was full dark. She could not even see the other women, she could only feel the press of their hips and shoulders.

She couldn't say how long passed like that. Hours, she supposed. Long enough for Mackenzee to work herself up to something, to get a few things straight in her mind. When her voice came out of the darkness like an extended hand, Sangye was surprised by it. She had forgotten Mackenzee was there.

"I'm not supposed to be here, you know," she said.

Sangye thought about saying that none of them were. Not precisely here, at least. Not in this exact situation. Instead, she kept quiet and let Mackenzee talk.

"Climbing was always his thing. Ben's. He said one day he was going to really accomplish something. Do something he could be proud of. Like his five children weren't enough for that. Like I wasn't enough. He was the best husband I ever could have asked for, but he let me know where I stood. I never wanted to come here."

At the moment, Sangye could understand the feeling Mackenzee had expressed.

After a long time, Mackenzee spoke again, subdued now, "Is it really a yeti?"

India shifted. Clearly, she had opinions on that, but she didn't give them voice.

"No," Sangye heard herself say. "Nyalmo isn't real. If he was, someone would have seen him by now."

And yet, could she be certain of that? Tashi had never seen Nyalmo, and, for all his tall and wild tales, Dawa had never claimed to either. But they didn't know what Sangye knew, about the ability of certain creatures to hide in plain sight, to be invisible even if they had been there all along. One of them might be with them right now, and they were not even bothering to look.

"Fuck," India groaned. "I have a splitting headache. My stomach feels like shit."

"Me too," Mackenzee said quietly.

The storm shifted. Sangye felt it before she heard it. Her ears popped painfully. Then the change was unmistakable. A sound was threaded through it, over and under the tide of the wind. It sounded like screaming, like no screaming she had ever heard before. It went up, up, up. One long sustained note, until it reached a crescendo and dashed apart. Then it started all over again, a low groan ascending up the scale of agony into a broken wail.

It was coming closer.

Sangye fumbled around the tangle of limbs in the bottom of the tent until she found her headlamp and switched it on. They were all left blinking in the sudden light. Sangye realized, a moment too late, that she had just lit up their location to anything that might want to know about it.

The screaming broke off.

Inside the tent, everything was still as the women held their breath. Almost a full minute passed. They were safe. It had only been the storm after all. India and Mackenzee started to relax. Sangye held herself alert a moment longer, out of a sense of responsibility.

But all was well. She was embarrassed to have been jumping at shadows.

At that moment, the mountain lurched beneath them.

The tent bowed inward, pressing against Sangye's back. The fabric cocooned her, as something massive and heavy pressed against it from the outside. However, even as it snapped the seams, pulled the pegs loose from the mountain and tilted the entire tent dangerously on its edge, Sangye was aware that the first jolt had come up from the very ground itself. She could still feel it vibrating through her, rattling her joints.

They landed in a screaming, yelping pile. Sangye realized that she could see sky, night sky. A high, bright expanse of stars, not a single cloud in sight, lapped over and under the blowing snow, the vortex of clouds, as if all existed at the same time.

The tent was torn open. She heard the rending of fabric, the metallic twang as the poles snapped. A massive arm reached inside. The hand had five fingers, and each was tipped with a nail, grown long, and gnarled like claws. Shaggy fur hung from it like moss from the branch of a tree. Where the fur was in contact with the snow, it was white, but where it dipped into the darkness of the tent, the color shifted like an optical illusion, like the colors in a prism, becoming a dirty black.

An unspeakable stench filled the ruined tent. For an instant, Sangye was too disgusted to even be afraid. Her eyes watered and she fought to keep from vomiting.

She caught a glimpse of something metallic out of the corner of her eye. Then there was an explosion next to her ear, so loud that it blotted out all else. Sangye's head spun and she thought she might faint. There was nothing but that sound, so loud that it took on the quality of a bright light, a flash that ate up her vision.

Somehow, she was out of the tent now, in the snow. Feeling the snow soak into her clothing, sneaking down the collar of her parka and over the tops of her boots.

India was on her feet, waving the gun at the sky and at nothing. When Sangye turned herself over onto her hands and knees, she could make out a spray of jetblack blood retreating from the shredded wall of the tent.

Mackenzee staggered over through the snow and then helped Sangye to her feet. Her ears were still ringing, and she heard the world as though through a layer of gauze. When India spoke to them, it sounded like buzzing. When Mackenzee replied, it sounded like nothing at all.

Then a sound came that penetrated even her damaged hearing. A kind of scream on the wind, rising up to a fever pitch, taken up by another before it could break off. Then another after that. And another still.

India and Mackenzee had frozen. They stood over her in exaggerated tableau for a suspended second.

Sangye didn't see what happened next. She scrambled to her feet, sending an arc of snow fanning behind her. It hung in the air for a beat too long, an uncanny moment in which time jumped its smooth and polished rails. She caught a glimpse of the gray clouds parting, and what she saw within them was not the mountain.

Then she was running, aware that India and Mackenzee had set aside their argument long enough to bolt as well. They were all in step when Sangye skidded down the incline of the couloir, but then she hit the slanted side and scrambled back up onto the mountain slope. The wind hit her full in the face, driving snow into her eyes. She staggered, blind now as well as deaf, but she could feel the mountain under her feet, pulsing up and through her, and she went on.

Her heart was hammering in her ears. The rush of blood was loud. At least she could hear again, though she certainly didn't like the sound that was building in her wake.

Head down, keep moving. It had served her well in the past. She was moving with swift surety over the mountain now. She had always made swift descents. Swifter than Tashi, swifter than almost anyone when she put her mind to it.

Dawa would have been pleased. Even him. He wouldn't have shown it outwardly, but it would have been clear all the same. Sangye thought of that pleasure like a beacon, a bright spot, leading her own down the mountain. She knew something had to still be down there.

She hit a steep slope that angled sharply and abruptly away under her feet. Sangye tested it with the side of her boot. It was chancy. She thought she could descend it, but she couldn't see the bottom. Another few degrees and she wouldn't be able to keep her footing.

A sound behind her made the decision for her. A wailing, a pulsing, like threads weaving over and under the air.

Sangye started down. Within a minute, she realized her error. The slope was ice underneath, and as smooth as glass. She stomped her crampons in hard, but they didn't slow her momentum much. There was time to reflect that this had been a mistake, before the earth dropped out from under her entirely.

It was a comical, cartoonish fall. She slid, thrusting her arms out to both sides, making herself large to slow the descent. It didn't help. She flipped over once, landed on her side.

Then the ground disappeared from beneath her.

Sangye had a moment to register that she was falling, for her stomach to lurch in the anticipation of fear that had not even wound its way fully up into her brain.

Then she hit the icy wall of the crevasse and tumbled the rest of the way to the bottom.

Sangye's thoughts fogged over. She wanted to cry, very suddenly and with seemingly no cause. The crevasse she had fallen down was shallow, and she could tell that she wasn't hurt. In spite of that, the tight knot remained in her throat, as the heat built behind her eyes.

Impossible. Unfair. Why did this have to be happening to *her*?

Because she was there, she thought bitterly. Then she choked back her tears and got up so that she could get moving.

A pair of eyes stared back at her from the ice wall in front of her face. They were milky white, wide-open in shock. The face they were set in was scummed over by glacial ice, locked into it by the passage of many seasons.

With cold finality that stubbornly refused to resolve itself into terror or grief, Sangye realized that she recognized it.

It was the clothing that gave it away. The corpse's blue-gray skin and mummified visage could not have looked like anything but a dead body, one of countless that littered the mountain. The discarded husks of what had once been very motivated people. People who had wanted to really make a statement.

This one, though, had substance beyond its thwarted wants, its dead desires. There was meaning inherent in the whisps of dark hair that hovered in the ice around its bare skull, in the parka torn open at the front in four parallel, bloodless gashes, ringed with old blood. The violence not of an avalanche, but of a creature that was not quite of the mountain.

Sangye did not know the eyeless sockets, the hinged-open jaw, but she knew that she was staring into Dawa's dead and screaming face.

She did not scream herself at the realization. Somehow, it did not even occur to her to scream. She doubled over, awkward in the tight confines of the crevasse, and put her hands on her knees and breathed deeply, but she did not scream.

For a moment, she felt lightheaded, as if cut adrift from her body. Then the moment passed and she was back in the present moment once more. At the bottom of a crevasse, cold and hungry and miserable, but not so far from base camp that she could not make it back on her own two feet.

Alert now, so alert it was almost painful to her senses, Sangye got her bearings. She was wedged into a tight slat between two walls of ice. Craning her head back, she could see the opening some three or four meters above. The sides of the crevasse were smooth like glass, but she thought she might be able to haul herself out with some creative maneuvering. It wouldn't be pleasant, but she could do it.

Bracing up, she pressed her back into one side of the crevasse and kicked her leg out so it was planted firmly in the opposite ice wall. She had seen Tashi do this before — showing off, as he so often did — and she thought she could also manage it. She didn't doubt her strength in this regard, only her finesse.

It was just as she stepped up when she heard a voice above her call down. "Hey! Hey!"

She craned her neck back. Her hood flopped over her eyes, but through the fringe of fur she could make out Mackenzee's face, peering down in what seemed more like annoyance than concern. It seemed she wanted to say, "What have you gotten yourself into now?"

Now that she was under Mackenzee's scrutiny, Sangye felt a fresh resolve. She dug in and began to ascend the crevasse. When she was high enough, Mackenzee grabbed hold of her parka and helped haul her over the icy lip and onto the slope.

"I don't know what happened to that freaking witch," Mackenzee panted. "I lost sight of her. She's probably halfway back to her treehouse retreat in Bali by now."

Sangye laughed, weakly. Bali had always seemed claustrophobic and chaotic to her, at least from what she had seen in pictures. Right about now, she wouldn't have minded it, though.

"We're close to camp," she informed Mackenzee. "We ought to go back."

"Sure." Mackenzee glanced up the slope one last time. There was a kind of obscure longing there. She had missed her chance at reaching the summit and she knew she wouldn't get another one. "Let me just..."

Mackenzee patted the pack strapped around her chest. The urn was still in there. Privately, Sangye didn't think there was much difference in whether the ashes were dumped on the waiting wind here or at base camp, but surely it would only take a second. She waited while Mackenzee climbed up a nearby ridge and removed the metal canister from her pack.

The storm had died down some, and there wasn't much chance of her being blown away. There was a lot of new snow, though. It had piled up as much as a meter high in places. Sangye had a sickening sinking feeling of disconnect. It was as though she had climbed up out of the crevasse and onto a mountain that was familiar, but still not exactly the same.

A knot of dread tightened in the pit of her stomach. It was as if she had swallowed something sour and unpleasant whole. Though the wind was still gusting, a curious stillness settled over the slope. Sangye felt still, still inside of herself, as she moved her eyes over the snowy expanse. All white and unbroken as far as she could see.

But that was not quite true. Further up the slope, a patch of snow was moving. It was sliding toward her, a single drift unmoored from the rest of the formless white mass. At first she thought it was an avalanche, but she knew it wasn't. This did not roll down the slope with gathering violence. Rather, it glided, moving effortlessly as though it did not even tread on the snow that was underneath.

It seemed impossible. Either her eyes could not quite make sense of what she was seeing, or else the image became garbled when her mind tried to sort it out. She saw something impossible, otherworldly, and her limited human senses could only try their best to graft onto it what they already knew.

The mass drew close. It still looked like nothing in particular, and she was so baffled by that. She had forgotten even to be afraid. Then it drew itself up to its full height, and for a moment, the underbelly that had been pressed against the snow was visible. It was covered in obsidian black fur, a pelt so thick that Sangye thought she could plunge her arm into it up to the elbow.

In an instant, the black patch melted white, disappearing seamlessly once more against the snowy slope.

The thing struck at her out of that illusion, out of the wind.

Sangye only barely stepped back to avoid the swipe of its massive hand.

The thing was above her. A white shape against a void of brighter white. She could see the form of it in vivid detail, but it was like a chalk outline. A rough sketch brought somehow into terrifying life. Not quite on the mountain. Not quite somewhere else, either.

It was three meters tall, covered in wild, white hair. It carried itself like a human, though its proportions were all wrong. The legs were stunted and short, the arms too long, slapping against massive thighs like a cartoon Neanderthal. Outlined upon the air and without detail, Sangye had the impression of a twisted and misshapen neck, broad shoulders, hips tapered to beguiling trimness. The comically bulbous penis and scrotum dangled between the nyalmo's bow legs, in defiance of the frigid weather.

The nyalmo drew back its massive arms. Its reach was enormous. Sangye braced for the weight of it. She could already feel it crashing down on her, the claws tearing into her flesh, snapping bone. Crushing her ribcage into a puzzle box of splintered bone and organs.

"God!" She heard Mackenzee's shriek over the storm. "*Fuck!*"

On the periphery of Sangye's vision, a metallic shape arced through the air. It moved slowly, so slowly that she was not even sure how it stayed aloft. After what seemed like hours suspended in the air, it clanged solidly against the nyalmo's skull.

The urn burst open on contact, disgorging its contents. The nyalmo reeled back, the ashes instantly covering its face and neck. They made a gray cast of its features, like a death mask suspended in midair. The features looked human, Sangye thought. And yet they also looked anything but.

The nyalmo snorted and then sneezed explosively. Slime splattered the front of Sangye's coat and her face. She tasted it in her stupidly gaping mouth.

Snorting like a dog that had tasted dust, the nyalmo turned. Sangye saw Mackenzee take a single step back, which was all she had time to do before the creature went for her. It surged over the snow in a single leap, leaving no tracks behind it.

Sangye did not see what happened next, though. She had already scrambled to her feet and turned. She was running when she heard the screams behind her. She was hurtling down the icy slope when they were choked into abrupt and stunning silence.

S angye ran until her head felt like it had been overinflated. Until she kept having to fight the urge to reach up and pull it back onto her neck before it floated away. The shadows came to eat at the edges of her vision, and she was aware of a presence. Not seen, but sensed, the way Shackleton had described it.

At least it was silent. At least it did not scream or cry out.

Smudges of black had appeared on the slope below her. These resolved into the arched tops of tents. There was smoke and the sensation of no longer being alone, even if she was a ways off yet.

It took her several minutes to realize it was camp two, wedged into a trough in the slope like a seed between two strong teeth.

The surge of relief she felt was muted by exhaustion, as if it had been wrapped in layers of gauze. Sangye tried to quicken her pace, but her legs refused. All they could manage was a steady pistoning, up and down, propelling her steadily closer.

She had drawn near enough to make out some of the scurrying upright shapes of people, when she heard someone calling for help.

Sangye froze. Though her legs still pulsed beneath her, wanting to keep moving, she pulled up short, held her breath, and listened.

The sound came again. Not far off, buoyed very clearly on the wind.

Sangye swore. Then she put her head down and went toward the shouts.

She found India half-buried in a heap of snow. A long track trailed after her down the slope, as if she had been brutally dragged there. She had almost made it back. Sangye was grudgingly impressed.

When she crouched down next to her, she immediately saw what the problem was.

India's left tibia had snapped cleanly, a few inches above her ankle. The sharp edge of the bone protruded through the skin. It was tipped with a piece of flesh, like a speared olive in a fancy cocktail. India had tied her scarf around her thigh to make a tourniquet, but Sangye could not say whether or not it had done much good. The skin of her leg, visible where her trousers had shredded, was greenish in color.

She was swearing continually, in a stream, scarcely able to compose herself to say, "Get me off this fucking mountain! What are we paying you for?"

"I can't carry you," Sangye said. "I can go down to camp and send help, though."

"So do it!" India, it seemed, had mustered enough strength to roll her eyes. "Useless bitch."

Sangye spotted the pistol in India's hand, and she must have eyed it a moment too long.

"Don't even think about it," India snapped. "I need it if those things come back."

Sangye wondered if India meant she needed it for the nyalmo, or for something else. Maybe it would be better, she thought, recalling Mackenzee's last spiraling scream.

Straightening up, Sangye scanned the sky. The storm had lifted now, though there was still a high white cover of clouds obscuring the sky. It was light enough, though. She would be able to make it to base camp. Arrange a rescue. There would be someone else to tell what she had seen, another voice to attempt to describe the impossibility of it all.

Having decided now, Sangye straightened up. Her knees popped in protest, but they held her alright. She would be able to make good time.

74

From one blink to the next, darkness closed around them.

Sangye froze. India caught her breath in a strangled gasp.

Then they heard it. A long cry that rode out the wind, over and under, carried in between the planes of the air.

"No!" India shouted. "No, no, no!"

There wasn't much use telling her not to. They had already found them.

A bank of fog rolled down the slope, a black wall not swept along on a tide of wind, but rather, steadily advancing. As if something from beyond had lapped over and subsumed their world.

Sangye turned to run.

"You bitch!" India called after her. "You Gemini *bitch*!"

Sangye threw herself over on her side, shrieking as she jarred her broken leg. She dragged herself down the slope, her leg rattling behind her.

She glanced back in time to see the fog sweep over her, hiding her completely. From within its roiling depths came cries not of terror, but of rage. Rage at a mountain, at a world that refused to be as tamable as she had long been led to believe.

Then, there was another sound. The sharp report of a gunshot. One, then another.

The advancing fog halted in its tracks. It broke apart, dispersing back into the mountain. India was gone. There was no sign that she had ever been there. Sangye was looking up once more at a clear slope all the way to the summit.

It was the kind of day where it felt like you could see for miles.

Then Sangye felt the ground tremble under her feet. The sound of the final gunshot echoed off the peaks, seeming to grow louder, not softer, with each return. Sangye looked down. The snow shimmered beneath her feet.

When she looked up again, she saw the avalanche bearing down on her.

It was a massive wave of snow. Like white water. That was the way it moved. A torrent that twisted around and overtook everything in its path.

Sangye knew she couldn't outrun it, but she tried, anyway.

She made it a few steps, then the avalanche swept over her. There was a moment of painless awe as it bore her up. She could see camp two below. Far away but approaching fast. Perhaps one or two of them would make it.

Then the snow rolled over her and bore her under for the final time.

5

LAST FLIGHT OF THE GLAMR
BY G.M. GRAY

Sven, captain of the Merry Swallow, pirouetted through the door in a gesture so laden with good-cheer, it forced Alan to glance up from his book. Sven's face was split in a pleased grin as he hummed a cheerful sea shanty and skipped to Alan's side.

"Alan! Alan, Alan, Alan!"

Sven peered over the back of Alan's book as if Alan had somehow yet to notice him, as if Alan were not already staring at him — albeit with reluctance. Sven's green eyes practically shimmered, and the pale tufts of his lavender bangs quivered in time to his bouncing.

Alan considered what it would take to ignore Sven, who was currently his roommate, sort of his boyfriend, and formerly his pirate captor, (but that was a long story, which Alan did his best not to think about) before deciding it was hopeless. Sven wanted Alan's attention, and until he had it, there was no hope of Alan finding peace and quiet. Alan replaced his bookmark before closing the book with a decisive *thump*.

"Yes, Sven?" Alan asked in an overly solicitous tone.

"You will not believe what happened!"

Despite his outward reluctance, Alan was a little curious about what had riled Sven. He glanced out of the room's porthole window, but all that softened the harsh, overwhelming emptiness of space was a smattering of stars. The Merry Swallow was patrolling the outskirts of a low population system situated near the edge of the Pyrean Outer Territories. Given that it was far away from any space shared with humans, and given that it was barely in range of the ma'jenn, the crew had begun this assignment with the expectation that nothing interesting would happen.

"Did you beat Valtra at cards?" Alan asked with sudden clarity. "Oh, that means you finally figured out she's been cheating." He gave Sven a sharp look. "You aren't playing cards while on duty, are you?"

Sven regarded Alan with a slightly offended look. "No, I'm not playing cards, and yes, I know Valt is cheating. I cheat too, obviously. She's just better at it. No, this is way more exciting. We found..." Sven paused for dramatic effect, "a ghost ship!"

Alan blinked. "A ghost ship?"

Ships sometimes went missing only to reappear dozens, if not hundreds of years later. Ghost ships, while not common, were always of great interest. He'd read about a number of ghost ships while working as an inspector in the Elite, an Earth anti-piracy task force. Alan still worked for the Elite, despite traveling on a known vessel in the Pyrean Navy's Piracy Division (but that was also a long story, and Alan did his best not to think about it either).

"I assume it's pyrean?" Alan asked, but it was more a statement than a question. He'd never heard of ma'jenn ghost ships, and there was no way a human vessel had made it to this sector of space. "How old?"

"He's over two hundred Standard Pyrean years," Sven answered. "Our sensors picked him up last night, but it took Ragnar a while to identify him. There's no name or registered code. He must be a smuggler's vessel. Built in the old style too. Pre-human."

"Over two hundred SP years" dated back to nearly the first contact between human and pyrean. After that initial cultural exchange, pyrean ship-building changed dramatically. They'd taken the curves and stylings of wooden tall ships from Earth from the Age of Sail and incorporated them into their space-faring vessels. That this ship had been built in the old style made it a historical treasure.

"That's quite the find," Alan murmured. "What are you going to do with it?"

Before Sven could answer, the door to their quarters opened again. This time it was Natalia's turn to flounce across the threshold.

"Ghost ship, ghost ship, ghost ship!" Natalia sang. She threw her arms around Sven and hopped onto his back. "We're gonna see some ghosts on a ghost ship!"

Though he was several decades older, Sven was the same size and height as his sister, so he immediately collapsed under her weight.

"Oof."

"Ghosts?" Alan asked. "You think the ship has ghosts on it?"

Pyreans had as many religions as humans did, but all of them were some flavor of animistic. Ghosts, therefore, were not a theoretical. Even the most atheistic pyrean would have concerns.

"Maybe," Sven groaned. He tried to shake himself free of Natalia, who remained happily seated on his back. "He might have been abandoned, but from the way he's drifting, it's just as likely the crew died while sailing. No way to know where their spirits went after that."

Alan paused. He didn't believe in ghosts per se, but he didn't *not* believe in them either. Space was vast, and he'd been raised as a pyrean for half of his childhood. "Aren't you worried they might be...vengeful?"

Natalia shrugged. "Isn't that part of the fun?"

Sven at last managed to push himself far enough onto his elbows that Natalia tumbled to the ground beside him. Sven rose to his feet, brushing out the wrinkles in his pants.

"You know there's no way you're coming, Nat," he muttered.

Before Natalia could protest, the good-natured amusement

drained from Sven's features. He looked serious enough (downright captainly enough) that Natalia fell silent.

"Ghosts or no," he explained, "this is a ship that has likely been missing for over two centuries. The cause of his disappearance is unknown. You're not official crew, Nat. Civilians stay here."

Sven glanced at Alan, also a civilian, as if to see whether he would protest. Alan shrugged. "Staying here suits me, but it sounds like you want to join the fun, Captain."

Sven's eyes gleamed, looking just a little sharp before they returned to a more even-keeled expression. "Aye. And we'll need a team that can deal with any sort of contingency — including the possibility of ghosts."

"**A**bsolutely not," Ragnar said. He waved his arms with almost comical intensity. "I went Communications track in the Academy for exactly this reason. I want to explore space from the comfort of my ergonomic chair behind this desk." He gestured to the communications panel in front him. "I don't do EVAs, I don't do space suits, and I definitely don't do ghosts."

"Your great-great-grandmother was a shaman, right?" Sven inquired casually. "It's always a good idea to have a shaman around if there are ghosts."

Ragnar's black eyes widened. Sven knowing this information came as a surprise, but he just as quickly realized who must have leaked that bit of trivia. He gave Gunnar a dirty look.

"Sorry," Gunnar mouthed silently. Yet from his conflicted expression, he appeared to realize the damage was done.

Ragnar sighed. It was very Fimmel of Sven to assume that Ragnar having even a tiny bit of Lenneel heritage somehow meant he'd inherited The Gift.

"I'm not a shaman, Capt, and ghosts or no, I get absolutely nauseous in zero grav." Ragnar paused. "Also I cannot emphasize enough how much I don't do ghosts." Having heard stories of his great-great-grandmother's work, the mere thought sent a shiver down Ragnar's spine. "Why not ask Sif. Isn't she part Lenneel too?"

"I am, and I'm coming," Sif said from behind Ragnar. She gave his shoulder a reassuring pat, but her smile, while kind, remained unyielding. "Don't worry, Ragnar, no one's expecting you to explore the ship. Just wait near the boarder and keep us in contact with the Swallow while we perform our survey."

Ragnar slumped. He knew a lost battle when he saw one. As the saying went, even cowards couldn't hide from the Fates.

In the end, the exploration team consisted of Sven, Ragnar, Sif, Reb, and Petr. Reb and Petr, as members of the boarding crew marines, were there as the muscle, while Sif, a senior engineer, would perform the actual survey and assessment. Sven was there purely for fun. Captain's privilege, Ragnar supposed. Which left Ragnar to play the role of unwilling, genre-savvy sidekick. However slim the chances of ghosts, Ragnar packed several protective tokens just in case.

Alan and Natalia were waiting by the boarder to see them off. Natalia looked displeased about being left behind, while Alan's expression appeared slightly apprehensive. He gave Ragnar a sympathetic look. As small as the glance was, it filled with Ragnar with a rush of gratitude. Never before had Ragnar felt such a deep kinship with the human inspector.

With the team assembled, Reb and Petr did one last check over everyone's suits before flashing thumbs up, and with that, the boarder's bulkhead doors opened. Only once everyone had shuffled past them did the doors slide closed. Ragnar both heard and felt the gangplank depressurizing as it recalibrated to the conditions of the other ship. As the atmosphere drained, the team marched in a line across the tube. Gravity lessened with each step until Ragnar floated off the floor. He flipped on his magnetic boots, which at once clamped to the gangplank.

"Did I mention how much I hate zero grav?" Ragnar muttered, slogging to the press-and-release tempo of his mag-boots.

Sif flashed an encouraging thumbs up, but Reb and Petr outright ignored him. They'd disengaged their boots so they could sail toward the ghost ship's hatch. Though The Merry Swallow had been built almost two centuries later, the basic dimensions of ship-to-ship boarders had been standardized for millennia, and this gangplank connected the two vessels without issue.

"Looks like we can open the hatch manually," Petr said, after popping off the side panel. "There's no power, but the mechanical emergency release is here."

By the time Ragnar reached the hatch, Petr had pushed open the hatch and floated inside, gun at the ready. Both Petr and Reb were armed with pulse rifles, while the non-combatants had only standard-issue daggers. Once Petr checked the hallway, he gave the others an all-clear to enter.

The ship's interior was claustrophobic. Much to Ragnar's dismay, he found such claustrophobia just as upsetting as the limitless expanse of space beyond the hull of the ship. Yet Sif and Sven seemed to harbor no such fears. Sif deployed her pair of autonomous drones to start the survey, before switching off her mag-boots. Sven disabled his boots as well, and both of them drifted down the corridor in opposite directions to look around.

"Will you look at that!" Sven breathed over the comm with obvious excitement. "This ship could be in a museum. Looks like they used some sort of metal alloy for the interior walls rather than fiberglass." The captain slowly spun in place as he touched the wall with a gloved hand. "That must be why the paneling is so blocky."

Indeed this ship did have a blockier appearance than the Swallow. On modern vessels, ship interior lines were usually sleek and bright. If Ragnar had one complaint, it was that those lines felt slightly too bright — too sterile. Yet sterile was better than the sensation this corridor exuded. The walls were painted a dark, pragmatic color that absorbed all but direct beams from their flashlights, while the paneling was jagged enough, the hallway lines severe enough, that it gave the place an unwelcoming, ominous air.

"Okay, let's check that comm links work within the ship, so we can split up to cover more ground," Sven said, after everyone had a moment to acclimate.

Sif's drones confirmed what Ragnar had hypothesized upon discovering the ship. While internal communications worked within the ship, the outside was painted in a way that blocked the Swallow's short-range communications. Whether this was due to it being older tech, or whether it was for the purposes of smuggling, Ragnar wasn't sure. Regardless, it meant that someone needed to stay close to the boarder to relay information between the Swallow and the team. Someone needed to wait here. Alone.

Sif and Reb disappeared around the opposite corner of the ship as Petr and Sven. Ragnar, having been left behind, slumped against the wall, but without any gravity, he just bounced off at an odd angle and half floated, half spun down the corridor. Nothing to do but wait. His helmet bonked against the opposite wall.

"Hmm," Sif said across the comm. "Looks like the systems are in hibernation mode. Everything's still functional. I should be able to restore basic life support and low gravity."

Without any atmosphere, Ragnar couldn't hear the ship engines purr to life, but he saw the emergency lights come on just before a low hum reached his ears. Atmo circulated through the ship, breaking the past two centuries of silence.

Ragnar righted himself to avoid face planting once gravity hit. Puffs of powder hissed through the ventilators near his helmet, and Ragnar wrinkled his nose in distaste.

"Looks like crud accumulated in the air ducts."

"Which is exactly why no one is removing their helmets even after we have minimal life support," Sif warned. After a pause, she added, "From these records, the ship's official name was G1MR-1034. Nicknamed Glamr by the crew."

"You found a terminal?" Sven asked.

"No, there's not enough power to restore the main system, but there are physical logs in engineering. No decay to the material, which suggests life support failed suddenly rather than the ship falling into disrepair."

"Okay, keep looking for answers. At least the Glamr isn't large. Smaller than the Swallow. Maybe a crew of twenty?"

"Could be," Sif confirmed. "There might be personnel records on the bridge?"

"Neither of you have found any...um..." Ragnar hesitated, his throat thickening around the words. "Um, no b-bodies, right?"

"Not yet," Sven replied cheerfully. "But I wouldn't count them out. Drones can't open doors, and we just entered the mess hall. Crew's quarters should be around here somewhere."

Ragnar realized how much he didn't want to know how the crew had died...if they died? Maybe they'd taken the escape pods, leaving the Glamr to drift for eternity?

"Hmm, only one escape pod was deployed," Sven observed, as if in response to Ragnar's unspoken hope. "It must have malfunctioned though. There are burn marks around its bay, and the emergency hatch is sealed."

"You think the internal doors blew when it tried to jettison?"

"Could be. It was the only one that launched either way. A ship of this size usually groups escape pods in one location rather than distributing them throughout the vessel."

With gravity established, Ragnar seated himself by the hatch door. He regarded the heavy space gloves encasing his hands as he tried to think about something that wasn't a missing crew or malfunctioning escape pods or creepy, abandoned ships.

"How's it going on your end, Gunn?" Ragnar said, desperate to make conversation.

"Good," Gunnar's voice was practically static even this close to the boarder. "I can barely hear you, though. Why don't you check back in a half bell?"

Ragnar's heart sank as he glanced at his watch. They'd boarded less than ten minutes ago. Another fifteen minutes seemed like an eternity. Ragnar would have killed for a tablet game.

In the end, Ragnar managed to restrain himself for a whole five minutes.

"Okay, that's enough silence. Let's talk, Gunn. We can play 'What is the other person trying to say?' maybe."

Ragnar waited, but only static answered.

"Gunn? Gunnar? Are you there?"

Gunnar didn't answer. It occurred to Ragnar that neither Sven nor Sif had spoken in a while either.

"Sven? Sif?" Ragnar's voice quavered as he spoke into the communicator. "E-everything's okay, right?"

Heart hammering in his ears, Ragnar tried to stop the tremors in his hands. *It's too early to panic*, Ragnar reminded himself. There were plenty of plausible reasons why no one was responding. It was too early to run screaming back to the Swallow and beg for someone else to rescue his teammates.

Footsteps echoed down the corridor, but the sound was not comforting. They were heavy, shuffling footsteps, accompanied by labored breathing. There was the faint screech of metal on metal, as if something metallic were being dragged along the floor.

It's a great time to panic, Ragnar disagreed. He flipped off his flashlight, loathe as he was to sit in the near dark of the emergency lights.

"Reb, Petr," Ragnar whispered under his breath, hoping that someone, anyone, might answer. "There's something here. Something...alive. Or maybe dead. B-but it's definitely here, and I definitely don't like it."

He tried to open the hatch beside him, but it didn't budge. There wasn't enough power for the electrical release to work, and the mechanical locks appeared to be stuck. As the footsteps drew closer, Ragnar glanced around, looking for someplace to run or hide.

"Please, please, please come and do something about it," he added before cutting off the comm. His eyes caught sight of the cargo bay entrance further down the corridor. Neither Sven nor Sif had bothered to investigate it, Ragnar realized. Had everyone failed to notice it?

Ragnar hated how loud his footsteps were. His heavy boots and thick suit left little room for stealth as he skulked toward the bay's service door.

He made a cursory attempt to palm open the door, but like the hatch, there was no power. Pulling off a side panel (and thank the Spirits at least this design had not changed in two hundred years), Ragnar tried the mechanical emergency release.

The footsteps were coming closer, the screech of metal growing louder. Any moment now, it would see him. Whatever *it* was.

He offered a desperate prayer to his great-great-grandmother, and at last the door slid open — whisper-quiet by some miracle. Ragnar slipped inside. Once the door shut behind him, he leaned against it, squeezing his eyes shut. He didn't want to linger, but he was afraid to move lest the creature would hear him. The sound of its footsteps was so close.

Thunk thunk screech.

The noises stopped before the door. Ragnar held his breath, willing his whole body to stop its trembling. But then the footsteps continued down the hallway. Ragnar didn't dare move or breathe until the sound was too faint to hear.

At last he took a deep, shuddering breath and opened his eyes. It took all of his will not to scream.

He'd found the crew.

Even without his flashlight, it was clear from the foreboding red of the emergency lights that the walls were stained with splashes of...something. The bodies must have been drifting for close to two centuries, but the low gravity had pulled them to the floor, forming crooked piles of limbs amid the cargo containers.

"Reb...Petr....anyone?" Ragnar's voice cracked. "Please respond?"

He kept his voice low, lest he wake the dead, but despite his best effort, there was only the faint sound of rustling in response. It came from the corner of the bay. Ragnar waited long enough to confirm that the rustling was real, rather than a fevered hallucination born of fear, before scrambling at the door behind him.

This time it stuck, the handle refusing to budge. In vain Ragnar pulled at the door — his prayers to his great-great-grandmother going unheeded.

The rustling grew louder and clearer until he knew they were undeniably footsteps.

Ragnar was still pulling at the door when he felt hands grab him from behind. This time, he didn't bother to muffle his screams as he was dragged deeper into the cargo bay.

Sif looked up from the stack of logs. An unpleasant prickle ran down her neck and spine, pulling her attention away from the ship documents. The cause of the Glamr's demise eluded her. The ship had indeed been a smuggler's vessel, and the last recorded manifest had been from its final (unfinished) run. The crew had smuggled ma'jenn goods from a distant port, and they were returning to pyrean territories when the records stopped. After running the napkin math, Sif decided that this sector was roughly where such a vessel would have drifted had the Glamr lost engine power shortly after his last recorded Gate hop.

"I doubt it was an engine malfunction," Sif murmured as she closed the final log book. The book ended abruptly, but there was nothing ominous within the records. Yet it was an uncomfortable feeling, knowing this final date and time was the last moment any of the engine crew had been able to continue their duties.

"I can't see anything in the records that would suggest an issue," Sif said on the comm. "Even two hundred years later, the engine shows no signs of damage. It must've been something else. Should we check the medical bay records? Sven, any luck on the bridge?"

Sven didn't respond. Reb, who until now had been wandering

the engine room and poking idly at the outdated ship fixtures, looked over at Sif. Sif sensed their concern even through their tinted helmet. Sif and Reb stared at each other for a long moment before Sif tried again.

"Sven, are you there?"

Silence.

"Ragnar? Petr?"

No answer.

Reb unholstered their rifle.

"You're going back to the boarder to make contact with the Swallow," Reb stated rather than asked. "Once you're safe, I'll search the ship."

Sif nodded. Any other time, Sif would be giving Reb their orders, but when it came to safety, her marine escort had full say.

As they moved toward the engine room's exit, Sif continued to check her comm.

"The comm says it's working," she muttered, unsure as to why communications would suddenly go down.

Sif was still checking the comm's status when the door opened, but she almost walked into Reb as they unexpectedly came to a stop. Sif glanced up. The corridor's atmo had been clear before, but now some sort of fine particulate filled the hallway, giving the impression of mist or smoke.

Sif remembered Ragnar's words — something about crud in the air ducts — but she'd dismissed them, assuming Ragnar was being melodramatic about a little dust. It appeared his words were an understatement.

Reb pulled out a braided metal cord from their suit's utility belt. It was for use during EVAs, but Reb used it to clip Sif's suit to theirs.

"Stay close, but if you lose sight of me, just follow this cord."

"Understood."

They started down the empty corridor. The Glamr was not large, and even with their heavy space suits, this walk shouldn't have taken more than a couple minutes tops. Yet every step felt heavy, and the farther they went, the thicker the particulate became. The corridor itself seemed to grow longer and longer.

Sif was just about to ask if maybe they were lost — if they'd taken a wrong turn and were circling some inner corridor — but then Reb stopped. They turned, looking past Sif and deeper into the fog. Sif didn't move, the sound of her breaths becoming uncomfortably loud inside her suit.

Abruptly Reb grabbed her by the shoulder and shoved her past them.

"We need to move," they said, raising their gun. "Now."

Sif did her best to run in the space suit, but it was awkward, even if low grav meant each step she took covered two or three meters.

One bound, then two, then three.

Sif had just hit her rhythm when she stumbled. She wiped out, gracelessly rolling down the corridor. A spike of pain shot through her elbow as her prosthetic forearm jammed against the ground. She winced, holding back a string of curses, and tried to rise to her feet. How in the bloody stars and nebulae had this corridor gotten so long?

"There's no time." Reb spoke with such low urgency, a shock of fear shot up Sif's spine. Reb rarely felt the need to talk, and in all of their time together as crew mates, Sif had never seen Reb hurry. "It's coming. You have to go."

Sif had barely recovered her balance before Reb unclipped her from their belt and shoved.

"Go!"

Sif still could not see or hear anything coming down the corridor, but Reb opened fire. Their pulse rifle's sizzling blasts filled Sif's ears. It was all she could do not to yelp before breaking into a run.

Sif ran until her breath became so heavy that it drowned out all other sounds — until she could run no more. Was the corridor quiet? Had the sounds of pulse fire faded? She listened for distant screams between her wheezing gasps and the hammering of her heart against her chest.

Don't think about it, Sif insisted to herself, gritting her teeth as she forced herself to stumble forward. *Don't think about it. Just get back to the ship. Everything will be okay if I get back to Ragnar. If we make contact with the Swallow.*

When Sif at last saw a turn in the corridor, a wave of relief washed over her. Around that corner was Ragnar and the boarder.

Almost there.

She was almost there.

Sif turned the corner and came face to face with a bulkhead door. It was closed, but when she reached out a tentative hand, it opened.

Unlike the foggy corridor she stood in, the room before her was clear and bright. At once she recognized the clean lines of the Swallow's engineering room — sleek gray walls and a shiny floor lined with terminals and stations. It was a Swallowtail-class vessel, yes, but not the Merry Swallow.

How...

"Sif, what are you doing? We don't have any EVAs planned."

Sif blinked. "Therese?"

Chief of Engineering Therese Fairson stood before her.

That couldn't be. Therese was dead. The Whistling Swallow had been lost decades ago. On instinct, Sif move her hand toward her eye. Her left eye was artificial as was her right hand — both lost in the Whistler's explosion. Lost in the same moment when Therese and the rest of the crew had been lost. Her fingers bumped against the polycarbonate of her helmet.

Why was she wearing a space suit?

"Time to get back to work, lass," Therese said, offering Sif the smallest of teasing smiles.

A flood of warmth, of relief, rushed through Sif. It had all been a dream. The Whistler was safe. Therese was alive. Herg and all the others...

Sif smiled. "Yes, that sounds wonderful."

She tapped the release clamps on the sides of her helmet, and the helmet emitted a faint warning beep as if this room didn't have full atmo. Sif hardly noticed. It was time to take off this suit. It was time to return to the life she'd thought lost.

~

Sven slammed into Sif. Given the Glamr's low gravity, he connected with more force than intended, and they crashed to the ground. The impact knocked the air from his lungs, but it also stunned Sif, giving Sven the time he needed to secure her arms.

He'd reached her before she had a chance to remove her helmet, he realized with relief.

Sif had gone limp, as if unconscious. When Sven peered through her tinted helmet, he could see her eyelids flicker, eyes rolled up to reveal nothing but their whites.

"Sif, what's going on?" He gave her a gentle shake. "Sif?"

No response.

If Sif had figured out what was happening, she was no longer in a position to explain. But without question, something was wrong. This whole ship was wrong. From Sven's watch, he could see less than two bells had passed since starting his survey, but events since boarding the Glamr felt hazy. He and Petr had started down a corridor. They'd reached the living quarters and then...

Sven's mind felt as if it were in a fog. Why was it so hard to think?

He shook his head.

"Anyone...is anyone there?"

There was still no response. Petr was missing, Ragnar was nowhere near the boarder, Reb wasn't responding, and now Sif was unconscious.

But what had possessed Sif to remove her helmet in such a place? When Sven had caught sight of her, Sif's motions looked so wooden, so trance-like, it indeed looked like possession. Evil spirits...hypnosis...Sven couldn't begin to guess.

Sven dragged Sif toward the boarder. As much as he wanted to find the others, he needed to contact the Swallow. If something had gotten into their minds as it had with Sif...if something was trying to destroy them...

"We have to get out of here," Sven muttered, as much to himself as to Sif.

The ship was small, so it didn't take long to reach the boarder. Ragnar remained missing, and in vain Sven tried to work the communicator that connected them to the Swallow's bridge. No response. On top of everything, the boarder's door was jammed.

Sven cursed, squeezing his eyes shut in an attempt to silence the low-grade headache that had begun to affect him since he had entered the Glamr's living quarters. The sound of laughter cut through the pain, sending a chill down his spine. It was low, self-satisfied laughter. Even with his headache, Sven recognized that voice at once.

Hadrian Steele.

The man who'd killed Hilde, Sven's older sister, so many years ago.

A cold wave of fear lapped at Sven's stomach. It was impossible. Steele was long dead. He'd executed Hilde, only to die moments later when the Crimson Monarch exploded. There was no way he was here. There was no way his spirit had flown as far as the Glamr.

And yet...

"Well, boy?" Steele's voice called out from the darkened corridor. "Congratulations. You saved that woman this time, but I wonder. Can you save them all?"

Sven bit his lip, willing himself to not get baited. That was what Steele wanted. Sven checked on Sif, who continued to twitch in her sleep.

"Chief, please," Sif murmured. "Please don't go."

"I'm going to find them," Steele all but purred. "I'm going to find your crew one by one, and I'm going to kill them."

Sven's whole body shook. Only when he felt a warm trickle drip down his chin did he realize he'd bit down on his lip hard enough to draw blood. Was this fear gnawing at him? Anger? Resentment?

For so long, Sven had tried to bury this past — to let go. And yet Steele's ghost followed him. He continued to haunt Sven. To hurt him.

"And once I'm done with your crew," Steele continued, "I'm going to take your other sister and that darling little human you have onboard."

A low, feral growl emerged from Sven's throat. Natalia. Alan. Steele had already taken so much from Sven — never again. Sven drew his dagger.

"No," Sven whispered, launching himself in the direction of Steele's voice. "No!"

The scream tore itself from Sven's throat as he dashed at Steele. Rather than donning a space suit, Steele wore plain clothes, and though he'd been dead for so long, his body seemed real enough as he evaded Sven's blade.

They scuffled, struggling for control of the dagger. Wrestling in low-grav meant bouncing against the sharp-edged walls and bulkhead after every impact, and Sven's head smashed against a wall as Steele tossed him aside. Sven's dagger skidded out of his hand and into the darkness of the corridor. The blood from his broken lip splattered across his face plate.

"Stay away from them!" Sven screamed with renewed fury, pushing himself off the wall to smash into Steele.

Sven wrapped his arms around Steele's suit, and together they bounced along the floor. This time, he'd kill Steele. This time, Sven would finish it.

Something slammed into Sven, sending both him and Steele careening down the corridor.

When Sven righted himself to see what had struck him, his eyes widened. It was also Steele. A quick glance at the person he'd pinned revealed a space suit — Petr's suit.

"How?"

The other Steele — the real one — bounded toward him.

"Enough, Sven."

Sven let out a desperate scream. He couldn't afford to lose. Steele would kill him. Steele would kill everyone. Sobs of terror threatened to overwhelm Sven, but he knew he had to fight.

"G-get off of me!"

Sven punched and kicked, but rather than respond in kind, Steele reached out, arms open, and pulled Sven into a tight embrace.

"No," he said.

Sven froze. The embrace was so gentle, so kind. How could this be Steele? Nothing made sense.

Tears spilled out of Sven's eyes, further clouding his vision. Was Steele alive or was he dead? Sven didn't know. He didn't know what was happening.

But Hilde...

Hilde was dead. He knew this with such painful certainty, it took his breath away.

"I...I want to go home," Sven whispered, pleading.

The person embracing Sven (not Steele, there was no way this was Steele) tightened their arms around him.

"Okay. Let's go home."

~

Alan was half-asleep when he felt a pair of eyes bore into him. He jerked awake at once.

"Sven!" Natalia exclaimed. She did her best to maintain a happy-go-lucky smile, but Alan could see the strain at the edges of her eyes and lips.

Sven remained prone on the med bay bed as he regarded Natalia and Alan with a dazed look.

"Nat...Alan..."

Alan felt a rush of relief. "Welcome back, Jiordson."

"What...happened?"

"A lot," Alan replied. The Chief Medical Officer entered the med bay, and Alan knew better than to interrupt her work. Rather than elaborate, Alan said, "But the summary is, everything is okay. Everyone is okay. I'll explain more once Katja gives you the all-clear."

Considering Sven had been unconscious for close to ten SP hours, Katja discharged him quickly enough once he awoke. Having already done this procedure on the other members of the exploration team, she'd gotten efficient at her testing.

Once back in their room (with Natalia under strict orders to busy herself elsewhere until Sven recovered), Alan did his best to explain what happened. The exploration team failed to check in on the half-bell mark, but the drones returned to report on time, giving the Merry Swallow its first clue that something wasn't right.

On a hunch, Katja ran a handful of tests to analyze the drone's samples of the atmospheric compounds that had been released when life support was restored.

"Space mold?" Sven asked dubiously.

"Space mold," Alan confirmed.

"Really?" Sven was resting on their bed, back propped up by pillows, while Alan sat beside him, his hand placed lightly on Sven's shoulder. Sven was still weak from the ordeal, but Alan could hear a slight whine in his tone. "I thought space mold was a myth? A stereotype?"

Alan shrugged.

In all honesty, Alan thought the "ma'jenn eat space mold" stories were made up as well, so he'd been just as surprised.

"Katja suspects the smugglers must have picked it up when they took their cargo out of the ma'jenn port," Alan explained. "It turns out this mold permeates through the materials used in pyrean space suits, so you were all affected shortly after boarding. The rumors say it causes extreme hallucinations in pyreans, which seems likely given what happened. That's probably what led to the demise of the Glamr's crew in the first place."

Alan didn't feel the need to elaborate. The recovery team found the crew's bodies on the bridge and in the medical bay — places the exploration team hadn't reached before the space mold sent them into full sensory hallucinations.

"Gunnar put out a distress call on ma'jenn channels, and fortunately one of their ships was nearby." Alan continued, "It seems they've had this region flagged since the Glamr's disappearance. They've been waiting for it to reappear after all these years, so they were more than happy to reclaim their property — and very graciously cleaned up the mold as well."

Sven's nod was shaky, and his words came out slowly and unsteadily.

"I got separated from Petr. I heard screaming. Sif was taking off her helmet, so I tried to stop her. Was that real?"

Alan nodded. "It was. Sif is fine thanks to you, but she didn't say much about what she saw either." Even after she returned to lucidity, Sif's eyes remained distant. She claimed not to remember anything at all, and despite his occupation, Alan was not one to pry.

Sven hands trembled, and he looked down at his lap. "I don't really want to talk about it either."

Alan touched the back of Sven head to run a gentle hand through his spikes of purple hair. "You don't have to."

"The others?"

Despite everything, Alan's lips quirked into a wry smile. "Ragnar was apparently living out a scene from one of his cult Earth horror movies. Space Reaper: Blood Moon's Harvest or something like that."

"Sounds like a masterpiece," Sven murmured.

Alan arched an eyebrow. "If it had tall ships, you'd watch it."

For the first time since waking, Sven smiled. "Absolutely."

"So Ragnar we found hiding in a closet," Alan explained. "Reb had reverted to some sort of survivalist action hero and was stalking the ship. The ma'jenn helped us flood the ship with a sedative so we could recover them."

"And Petr?" From Sven's fearful expression, he must have remembered quite a bit.

Alan hesitated. He kept his tone as neutral as possible. "Petr is fine."

Sven's face tightened. "I hurt him. I remember hurting him."

"Both of you were confused," Alan insisted. "As I said, Katja already cleared him, and whatever he saw in his hallucinations shook him more than his scuffle with you."

Sven nodded. He squinted up at Alan as if noticing something for the first time. "Alan, why do you have a cut on your forehead?"

Alan cleared his throat. "Well, time being of the essence, I used my Elite inspector privileges to bypass Valtra's orders to wait on the ma'jenn."

Sven blinked. "You...boarded the Glamr. Alone?"

Alan unconsciously touched where his head had smashed into the space helmet. When Alan tried to restrain Sven, the captain had fought back like a cornered wild cat. It took all of Alan's strength to pull him off of Petr, but as much as his head hurt, Alan considered it good fortune he'd returned as unscathed as he had.

Sven's eyes widened. "Alan, you're part pyrean! What if you'd been affected?"

"I'm barely pyrean," Alan observed. "Only an eighth, and human enough to be allergic to poison ivy. I decided it was worth gambling."

"Poison ivy?" Sven asked with a blank expression before understanding flickered across his face. "Ah, you mean dawn's blush vine. Humans get so weird about it."

Pyreans loved cultivating plants and animals from other planets, and much to humanity's chagrin, poison ivy was one of their favorites. Since pyreans had no allergic reaction to the urushiol oil, they cheerfully and safely experimented with poison ivy's colors, form, and growth patterns. Since he had lived on a pyrean planet for most of his childhood, Alan had far too much experience with poison ivy cultivars, which pyreans often showcased in their luxuriant botanical gardens.

"Yes," Alan replied in a flat tone. "We're the ones who are weird about it."

Sven ignored the joke. His face was serious as he touched Alan's cheek. "Thank you, Alan. Thank you for helping Petr. And...I'm sorry. I'm sorry I hurt you."

Alan took Sven's hand in his own, giving it a gentle squeeze. "As I said, everyone is fine. No more worrying, okay? You need to rest, Jiordson." He leaned over and kissed Sven's cheek. "So rest."

Although Sven settled back onto their bed, his face remained pensive.

In answer to the unspoken plea, Alan added, "I'll be here, Sven. I'll keep you safe from ghosts, and space mold, and whatever else comes your way."

"But not dawn's blush."

"Yeah, no way," Alan agreed. "If it's poison ivy, you're on your own."

Sven smiled. With that reassurance, he at last fell into a deep, dreamless sleep.

6

THREE ALGORITHMS
BY G.M. GRAY

"Got a job lined up," I say to the night air. "Gang business. Good pay. Nothing hard."

"Don't need another toving job," RAIDer retorts. "We're still flush from the last one, yeah?"

I expected her to say as much, but I couldn't help asking. Never mind that RAID blew half her cut tonight. She's the type that lives in the moment. A real bodhi that way. The thought almost makes me smile.

As I fumble around in my coat pocket for a lighter, I reflect on this latest beating. Going out with RAID means drugs and fighting, and tonight she's had both in excess. I'm not much into either, but it's better than the other option, which is not going out with RAID. That means being alone, and being alone means facing the darkness. As bright as the corp-state shines, it's steeped in dark.

I used to keep the shadows at bay with liberal doses of morpho-dyn, but I've been clean for over a year, and I want to stay that way. The cravings still hit fiercely whenever I dwell on the emptiness gnawing at my insides, but that's why I've got RAIDer. She's nothing if not a pillar of fire, and it's worth the nicks and bruises to stand in her light.

I check with my tongue for loose teeth, but everything's in place. My face is mostly in one piece as well, though my knuckles are tattered, and my sides ache with what's likely broken ribs. It wasn't the worst night I've had, though. Hackers rely on their brains and skills for jobs, but we can fight with the best of them — my junkie physique notwithstanding.

"I can work it alone," I shrug, lighting my cigarette. The breeze is chilly but pleasant on the roof of our safe house.

We sit amid scraps of concrete and discarded metal, and they make for plentiful, if not comfortable, seating. It's well into the night, and Zephyr's Tiers gleam in the distance. Tier residents have a more stringent curfew than us Outskirters, but the towering buildings remain lit day and night. Out here, nuclear is contraband so the best we get are the dim flickers of gas and petrol.

RAIDer snatches the cigarette from my lips and takes a long drag. The tip flares in the darkness. She sucks greedily until a bit of ash hangs on the end. She's a grisly sight in its glow. One of her amber eyes has swollen shut, and the other is dark and glistening from a burst capillary. There's dried blood caked around her nose and mouth, but a gleaming trickle still flows over her lips and down her chin.

She hands the cig back to me, and I regard its butt, now sticky with globs of blood. It's reminiscent of lipstick smears.

"Keep it." I wave.

RAID chuckles before taking another drag.

"This place is such a shit hole," she remarks. Smoke trickles out of her one functioning nostril. "Wish it'd tovin' burn."

She says those words so often, they've lost all meaning. This annoys me, but most everything RAIDer says annoys me. I get how slagging awful life is, but I have the decency not to bitch and moan at every opportunity.

Most nights, I'd just nod and listen to her rant, but something must be stirring inside of me, because I snap, "Then set it on fire."

RAIDer looks at me in surprise. Her one open eye narrows, and for a rare moment she regards me with something close to respect. "You serious?"

I snort, because it's too absurd to be serious. Yet it's not entirely a lie, either. I run a hand through the thin strip of hair down my head in frustration, as I regard the hazy gloom around us.

The sun and moon aren't visible from the Outskirts or lower Tiers. There's a perpetual blanket of smog smothering out the light of the heavens. Beyond Zephyr's walls, they say it's possible to see stars more plentiful than the lights of a city, but from here, even the craggy mountains surrounding Zephyr Corp's valley are concealed.

Not for the first time, I wonder about the world outside. Not life in Zephyr's sister cities, which would no doubt be as tript as the shit here, but life in that unknown territory between — life in the wastelands. Zephyr does business outside the walls, but only for Tiered citizens. For Outskirts rats like us, leaving the corp would be a one-way trip into exile.

Supposedly, hackers do well out there, but "well" is surely relative. In the wastelands, tech is scarce and resources are limited. The only things they have in plenty are gang wars and empty desert. I tell myself that's the sort of trade I'd be willing to make, but even I'm not dumb enough to believe it. RAIDer has made it clear she'll never give up her gig in Zephyr for second-rate dirt jobs, and I can't leave on my own. I've never been good at alone.

I pull my knees to my chest, and admire the weighty oppression of the city around me. On the best of days, Zephyr feels like a prison, but in this moment, its bars, filth, and despair overwhelm me. The Outskirts are Zephyr Corp's latrine, and everyone knows it. We sit here and take it because there's nothing else. No other choice.

"What's there to be serious about?" I say, wanting end the too-long silence. "Zephyr'd just stomp the fire out and us along with it."

RAIDer settles beside me and curls a fist into my jacket. Maybe she means to be comforting as she presses against my ribs, but I hiss in renewed pain. Yet I don't try to move her. Instead, I shrug an arm over her, as much to ease the pressure on my shoulder as it is to huddle against her. Nights are cool, but Zephyr is just too crowded, too enveloped in smog, to get cold.

"So long as we get paid, it don't matter," she murmurs, and I wonder if she believes it.

She soon falls asleep, her breaths harsh and uneven from the blood in her nose, but I stay up till dawn. The sky grows light. No doubt the sun is rising in the east.

We spend the next day honing our arsenal of scripts and checking on zombied machines. It's not the most exciting work, but maintenance is important in our business. I recline on dusty cushions, while RAIDer sits against a crumbling plaster wall by the leaky kitchen. In nothing but undergarments, her dark skin appears even darker from the thick, crude lines of cheap tattoos. They're scrawled across her body and shaved head like amateur graffiti. She has on earbuds, but I can hear savage screaming and frenetic pounding of drums all the way across the room.

It's not long before OverByte breezes in without bothering to disarm our security measures. He must have bypassed them completely, which is typical. RAIDer glances over at him before cranking the music player's volume. She makes no pretense about hiding the gesture or her disdain. He just smiles, as if he thinks her hatred is hilarious.

OverByte has good looks, a charming disposition, and undeniable brilliance. In a word, he's insufferable. But he's a buddy, and that means more than any list of personality defects. A buddy will be there when things get rough. A buddy won't screw you for a piece of the cut. In our business, a buddy is hard to come by.

I give him a nod of acknowledgement even if I can't bring myself to smile.

"Hey Nexus," he says, ruffling my 'hawk as he settles beside me.

I ignore the mock-affection, but with him so close, I can't work anymore. Against my better judgment, I give him my attention.

"Bytes."

He props his chin on a hand to regard me with his honey-brown eyes. "You're looking handsome. Pink this week?"

I shrug. Rarely do I settle on one hair color for long. "I wanted something visually offensive." I raise an eyebrow. "Is it working?"

He grins. "Oh yes."

Despite myself, I feel my lips quirk. Self-absorbed as OverByte is, his easy-going humor and wit is a pleasant change from RAID's violence and my ceaseless wallowing. He's undeniably fun, even if I know better than to trust his motives when making small talk.

Bytes is too polite to stare outright, but I see him eyeing my screen. I don't have anything confidential displayed, but it makes me nervous to know that he's looking. He's a better coder than me, and a better hacker in general. But one thing he isn't better at is being gracious. I'm not in the mood for a lecture on best practices as he finds reasons to talk down to me.

Yet instead of offering critique, he asks, "You managed to access Third Tier transport schematics, huh?"

I keep my tone neutral. "Yeah."

"That's quite the feat." OverByte's tone remains cheerful, but when I glance at him through lowered lashes, I see the tension in his smile.

It had been his job, but he had to scrap it when security had gotten too close. No doubt it burns him that we succeeded where he had failed, but if he's looking for comfort, I'm not his man. No way in hell am I gonna assuage his wounded ego.

"It wasn't too hard," I say with a dismissive shrug.

"How'd you do it?" Bytes is no longer grinning, and I can see him trying to keep his jaw from clenching.

I flash a small, sardonic smile. "Teamwork."

He forces a laugh, as if it's a joke. Maybe I even meant it as one, but it's still the truth.

Hackers are notoriously vain. While it's not unusual for them to run in loosely affiliated circles like the three of us do, most prefer to work actual jobs alone. RAIDer and me are different. We do our best work as a team.

Even on her good days, RAID is a wrathful jinn - unpredictable, fierce, and petty in her cruelty - but on jobs, I know exactly how she'll move, and fight, and think. This property is symmetric. RAIDer can dismiss me, hurt me, hate me, but at the end of the day, I'll have her back. She can count on me for anything. We've always been like that — two halves of a whole.

Once I told her I thought we were soul mates. RAIDer laughed in my face and told me to keep my faggoty feelings away from her, but she must have liked the idea. Later, while she was getting high out of her mind on her usual cocktail of alcohol and amphetyn, RAIDer lavished me with her version of affection. For anyone else, they'd be laughable attempts at tenderness — nails but no fists, holds but no pressure — but such caresses coming from her meant all the more for their inadequacies.

I regard OverByte's grimace and realize that despite his talent and intelligence, Bytes can't compete when RAID and me are together. RAID and me have something special - something that binds us tighter than blood or sex or camaraderie. She's my light and I'm her dark, and together we're actually worth something.

When Bytes starts pointing out the flaws in my work, couched under the guise of advice, I know he knows too, and this knowledge makes his jealousy that much sweeter.

RAIDer and OverByte are fucking again. They don't really try to hide it as they emerge from a back room. RAID's clothes are in disarray but she looks satiated, and when she comes to sit by me, I can see blood under her fingernails. Bytes is covered in bruises and scratches. He looks put out, but he knows as well as anyone that RAID likes a little violence with her sex, so I have no sympathy.

Bytes will fuck anything warm, but he and RAID never get along on any level, personal or professional. As far as I can tell, sex between them is more of an arms race — a need for mutually assured destruction. It's just one more act of defiance in the swirling cesspool of our lives. If they're getting anything out of it past that, I can't imagine. But then, I wouldn't fuck either of them.

RAID sits beside me, slinging an arm around my shoulder. The gesture might have been meant as affectionate, but just as likely it's possessive. "Bytes has a proposition."

I narrow my eyes. "If it's a threesome, the answer is 'no.'"

OverByte bursts out laughing, "What, Nexy? I thought you were into boys."

I raise an eyebrow. "I'm not into egotistical pricks."

Now it's RAIDer's turn to bark with amusement. OverByte winks. "Never fear. There'll be plenty of time to change your mind later. No, for now, I thought we should all play a game."

I look between RAID and Bytes, and I feel the hairs on my neck rise. RAIDer is practically quivering with predatory anticipation. OverByte's smile is a bright slash against his dark, handsome face. I don't trust either of them.

"What sort of game?" I ask with caution.

"A graffiti battle. First to a Second repo wins. Should be right up your alley."

My lips flatten into a thin line. I've always had a flare for tagging, but Second Tier repositories aren't on the wider Zephyr Net. This means physically infiltrating the servers, and it's a long walk up to Second. I regard RAIDer. She stares back at me with confidence.

"I gotta talk to RAID," I say softly. "Alone."

Rather than question me, Bytes bows before collecting his gear. He pulls his headphones over his ears and then wanders toward the roof. I turn back to RAIDer.

"You won't take a toving gang job for cash, but you want to poke at Zephyr for giggles?"

She plays with one of the many piercings in her ear. "Don't be so uptight, Nexy. It'll be fun."

"Bytes is just pissed that we finished a job that he couldn't."

"So what? We'll piss him off again. It'll be great."

I feel my hands clench into fists. "Is this really enough for you? Playing stupid games that waste away your life, because it's already so meaningless? I'm toving sick of it, RAID."

RAIDer stares, but then her bright eyes turn hard and angry. I wonder whether she'll decide to punch me or smash the junk around us, but instead of doing either, she rises to her feet.

"Then go."

"W-what?"

"You heard me. Fuckin' get out of here. You think you've got everything figured out? Maybe you're better 'cuz you never lose your cool or need to prove nothing, but guess what? You're made of the same meaningless shit the rest of us are made of. Just another mopey, loser junkie clogging up the Outskirts."

The word "junkie" has a special sort of sting coming from her.

I'd like to pretend I kicked my habit out of sheer strength of will, but in the end, it was RAIDer who did it for me. After beating me senseless, she locked me in a room and refused to open the door no matter how much I screamed and kicked and bled.

After coming down in that awful shit hole, I lost my taste for easy, perpetual bliss. The constant bruises and cuts of RAIDer's fire probably make me a different sort of junkie, but as humiliating as that may be, it's better than the darkness.

I think about what it would mean to leave her. Life doesn't begin and end at corp-state walls. Beyond them is the promise of something different, if not something better.

I meet her eyes. "You want me to go? Fine. Maybe I will."

RAIDer scoffs. "Yeah, right. You're too much of a pussy. You gonna find a different crew? Maybe ditch Zephyr completely? You always talk like you'll do it, but you ain't gonna leave without me. You ain't got what it takes."

I want to prove her wrong. I want to collect my gear and never come back. I tell myself I never want to see her or OverByte again. I tell myself I hate everything in this city. I hate this place. I hate this life.

But RAIDer is right. I can't leave without her. As long as she's trapped, I'm trapped beside her. If Zephyr's a prison, RAIDer is my personal cell. I stare at the grimy floor beneath my feet and admire how there's something comforting in the familiarity of self-loathing. Like an old friend, it's always there for me.

RAIDer folds her arms, and her hard features soften a fraction. "This can be it, though." When I don't respond, she clarifies, "Our last job in Zephyr."

I regard her with uncertainty, because it's too much to hope that her words mean what I think they mean.

"If you help me beat Bytes, I'll help you ditch Zephyr," she continues. Her face is honest in a way I've never seen before. "You know I can't do it without you. You need me, and I need you. That's how this works. We're soul mates, remember?"

She extends a hand. I realize something's changed. We're going to leave — actually leave. The prospect is more frightening than I had imagined. But as long as we're together, RAIDer and me are unstoppable. I grip her hand in my own.

"One last job, and then we're gone."

It takes a couple months of planning and a handful of smaller jobs to acquire the gear and hacks we need to get around Second's physical defenses. OverByte is all but silent during the process, which gives us confidence.

The job goes well. It goes frighteningly well.

Once Zephyr's clean, precise archives are overwritten with our digital art of questionable content, it's easy enough to slip back into the anonymity of the Outskirts. A couple of arachnids pick up our scent and trail us as far as the Fourth Tier, but we lose them in a maze of shops and tenements. All in all, it's barely a challenge.

Only when we fail to contact Bytes do we realize things have gone wrong.

"You think they got him?" RAIDer asks. For once, she's not trying to hide her fear.

"No," I say more adamantly than I feel. "He's not gonna die that easy."

But I imagine poor Rewind, who did die that easily. She was as good as OverByte when it came to hacking, but that didn't stop those loan sharks from smashing her brains in at a bar. At the time, we'd forced ourselves to laugh. We'd joked how her favorite color had always been red, and she at least got to die covered in it, but that's not funny anymore. It never was funny. The thought of her dead, and now OverByte possibly dead as well, makes me sick.

If he really didn't make it, that means we're alone.

"It's just the two of us," RAIDer says, as if echoing my thoughts.

I mumble, "Then...we should go. Get the fuck out of Zephyr ASAP."

RAID shakes her head. "We hafta find Bytes. We find him first, just in case."

And though I never liked OverByte, I realize RAIDer is right. OverByte's a buddy, and buddies watch each other's backs. And if he's still alive, he needs us.

I nod. "We'll find him."

~

After several weeks, we track down Bytes. I'm the one who retrieves the final piece of information, and that means I have the honor of telling RAID. My stomach turns as I relay the truth to her.

"He sold out."

RAIDer doesn't look up from her portable, but the clacking stops. In this skeletal belly of a defunct factory, even the smallest sounds fill the space, and it's suddenly too quiet.

"No." RAID shakes her head with a childish petulance. "No."

She shoves aside her gear and stalks toward me. I'm sitting on the floor, and without bothering to ask, she bends over and seizes my portable. Over and over, her eyes scan the files acquired from a security station in Third.

Whether or not Bytes finished tagging, foot patrols detained him as he passed through the Tier. They held him for just over 24 hours before a special unit from Zephyr proper arrived. Five hours later, OverByte and the unit left the station.

RAIDer shakes her head. "They forced him. He wouldn't sell out. Not to Zephyr."

"There wasn't an official report," I murmur. "No one roughed him up. And after he walked out of there, alive and unrestrained, a security team retrieved his belongings from a safe house." I feel my fingernails dig into my palm as I meet RAIDer's eyes. "He sold out for a cushy gig in 'proper."

"Sell out" is the dirtiest word you can sling at an Outskirts hacker. It means betraying comrades and ideology, and giving up proud, hard-earned freedom for the pampered shackles of corp life. It means serving the enemy and all that the enemy represents.

But there's an undeniable allure to it. Selling out buys all the luxuries of Tier life: access to the latest and best tech, and most important of all, the promise of safety and security. Anyone in the Outskirts who claims not to covet those things is either a liar or in denial. But our desire for the very things we despise is what makes that the bitterest of truths. Our desire is what makes corp slavery that much more repugnant, and sell outs that much more revolting.

RAIDer is quiet for a long time before she slumps down beside me.

"What about his woman?"

I think about Bytes' woman — a quiet prostitute with a sad smile. I remember her only vaguely. Nothing about her is exceptional, and beyond the occasional times Bytes brought her along for an evening, she hardly figured into our lives at all.

"What about her?"

"I dunno. I just," RAID trails off. "I guess I thought he was serious for once. He really tried to do right by her. Like maybe it was love."

"OverByte only loves himself," I retort. "And he didn't love her enough to stop fucking you, did he?"

RAIDer stares at me like I'm an idiot. "What's sex got to do with love?"

Any snide remarks die on my tongue, and with a grimace, I slam shut my portable. "Yeah. Love's got nothing to do with nothing."

It occurs to me that both of us had indeed fallen in love, not precisely with OverByte, but with the idea of something that runs deeper than money, drugs, or the cheap thrill of breaking things. We'd never believed in friendship, but we'd craved it. Like children, we'd unknowingly and naively chased after it.

We gave OverByte pieces of ourselves not because we liked him or had any obligation to him, but because sometimes it's good to give pieces of yourself away without hope of getting something in return. It's good to feel human. Thus we fought for him, trusted him, loved him.

But OverByte hadn't loved us. When he saw something better, he took it and ran. And the sting of this isn't so much because of his betrayal, but because we allowed ourselves to be betrayed. We marched around in our armor of world-weary nihilism, but in the end, it was nothing but a facade.

RAIDer stomps to her feet.

"I hate this place," she snarls. For emphasis, she chucks my half-empty bottle against a wall. It smashes in a satisfying explosion of glittering shrapnel. "Everything smells like shit. Have you noticed that, Nex?"

I shrug.

"This toving city," she growls. "What's so great about it? You don't see those wasteland assholes clamoring to get in, do you? Maybe that's because the joke's on us. We think we're on top, but really, we're the world's shit hole. Everyone's laughing at how tovin' self-important we are, because we're nothing. Nothing!"

She kicks a pipe for emphasis, and its hollow *thong* reverberates through the room in harmony with her echoing screams.

"We can leave," I say on impulse.

I expect RAID to turn her fury my way, but instead she stares, as if noticing me for the first time.

"Leave?"

"Yeah."

She stalks over. As well as I know her, I can't begin to imagine what she'll do next. I tense up in case of violence but despite gripping me by the neck, instead of striking, she presses her forehead against mine.

"We'll leave," she mutters, and it's almost a plea. "Me and you."

"Yeah." I smile. With caution, I wrap my arms around her and she allows it, curling into me. I continue with more insistence, "We can just go, right? Just the two of us. We don't need OverByte or anyone else. Fuck him. Fuck 'em all."

"Yeah. Fuck 'em." She's become kittenish in her docility, and it frightens me. "Just me and my better half."

To hide my nervousness, I ramble on, "We'll go tomorrow. Just gotta pack up some supplies, and then we're gone. We're unbeatable when we're together, remember? Plenty of opportunity in the waste-lands. Why stay in this dump?"

"I want to go."

"Y-yeah. We will."

We huddle together, and I continue whispering how we'll leave everything; we'll just walk away from it all. The two of us is all we need. Zephyr can't stop us. No one can. RAIDer doesn't say much, so I convince myself she agrees. I am certain it's finally going to happen.

Not that I'm surprised when she's gone the next morning.

A few days later, I hear she's taken a job stealing corp tech from one of the inner Tiers. A few weeks after that, I hear that she's dead. She got shot up by patrols on the way back and she left a trail of blood all the way to the Outskirts. The arachnids, with their canine sense of smell, had no trouble following her. They tracked RAIDer to a safe house where she was dying of blood loss and retrieved the payload. They didn't bother to kill her. Didn't need to waste the bullets.

I don't know what I hope to accomplish, but I go to find her body. I walk up the familiar, crumbling stairs to enter a room painted with the dingy browns of dried blood and that smells of rotten meat. RAIDer's body is decorated in a similar fashion. I've never seen that much blood. In death, RAID has become a grotesque sort of quiet. She's so still, it leaves me numb all the way to my core.

At some point, I must have collapsed to my knees. My eyes never leave her corpse. I've lost my soul mate. She was not my better half, but she was a part of me — my wild, strong, hateful half. She'd escaped Zephyr the only way she knew how, and it hadn't involved teamwork or walking away. OverByte had abandoned both of us, and now RAIDer had abandoned me.

I dimly wonder about my own escape. A blaze of glory wouldn't suit me as well as it suited RAID, but there's always sweet morphodyn to dull life or benzo to silence it. Still more cost effective is the wrong end of a gun. That thought is enough to make me smile, but OverByte was into optimization more than me or RAIDer. Efficiency never suited us. It certainly never suited me.

I never had RAIDer's defiance or Bytes' adaptability. The most I ever accomplished in my life was a series of addictions and the paralysis of cynicism. Take those things away, and what's left?

I stare at RAIDer's face, still frozen in a grimace of pain, and I realize there's nothing left at all. There's nothing left to hold onto or to love, and knowing that emptiness is agony. There's also nothing left to tie me here. It's the same as coming off of morphodyn and breathing for the first time. It's realizing that the only chains that matter are the ones in my own hands. All of this torment is because I'm free.

I have the same choice in this moment that I've had in every other moment of my life. I can let myself die, or I can try to live. I can bury myself deeper in this pit, or I can attempt to stand.

Whether or not I succeed is uncertain. For so long, RAIDer stood for both of us. She had the strength to bear two, but that doesn't mean I don't have enough for one.

I wonder what it would mean if, just this once, I could manage to live on my own. Alone.

In the end, leaving Zephyr isn't hard at all. It's as simple as breathing, or eating, or sleeping, or fucking. It's as simple as all of those things that are supposed to come naturally, yet we manage to muck them up anyway. This time, at least, I manage to get it right.

The algorithm is simple. Put one foot in front of the other. Repeat.

7

THE BLOODY SHOW
BY ELLY CALL

R ichmond, Virginia loved a conversion. The Belle Isle
hydroelectric station revamped into an outdoor gallery.
The downtown restaurant strip became the borders of
Kill Mouth tour, and Amanda the high school prep transformed into a
college goth.

The crowd around her howled, sardined into sweaty, fleshy froth.
She was too far to see the members of The Lamb herself, but their
guitars snarled dominance from all directions, gathering the lot of
them up in triumphant riffs just to smash the mash of bodies into
Broad Street's dirty asphalt. Life-changing, sober. With mushrooms?
Sublime.

"Bitch, we're *sarchovies*," she breathed to her friend Christian,
mid-headbang to her right. He lifted his white-painted face and the
stage light strafed the wing of his cheek. Was the cheek flapping or
the light wobbling? Over its motion, his dark-lined eyes searched
hers with beautiful concern.

"What?" He inclined his curly-haired head. Her lips were right at
his ear.

"Your eyes," She said, her lips teasing its shell. *Oh no. Oh god, that wasn't platonic.*

He pulled out his phone in an instant, but not to photograph the evidence of her thinking of him as more than a friend. Instead, he checked his eyeliner with frantic worry. It was perfectly applied. He was as achingly attractive as he'd always been.

"They look fine!" He shouted over the music — then he smiled in realization.

"Ohhh I get it," Christian said, teeth flashing, "faces are always weird on it! Don't look too long!" *This was a mushroom thing.* It was funny, but her body was too heavy for the laugh to leave.

He clapped his large hand on her shoulder.

The warm impact rippled downwards, warping her like a fun-house mirror. *I am a cartoon,* she beamed his way, but he didn't seem to hear it like she'd heard his thoughts earlier (just snippets, but she knew). Instead, he stared. She held those wide eyes. Doe eyes. She could cry into them and they'd catch the whole thing.

"Amanda?" His voice melted into the space between the drone of her heartbeat and the heaving music. Like he was crawling down her throat, but in a good way.

"Oh," she said.

"Oh...?" He searched her face. Ultimately, it was okay to be in love with one's only college friend. Especially if they never found out.

But the guilty must confess.

Grrng Grrrng Grrng EEEE!!! Agreed the guitars of the Lamb.

The violet lights traced along Christian's jawline and slid over the plush of his lower lip. He nodded his head, and she discovered midway to the edge of the crowd that he was walking her to a brick-walled alcove next to a dumpster. It was only a little quieter.

"Don't worry," She twined her fingers into his knot of curls. He stopped her hands gently, the cords of his throat flexing as he swallowed.

"'Don't worry' like you feel fine, or 'don't worry' like I should worry?" he said. When she didn't answer (*his eyes were wide as moons!*) he continued, "I think you should have just micro-dosed. The heroic dose only *sounds* cool. In reality, it's just, like...a shit ton of material."

She put her finger to his mouth. Christian inhaled, the cold air wooshing past her top knuckle. The pink of his lips and the pink of her pointer-nail *wom wom*-ed together.

"Electric." She breathed.

"Well, yeah." He spoke with slow care around the pad of her fingertip. "That's the...whole point of taking it."

When he stopped talking, his mouth was still a little open. There was a line at which his outer lip gave way to a spit-slicked interior. Queer... she touched one finger to the meeting place. He was a glory of textures. She moved her other hand to the soft hairs at the back of his neck. He stilled. He was afraid to scare her away with a movement. Or...*oh, no.* The words echoed in her throat, clanging the whole way down. She'd misread.

She dropped her hand.

"No," he said.

"I shouldn't — I'm sorry." Her wretched words slunk, embarrassed, to nest in the front of her black mesh festival shirt.

"That's not what I meant," said Christian. And he dipped his head to press his lips to hers. She nearly sobbed into their softness, filling her hands with the yoke of his shoulders, his waist. His nose pressed into the divot of where her cheek met her nose. She could see their mouths burrowing into one another, the slide of cheek-turning-tentacular spectacular. Their two faces becoming one.

"SICKOS!"

There was a blinding flash.

A leering man from the crowd in front of them lowered his phone then disappeared into the thrash of other crowd-goers. Amanda lifted her head to yell after him, but Christian pulled away and looked at her so earnest and awestruck that all she could do was clumsily pull him back to her mouth. Christian's arms swooped around her neck and waist and he walked her back against the brick of the building. The rest of the crowd was thrashed, oblivious.

He thumbed up the hem of her shirt to finger the crest of her hips — tease forward, firm tug back, then tease again. An involuntary noise fluttered in her throat and he answered, a chant in breaths that the screams of the singer and the rata-tat of the drums quickly consumed. *Could wetness wash down a body's thighs and reach the ground in a flow strong enough to water a plant?* She reached for his waistband and his phone fell out of his hoodie pocket.

"I'm sor—," she said into his mouth.

"Stop it." His hands slid into her hair, then he broke the kiss with a lingering peck on her cheek. But he did not bend to get his phone — instead he held her gaze and sank, his back to the enormous crowd. Eyes still on hers, he kissed down the underside of her rib cage, her waist, and finally to the crest of her hip just above the waistband of her skirt. Her hips rolled after the touch, seeking him as his knees reached the cracked pavement. The back of his head was almost hit the hem of her skirt as he finally looked down to pocket his battered phone. It would only take him one look up...

She put her hand on his head in benediction, and he allowed her to push his head entirely back in surrender, eyes on hers. When his eyes drifted down under her skirt, his lips parted with naked reverence at what he saw.

The shock of her arousal wrenched her pelvis into sure alignment, irreversible machinery at the top of a precipice. Certain and chambered, her heart drummed in her ears. *Closer, closer* — he smoothed his hands up her torn fishnets. The hairs at the back of his neck were as fine and soft as she thought they'd be, and then his curls disappeared under her hem. He gasped into the join of her legs.

The air shattered. The roar of a gunshot ripped through her eardrums, rattling Amanda's teeth like a punch in the face. She clapped her hands to her head — *had she been shot?* Christian's head dropped forward almost through her legs in the same instant. She stumbled back, legs tangling in his arms. Struggling for balance, she failed and hit her shoulder hard against the dumpster, spilling both of them into the rest of the crowd.

She swam her arms to stay upright but the forest of flailing limbs clawed back, crazed and desperate. A woman screamed to her right. The crowd swelled and Amanda and Christian hit the ground. As the crush loomed overhead, a hand yanked Amanda to her feet.

"— Cover!" Shouted the man who'd pulled her up, spit flying from his lips and beard. He tried to yank her deeper into the alley, out of the way of the shooter, but Christian gripped her thigh, leaning hard. The bearded man let go. With one last wild-eyed look, he sprinted behind the building and out of sight. Amanda pulled them both back into the corner of the dumpster and the brick building wall.

Amanda detangled herself from Christian as the crowd swarmed past, a confusing stream of color and noise.

"Christian? Is there a shooter? This trip is... " her vision rippled, fuzzing with black spots. She was losing control. He didn't move.

"Christian!" His head lolled back, nearly into the surge of the crowd. She caught him in time, but barely. The crowd was screaming, crushing others in its path.

"Hey —!" Her hand at the back of his neck was warm and wet. She tried to stabilize her vision but it appeared he had two heads, the dark of his curls eddying, coiling.

"Stay still," she said, her lips numbing, pulling them both against the dumpster and hopefully out of sight. If there was a gunman, he'd be on the rooftops. Broad Street was full of mid-height office buildings all with openly accessible roofs. She would know. She'd climbed them with Christian nights before.

"You know how if it's going bad? Dude, please —"

He didn't look at her, his head was still down, his hair over his face. Over his eyes.

"How big can hallucinations be?"

She shook him, hard. "Dude!"

He flopped against her side then fell forward, deadweight on the ground.

"Stop...stop...stop..." She pulled him up, her breathing hitching. An itch was beginning under her skin, one that made her want to move uncontrollably, but she couldn't risk getting the gunman's attention. The boundaries of the buildings marched like ants. Even though there was a moon, seeing anyone atop the buildings was impossible.

The venue was nearly cleared, people hiding behind cars. The number of screaming faces tilting past were thinning. Shafts of streetlamp light shone down on Christian's curls and her knees. *If he passed out, it's up to you to help him*, she told herself. Resolute, she put her hands on the sides of his face and pulled his head back. His wide dark eyes were open completely, unblinking and unfocused.

Reality tore into white thunderous noise, shards of asphalt slicing into Amanda's shin. She scrabbled back, an animal noise fighting out of her heavy throat. There was a gunman. He could see them. If Christian wasn't hit, he was in shock.

She kicked the dumpster away from the brick wall with her legs and pushed Christian's body behind it. Her breathing screamed out from between her chattering teeth and she tried without success to stop it. She checked his arms, legs, torso — all completely untouched, aside from mud here and there from their fall onto the street.

"Christian — please it's so bad, when do shrooms end?"

He leaned against the dumpster, saying nothing. Shudders muddied her vision further, the air and colors loud in her ears and skin. She wedged herself next to him to hold him against her, his head tipping against her shoulder.

"Are you ok?"

He didn't make a noise. Roiling dread swept her body, yawing, needling, and unreachable. She steeled herself, and then checked his face again.

The sides of his face melted, moving like the sides of the buildings. But his forehead, in the center of her vision, was still enough. Above his white-painted nose was a perfect, dime-sized hole haloed in grey residue. It looked like Christian had been shot in the forehead.

The mushroom-induced dread wasn't an emotion now. It was an unbearable spasm, crawling in her muscles and bones.

"I'm sorry, I'msorry I'msorryI'msorry. You were right, the heroic dose was a bad idea," Amanda pulled his face into her neck, her surroundings spinning and pulsing. *If she could just get in close enough to hear his heartbeat...*she held his head to press her ear to his chest, but her hand at the back of his head sunk, then continued to sink. Her hand was braced against a gaping head wound.

Her breathing grated raw from her throat now, sweeping hair from from behind his ear in a pantomime of tenderness.

"Help!" She screamed, then shrank back into the opening between the dumpster and the wall. The gunman wouldn't be able to target them by sound—why had she waited so long to say it? She fumbled for the phone in her boot with her free hand, the numbers swirling on the screen. One by one she caught 9-1-1. Impossibly, the call went through. But as the operator began speaking, Amanda's words died in her mouth.

At the corner of the building the formed the back of Amanda and Christian's hiding spot, right where the dark opening to the ally beyond them began, a shape burbled up from the size of a spent bullet to an infant. It shifted and stretched on two legs to toddler, child, and then teen height. As sirens sounded, too late, from downtown, the transformation of the figure slowed.

"Ma'am are you there?" The operator prompted.

"There's..." Amanda's throat clenched so tightly that her voice came out scarcely louder than a pained breath. She tried again.

"There's been a shooting. It's right in front of the National. Like, by that...Italian place. There's a shooter. I think he's on the roof."

"I gonna need cross streets. Ma'am?"

The figure on the corner had become an adult man, naked and

staring at his hands in wonder. If he wasn't a hallucination, he was a lone target in the middle of the now-abandoned parking lot where the crowd had stood. Should she keep watching, Amanda would see a man get shot.

Christian's doe eyes gazed starward, empty. Her hand was deep in his head. Would letting go mean releasing a deluge of blood and killing him? He wasn't cold yet. A red rivulet ran down her forearm to drip from her elbow.

"I won't move," she buried her nose in the curls on his forehead. "You're doing good. You're okay —" then her mouth shuddered to hard for her to continue and her breathing hitched, uncontrollable. Too fast, no purchase — she'd dropped her phone. Over Christian's curls she could see the 9-1-1 lady had hung up.

Blue and red lights flooded the streets and the figure at the edge of her vision walked into the night as another burbled to adulthood by its side. The two figures walked towards the stage together until they melded with its swirling, jumping spotlights. Their silhouettes were quickly crowded out by an advancing line of police officers.

"Hi, hi, h—," she stopped herself, the word wanted to come out as a loop. "Officers please, could someone tell me if this is real?" She said, her lips cold and her body shuddering. They didn't answer.

"Can you please tell me if this is real?" The man who'd said 'Sickos' earlier watched, furtive, from behind the line of officers, phone camera pointed her way over their shoulders.

⁓

"*C*an *you please tell me if this is real?*"
       "*Can you please tell me if this is real?*"
   "*Can you —,*"

"Can you turn that off?" The female officer from the desk said. The recording began to play that unsettling recording again and Amanda opened her eyes. She was leaning against the bars of a holding cell. A cheap blue fleece blanket was draped over her. The female officer stood up, and the recording paused.

The recording was her own voice, Amanda realized, and it was coming from three male officers huddled around a phone in the corner.

"Come on Carla, ain't nobody cares about a killer," said one of the men. He was an officer with blonde hair, pale skin, and a name tag that read "Jones." The female officer (nametag "Heins") blinked, seemingly surprised to find herself standing up.

"Ain't about her. It's about my damned peace of mind." Officer Heins said, sitting. In doing so, she caught Amanda watching her. Heins engrossed herself in her smartphone.

"Excuse me, Ma'am?" Amanda said.

The female officer stiffened. For a moment, Amanda worried she'd pretend Amanda hadn't addressed her. Finally, she looked up, raising well-manicured and expectant eyebrows. She was somewhere in middle age, and for a moment she reminded Amanda of one of her aunts. It was strange to see a familiarly-shaped face filled with such breath-taking loathing.

"Can I have my phone call?" Amanda said. Heins looked back down with pursed lips, not answering.

Panic pushed Amanda's voice forward. "I need to tell someone where I am, I've got someone who'll be worried." She hadn't spoken to her parents in two weeks, they were worried but she'd wanted to enjoy the independence of being at school just a little longer. If Christian heard about this, he'd never let her live this down. *If he's alive.* The dark cold voice made her freeze so completely she did not hear Officer Heins' response, though her mouth moved.

"You don't get a phone, but want to see your video?" Officer Jones's voice was gentle, caring like someone trying to win the trust of a wild animal.

"Jones —," Officer Heins said from the desk, starting to rise again but catching herself. She sat back down, arranging her face into tired apathy. But her eyes were too wary for Amanda to chance any answer to Officer Jones.

"What?" Officer Jones said, his eyes bright. The flush in his cheeks was too high. Was he on something? She hadn't done enough drugs herself to know.

Jones walked up to the bars, so close Amanda got to her feet to stand away from them. He held his phone out to her and it began playing as, behind him, on the television screen, the same video appeared: A girl leaned against a wall while a young man kissed her. Christian. There he was, kissing down her side. A frantic hysteria seized at her throat at the intimate act onscreen, the obvious enjoyment on her face, then him bending his head to the ground — a body briefly blocking the camera's view, but the awful video wasn't over yet — then his head was pushing up her skirt — a flash from between her legs, the shock of his head caught in her skirt, his body beginning to completely fall back. The image was blurry but even as the phone holder jolted back with the sound of the gunshot, Amanda could still make out the explosion of material from the back of Christian's head as he slid down her leg. Then, finally, the video cut to the high-gloss, sympathetic but serious face of a male newscaster.

"Where did it come from?" She asked, unable to make her voice louder than a shaking whisper.

"What? Gonna, shoot the photographer too? Fuck no, I'm not telling you his name." Jones laughed his way back to the two other men in the corner, both watching her with wide smiles. *The bullet, where did the bullet come from?* She wanted to clarify, but her stomach reeled and she stepped back from the bars, fighting nausea.

The banner under the video on the TV answered the question instead.

"HIDDEN SKIRT GUN: TRAGEDY AT THE NATIONAL"

Christian fell back exactly like in the bad trip. His painted face blank, his body ragdolled on the ground as the girl onscreen shook him, pulled him close — Amanda vomited on the floor.

"*Bitch*," Heins hissed from the metal desk. She stood up slow and tired.

"*Hoooooo* you didn't tell me she was unstable!" said Jones, his phone already out and recording.

"You really needed to be *told* that?" Heins snapped. "And put that away."

"You fuck up, you clean up, Amy. Also, Virginia's one-party consent." he said to Heins, grinning. Amanda's vision reeled, her heart rate spiking. *What a shit way to die...a heart attack in jail...*

"I'm okay..." Amanda said from far away, the beginning of an iron hardness forming in what felt like her very womb. Even the touch of her own awareness on her lower body felt unwelcome. The more she leaned into the feeling of no feeling, the oblivion...well, that was certainly easier.

Heins's voice cut through the peaceful fuzz.

"Nope, I'm done. Not my time shift." Heins snapped, already at the door out of the room of holding cells before Jones could say otherwise. But Jones only smiled.

"We'll cope," he said. Amanda would be left alone with the three of them.

Heins looked at Amanda long enough that Amanda felt a small flutter of hope. But Heins's eyes slid off of hers. *Limited sympathy,* Amanda realized. Like the sympathy one would give an injured animal. However sad the animal was, it wasn't like it was a person.

"I'll get a supervisor to relieve you boys," said Heins over her shoulder. Without Heins, the room was quiet, secret. There was no one else in the holding cell. The door to the rest of the precinct had only a thin window in, paned with thick glass and criss-crossed wire. All she could see through it was the wall beyond.

The three male officers blurred into one large shadow at the edge of her vision as Amanda tried to focus only on the security camera at the corner of the room. Whatever happened would be recorded.

"You hear me?" hissed Jones. *Oh no, they'd been talking to her the entire time.* Why was she here?

"Oh, I'm sorry, Officer Jones." She almost sounded normal.

"There. That's what I thought," Officer Jones said, and he opened the holding cell. The two other men stepped through. Behind their heads, her face took up the entirety of the TV screen. It was her senior picture from high school. She'd always been only a semi-confident smiler at best.

"Ma'am, I don't want to have to use force!" Officer Jones's near-yell startled her enough that Amanda's teeth clacked together, her heartbeat hammering as he put his hand on his waist next to his baton.

"This is a routine medical check. Go sit on the bench," whined one of the male officers. Also white, with watery blue eyes. His nametag read "Evans."

Is it? Amanda's galloping heartbeat took on an irregular stunted pace, like it was having difficulty turning over. The floor was getting fuzzed over by black dots and she held out a hand for the bars of the small cell.

"I—I'm—I think I'm having a heart attack," Amanda managed to mumble out through her quickly numbing lips.

"You're in good hands, I have partial EMT training," said Evans. His voice sounded so forced-casual it made her hands go cold and sweaty. When he touched her waist to navigate her back to the bench, she jumped.

"*JE-sus,*" snapped Jones.

The very fact of the officers' shepherding made the bench a wrong destination, a place where only bad things would happen. *HIDDEN AK?* blared the TV over Jones' head as the other white cop, Evans, looked through her.

"You owe Officer Jones your trust," he said. She stepped back, adrenaline spiking, and the back of her leg hit that very bench. The officers had successfully maneuvered her into the corner of her cell, right in front of it. Officer Nadar, the only brown cop between the three of the men, blocked the free end of the bench, looking away, but Officer Jones knelt on the floor in front of her with interest.

Evans completed their little quarter circle around her and the cell corner.

How had she ended up here if she'd been paying attention? Was it alright to kick a police officer? Was it alright to say something? Probably, if she didn't they might say she agreed. But fighting at all could be resisting arrest. *Aren't I already arrested?*

"Did you hear Officer Evans?" Officer Jones said, his eyes even shinier, his skin even more flushed.

Don't don't don't whatever the three of them had gathered around her for don't —

"Don't!" she said.

There, the word was out. At least she knew for herself that she'd managed to say it.

"Come on, don't flatter yourself — this is a routine check and no one thinks you're attractive. Sit," snapped Jones.

She sat immediately with a bolt of self-hatred. So they were going to look for the hidden AK being discussed in confusing snippets of closed captioning on TV and she'd sat out of surprise. Was it possible to move her legs closer together to block any view up her skirt? She needed to stand again. *Did it hurt to be tased or would you be too shocked to tell? Badum-ch.*

"Ma'am, did you hear him?" That was Officer Nadar.

"What?" Her tongue was leaden, slow in her mouth. Officer Jones was in the same position Christian had been in, only Jones was craning his neck with a look of revulsion.

"Shut up, this'll be quick anyways," Officer Jones replied. He reached forward towards —

"Kyle, don't be an idiot," said Officer Nadar.

Officer Evans and Officer Jones all but recoiled from him. So this wasn't routine. She knew it hadn't been. *Why had she believed them?*

"I want my lawyer." She wanted it to sound strong but her voice was high, afraid. *Damnit.* This room was surprisingly large with all four of them bunched in one small corner, the door so far away, the camera obscured by their height and her lack thereof.

"A lawyer, Ma'am? For standard procedure?" said Evans, his air of hurt almost practiced.

But Officer Jones ignored her from between her knees, saying instead, "You must've stuck that shit way up there to not see any evidence." He'd leaned so close she could feel his fetid breath on her lower knee. "Take this," he indicated her crotch area, "off."

Take off my vagina? Her mind swam for a moment before she realized he must've meant her underwear.

"Kyle! You said —" Officer Nadar said, looking up from the ground.

"Amir, remember how we have to do our fucking jobs? Gynos are money. I promise this won't bring her any closer to fucking you."

"It's Dinesh," said Officer Nadar.

"What?" Office Jones replied, incredulous.

"My name is Dinesh, not Amir."

"Your pronunciation was *really* close, though. I think we can all admit," jumped in Officer Evans, rubbing Officer Jones's shoulder.

Officer Jones snorted and put his tongue in his cheek, smiling and nodding.

"What the hell is wrong with everybody here tonight?" he said, finally. Officer Nader and Officer Evans jumped and looked at the ground. "Any other murderer would be shot on the scene. Why the hell are we still bringing in these people alive?"

"Due process?" mumbled Dinesh.

"Stop thinking with your dick." spat Jones.

Officer Nadar went still and Officer Jones snorted, shaking his head. Then, to Amanda, he said "Alright, you gonna be a big girl or do we need to do this the hard way?"

If there were a gun up there, the hole in his forehead would have a halo of ashen residue too. Amanda could see it. The flush in his face, the beads of sweat on his forehead, the twitch at the corners of his mouth razed for good.

Amanda sloughed off her underwear in as un-sexy a way as she could, not standing from the bench and Officer Jones flinched at the suddenness of the movement. She dug her nails into her palms. *There was no gun. This is a disgusting joke. They'll see —*

"God, fucking disgusting." Officer Jones squinted under her hem and took out a pocket-sized sanitizer, applying it to his hands quickly. *I'll be alone and able to claw her skin off soon enough.* She adjusted her feet.

"Any sudden moves and I will use the baton," said Officer Evans crisply, almost self-righteous. Maybe that sentence was why he'd joined the police. Amanda tried to nod, but her uncontrollable shaking had returned. Where did any of them imagine a gun would fit? *There was no gun. Christian was a bad trip, Christian was alive, Christian —*

"Woah, what is..." Officer Jones leaned in, his breath on her lower knee. But before he could get any closer, Officer Nader spoke:

"What happened to calling the gynecologist?"

"You want to leave? Fucking leave, dude. We're actually protecting people. What are you fucking doing?" Officer Jones sat back, spots of color high on his cheeks now.

"Kyle, where would the gun even *go*?"

"That's what I'm try to *fucking* figure out!" Officer Jones stood in an instant. "There's something metal between her fucking legs, I saw it myself. I'd say I'd show you but I bet you'd love that, right?"

Officer Nadar strode past him, wrenching the cell door then clanging it shut behind him. The door to the room slammed. The three of them were alone but for the high whine of TV static.

"Don't worry man," said Officer Evans, rubbing Officer Jones's shoulder again.

Office Jones batted his hand off. "Shut up, faggot."

He leaned forward again and Amanda looked at her pile of vomit next to his ankle. *If there is a gun, let it shoot. Then they will shoot. If there's no gun it could not have been me. Christian at least wouldn't have been because of me.* Officer Jones' finger made contact. The silence in the room stretched, Amanda's stomach turning, clicking over in revulsion — no shot. There was nothing in there. She breathed a sigh of relief.

"Fucking freak, you should *not* be liking this," said Jones. The flush in Jones's cheeks had turned into high red patches and his breathing hitched, his eyebrows inching up, eyelashes fluttering, mouth opening.

"Uh, what are you seeing, man?" said Officer Evans. Officer Jones sat back on his heels, wiping his hand on the dusty concrete.

"It's all metal."

Her stomach sickened and swooped. He just wanted to make Officer Evans complicit. *My gun would have shot. There is no gun.* Officer Evans had gotten out his phone light and stooped too. Now would be a good moment to sit up.

"I can see the barrel, but it's tough to say…"

"Get in there, man. You know better than to shoot us huh, sweetie?" said Jones, patting her thigh like the hindquarters of a horse. She could see herself saying don't again, but this time stronger — sitting up like a cadaver folding up at the waist.

"WHAT THE HELL I THOUGHT AMIR WAS MAKING SHIT UP."

A white-haired, compact man in full police regalia of a colonel rammed his hand into the side of the holding cell, Officer Nader at his side. Jones and Evans stood in an instant.

"Put your fucking phone down asshole, where the hell is Heins?"

"Amy took her break, sir," said Officer Evans. "We were—"

"Desperate to lose our precinct more money? You couldn't have found a *female* officer? 'They're everywhere now,' isn't that everyone who doesn't ask, Jonathan?" said the colonel.

Officer Evans balked, his hand on his baton again, but this time for comfort. Officer Jones stilled, his jaw flexed.

"You can sit up," the colonel added to Amanda, curt. She folded up at the waist, but the emotions were gone. She reached around and finally, under the bench, found her discarded underwear.

"Jesus," the colonel turned away, rubbing his face as she put them on.

"She took them off herself."

"After you threatened her. Amir told me that too," said the colonel, then he stopped, sniffing the air until he saw Amanda's vomit. "You couldn't even be bothered to call a *janitor* you were so focused on —?"

"Colonel Johns, there's good reason." Officer Jones held out Evans' phone. The colonel slapped it out of his hand and it fell to the ground with a *crack*! At the noise, the colonel turned. Whatever he saw was enough to make him pause in earnest.

"Metal," Officer Jones said.

"I don't care if there's an AK shoved up there. We don't do medical exams and even dear old *dad* knows that."

Impossibly, Jones' sneering face went blank. *Was this his version of contrition?* The colonel drew himself up to his full height and then said, with great loathing, "Bookkeeping. Both of you."

Officer Jones opened his mouth, mutinous, and the colonel continued, "until the end of the year."

Bookkeeping was business. Her major, Amanda thought with a rising, almost-giddy hopelessness. Her regular, one-day job and goal was someone else's punishment for...whatever had just happened. *There was no gun on the screen, there was no gun on the screen,*

"Amir's called for an armored vehicle to Planned Parenthood. They'll look for free," continued the colonel. "Now clean up that fucking mess."

As the Colonel turned away, Officer Jones made eye contact with Officer Nadar and, with slow deliberation, made the motion of shooting himself in the head.

~

"He shot it to the press. There's no other way," said Officer Nadar to the armored vehicle driver.

Amanda had never been to Planned Parenthood, but her parents forbade it with enough specificity that she knew exactly which way not to go: up Hamilton, where the cheap cars started looking more expensive, and the hodgepodge of brush and knobbled old maples gave way to ornamental hedges and manicured evergreens.

"So he's finally out," said the driver. Hidden as he was by the seat, Amanda could discern nothing about him aside from that he pronounced his "o"s like a midwesterner.

"It's *Kyle.*" Officer Nadar, it seemed, was a frenemy.

"Is Kyle not on probation or…?" It was the officer next to Amanda who'd spoken, a tall Black woman whose skin glowed in the red of the stoplight ("Officer Laurence" on her name tag). At Officer Laurence's words, the four other officers shifted their shins against their riot shields.

"No, he is," said Officer Nadar, carefully.

"Ah, daddy's influence prevails," said Officer Laurence.

Amanda's palms sweated at the silence the rest of the police officers responded with. It was only okay for the other officers to talk about Kyle. Did Officer Laurence know? The vehicle was close to Planned Parenthood, but not close enough to leave the car.

"There was too much public support," replied Officer Nadar to Officer Laurence, finally, his eyes on the crowd of people lining the road to the clinic with signs under their arms. Officer Laurence snorted, to which he added with a sigh, "…plus the dad thing."

The pregnant silence returned as the officers tried, without success, to fit their legs around their shields in the small space.

"Jonathan vouched for him, too." Said the officer to her other side.

Officer Laurence snorted again — then a change came over the vehicle. The police officers' eyes went flat like sharks, their hands gripped their shield backs, patted their holsters, put on sunglasses, and slapped down helmet visors.

"Are we here?" Amanda looked out the window and there was her reflection. No — it wasn't her reflection after all. It was a photograph of her own face wreathed in uterus cutouts and marker-drawn rifles. *Come and take it.* The entire thing was half the size of a door.

The white woman who held it glared at the bus. Other signs vied for the armored vehicle's sight line, "unborn lives matter" and "spare the gun spoil the child."

As Officer Nadar opened the door, a silence impressive for its crowd size fell over the packed parking lot. But when Amanda emerged, her hands cuffed in front of her, the sea of heads exploded in cheers.

From the parking lot to the office exit into the long hall of exam rooms, the officers of Amanda's escort peeled away in pairs. When she finally found herself in the furthest examination room from the front with only one officer, Officer Laurence the lone female cop, she almost felt naked.

"Has anyone called?" Amanda asked. Her voice sounded like dry wind out from under a drier rock.

"I don't get notified." Officer Laurence eyed the two covered windows into the exam room. Unsatisfied, but resigned to their presence, she patted the gurney. Amanda barely had time to beach herself awkwardly onto it, tearing the sterile paper cover in the process, before the officer undid Amanda's pants without preamble and lay the supplied sheet in a nearby chair over her legs. Then, the officer bent, unlocked one cuff, and secured the other around her own wrist. Amanda stared at her.

"Beats the bed frame," Officer Laurence said.

Then she took out her phone to start a game of snake with her free hand. Normally this exam room would be a devil Amanda knew, but now she interloped on the familiar "gynecology visit" dance as a maybe-dangerous partner. In another life, the worst part of the visit would be that the stirrups would be harder than she remembered. She'd scoot as far forward on the table as she could and it somehow wouldn't be far enough. She'd apologize. The speculum would be too cold. She'd hope this time wasn't a pap smear time. It would be. This time she was either a killer or the cause of a death and the gurney pointed her vagina-first at the seahorse curtain that offered a polite layer of privacy from the exam room door.

In a flurry of marine-print, the gynecologist arrived.

"Ah, the celebrated 'visit with a friend.'" The gyno was an older white woman with a pleasant, warm voice. Beyond the crow's feet that normally would have heralded a generous smiler, her eyes were flinty.

"Ma'am, we have reason to believe she has a deadly weapon concealed on her person."

"'*In* her person' your colonel's wording, and I understand she sent pictures of it to the police. From jail, too! Quite the feat." The gyno's emphasis was so syrupy and cruel, and Amanda almost pitied Officer Lawrence, who's mouth stuck open in response. "Don't they confiscate phones in the holding cell?"

Officer Laurence found her voice. "Ma'am—" but the gyno wasn't finished.

"Are YOU even aware of this news story?" she asked Amanda.

"Uh..."

Was there a way to say she wasn't surprised and hadn't taken the pictures herself and was there any way to stop them from showing them on TV...all without angering Officer Laurence?

"Of course you aren't. Coeds don't 'sext' the precinct." Even the visage of the gyno's warmth was gone.

"Not everyone thinks the same on the force," Officer Laurence replied, stalwartly staring again at the windows. When Officer Lawrence said no more, the gyno turned to Amanda.

"I am sorry for the handcuff, dear. It's out of my hands — hah! Now, if you please, *scoot*."

The gyno continued to talk so animatedly about how quickly people forget things that her nervousness started to stoke nerves in Amanda, too. On the TV behind the gyno's smiling head was a blurry shot of Christian slumped against her leg, his head falling from her skirt.

"Ah! I fear I'm looking right down the barrel." The gyno's voice attempted brightness, but shook. *No.* The noises in the room blurred into one high ringing sound, and the roiling terrible itching under Amanda's skin lifted its head, promising mind-wiping panic.

"Care to take a gander?"

The gyno did not wait for Amanda's answer. She took up the hand-held mirror on her set of table tools and positioned it a little just away from Amanda's vulva.

There, under the paper of the gown and against her regular dusky pinkness was the tip of a cold, circular barrel. Amanda breathed a deep breath to loosen to muscles there as much as possible, the image on the mirror shaking.

"It's a gun, sure as daylight. Though you'll find me at a loss in regard to type." The gyno's voice, so warm and comforting before, was now fainter and higher.

Why haven't I felt it before? How did it get in there? The questions flew fast, faster, her panic rising until finally Amanda managed, "Can you get it out?"

"'Get it out', dear?" The gyno looked at her over the rims of her tortoise-shell reading glasses in earnest concern. "You don't want to keep it?"

The fluorescent light buzzed, Officer Laurence closing the game of snake on her phone.

"Never let anyone tell you that you aren't made exactly as you should be," said the gyno, nodding assuringly, "and if you haven't notified your parents, do. They oughtta be proud."

"Ma'am, can you confirm there is a weapon in place?" Officer Lawrence extended the arm connected to Amanda as far as she could in effort to see into Amanda's vagina from the gyno's position.

"I—I haven't been able to call." Amanda's awareness was lifting, hovering away from her body. This wasn't the horror she expected, or the urgency she needed. Keep *what?*

"Why would I not want it out? I don't know what it is!" Amanda tried again.

"Nor do you *need* to know." A soft smile played over the gyno's wrinkle-edged lips. She put her hand on Amanda's shoulder, rubbing it gently before Amanda could squirm away. The gyno gently took the mirror from Amanda's hands and turned her attention to palpating the skin just above and beside the crests of Amanda's hip bones.

"No matter what the media says, your body is no accident. To change anything about it —" she chuckled, her shaking uncomfortably jostling Amanda's stomach. "Why, that would be to deny your very womanhood. Curses aren't curses, but unrevealed gifts from above. My dear, the safest abortion is *no* abortion."

"I —" Amanda fought to form words with her quickly numbing mouth. "But it's not a baby."

"No," agreed the gyno, "it's something far greater."

But before she could say more, the marine curtain swept back again. A short Black woman in a lab coat swept in. "You're needed at the front," she said, revealing a winsome gap between her two front teeth. "Something about —"

"I'll see for myself," the gyno said frostily. Then to Amanda, "Sit tight. I won't be a second."

The smiling woman in the lab coat dropped the smile immediately as the gyno passed to glare at Officer Laurence.

Officer Laurence held up her hands immediately, yanking Amanda's with them.

"Sorry Dee, it wasn't my idea."

"I *know* I made myself clear." The new nurse's voice was low and furious. Her name tag read 'Didi Johnson'

"I can't say no and gripe about some ex," snapped Officer Laurence.

"*Some ex—*" Didi's eyes widened, incredulous, and then she saw the cuff.

"She's *handcuffed?!*"

"It's standard procedure!"

"I will *standard* your *procedure* right out of this goddamn *building*, I swear to —" Didi went quiet as footsteps approached the door.

They passed, a false alarm, and Officer Lawrence's stony face bent in earnest concern.

"You've got a plant on your staff," she said.

"Who?"

"That gyno. Something about 'best abortions are no abortions'?"

"Yup, we know," sighed Didi. "We've *been* gathering evidence."

"Nobody can fire anybody, right? Similar thing on my side but...yeah. Nepo baby."

The two women laughed together a moment then looked away. Officer Laurence gave Didi a sly look. "Still got that laugh, huh?"

"Yeah, like how you still stupid. " But the corners of Didi's mouth twitched. They were so wholesome, so in love. And Amanda's heart was a creature that'd broken into the house of her rib cage, gotten lost, and died. The best it could do now is stink up the place. *If I'm the gun, then...*Christian's beautiful face turned up to the sky, empty, sightless, hazed terrible and heavy over her vision, over her clarity of thought.

The gyno returned, batting the marine life curtain out of her way. Auric black dots danced in Amanda's line of sight.

Didi offered a cherubic, expectant smile to the harried white woman.

"Don't give me that look. You knew what they wanted," the gyno snapped. Even her harsh tone of voice wrenched at Amanda's throat. Her mind was going to break. She was going to crumple.

"There *is* a militia. Happy?" the gyno finished.

A militia. They could decide when they shot. They probably prided themselves on never shooting their family, on defending their loved ones. A pin of panic stabbed at Amanda's throat, igniting a certain contraction in her stomach that clicked into place, roiling outward —

The gyno swore and leaped back, spilling her roller chair onto its side. Officer Laurence jerked back, wrenching Amanda's arm with her. Something was going on between Amanda's legs — but around the wrenching in her arm and the sheet Amanda couldn't quite make it out. The gyno carefully extended an arm to grab a hand-mirror from a drawer by her overturned chair. She pointed it between Amanda's legs.

"Lord above — *there!*" Her eyes were wide, her wrinkled face slack. She dug in her coat pocket and extended her own phone to Amanda.

"Point the screen at the mirror from the side, child."

Amanda took the phone with her hand. It wasn't locked. She pointed its camera at the mirror the gyno tilted her way, panic wom-womoming with growing intensity. *If I have a gun, I killed him. If I have a gun...*

"I'm sorry to interrupt, but Dr. Gilmer, we need to evacuate," Nurse Didi said, touching the gyno's shoulder gently.

"Have the patients left?"

"No, but —"

"In a moment. She should at least get to see her body for herself."

Between Amanda's shaking hand and the similar shake in the mirror the gyno tilted her way, the pink of her flesh blended with the sheet—until she caught a streak of silver. Amanda stilled her hand. The slim, carbon-grey barrel of a gun extended from the shadowy folds of her sex. Amanda's stomach lurched and with the feeling the long, thin, fluid-covered muzzle extended, tapped at the glass of the gyno's hand mirror. Dr. Gilmer hastily pulled the mirror, and her hand, out of harm's way.

"You have to get it out. Please —" Amanda said, her voice rasping as her stomach and chest clenched harder with disgust, fear. She pulled herself up on her elbows, lowering her knees slightly. She could see the muzzle. "Oh God —!"

The gyno grabbed her shoulder and shook it.

"No more movements. Relax, and stop making the rest metal. There's no need. "

"The *rest*? I'm trying to stop!" Amanda cried.

"Dr. Gilmer, please! " Nurse Didi said, her voice high and shrill.

The gyno only returned to Amanda's knees, yanked back the

sheet, and slowly extended the hand mirror again. Hands shaking, Amanda focused the phone's camera on it again. Sleek chrome-y metal that now flowed over her chronically uneven labia minora and covering her entire pubic mound like a cool second skin. *I killed him, I killed him —*

"Miss Anderson. Explain this metal." The shock of hearing her own last name from the gyno's mouth lashed Amanda briefly from her accelerating spiral of panic.

"I don't know!"

The gyno set down the mirror and approached again, this time feeling again at Amanda's midsection, massaging something at the underside of her ribs. Dr. Gilmer's face transformed in an instant from terse fear to fascination.

"I can feel the stock corner. Truly an entire gun does seem...ah, and, here's the rest. Like a second, steel spinal column."

"Ma'am. The threat was already immediate. If we don't leave, we will die," said Didi, this time as much to Officer Laurance as the gyno. But the gyno was lost in the process of transforming Amanda from person to specimen.

"Their hearts are in the right place. They're men of God. You truly think she'd be safer out there?" Dr. Gilmer's eyes blazed with determined righteousness. "Traditional medicine would teach her to maim her god-given body. All those boys need is the right voice to show them the light"

"The *light?*" Nurse Didi's hiss was venomous. "Martha, these *boys* ain't yours. You're nothing to them. They will shoot you if you talk to them."

Dr. Gilmer turned to her with a mouth so terse her cheek wrinkles shook with its barely contained rage. Nurse Didi stared her down, cool and level.

"What did you just say to me?"

"I ain't dying next to you, Martha." Nurse Didi stripped off her gloves. Static crackled at Officer Laurence's walkie talkie.

"Code —"

The gunfire shattered the Planned Parenthood building, rattling the door on its hinges and the teeth in Amanda's skull. Amanda tried to remove her feet from the stirrups but the gun was still extended and heavy. She tried to relax — *hadn't that put it away before?* — but the hammering of her heart only seemed to grow it longer.

"Have you been baptized?" The gyno took her hand, fervent.

"Shut up, Martha." said Didi flatly. "How many militants?" she asked Officer Laurence.

Dr. Gilmer took off her glasses and began to cry. "They're here *for* us, can't you see?!"

The gyno's scream and her tear-stained face hung in the silence, then the walls of the Planned Parenthood roared.

The force of the gunfire drove her heartbeat to Amanda's throat — then as quickly as it started it was over, Amanda's ears ringing. Officer Laurence mouthed something to Didi and she cut the lights to the room, dousing the weeping gyno in darkness. They waited.

Screams tore from a room down the hall, bursts of gunfire hammered the walls. Officer Laurence flew toward Didi, nearly yanking Amanda off the table with her.

Swearing at the cuff connecting them, Officer Laurence shouted over the gunfire, "Barricade the door — the chair!"

Nurse Didi swept aside the curtain and tried to fit the chair under the doorknob as Dr. Gilmer lowered her coiffed head and began to pray under her breath. Nurse Didi's scrabbling with the chair wrenched the door open. She shut it, with a breath like a scream coming from between her teeth. The chair fell on the ground. Didi stumbled, managing to right the cheap wooden thing.

"DIDI!" yelled Officer Laurence.

"I DON'T KNOW HOW!" Didi screamed back, her brown eyes sparkling with tears in the dim light from the frosted windows. "And don't you *dare* raise your voice to me!"

Officer Laurence's face collapsed in agony. She started towards Didi again, wrenching Amanda's arm so hard she yelped.

"Okay," Officer Laurence fumbled with the key at her other side.

"You know you're ok. I know you're ok." She stabbed the key at the lock of the cuffs connecting them, "But move from this table, see what happens." The key turned in the lock and the handcuffs clattered to the floor.

Officer Laurence was at Didi's side in an instant. The gunfire bursts ceased, but the extended silence was no comfort. Officer Laurence froze as Didi collapsed, sobbing, into her chest. Noticing her stillness, Didi clapped a hand to her own mouth. Even the gyno stopped praying aloud, mouthing the words with increasing fervor. The officer leaned with a silent step back and fitted the chair under the door handle, turning the two of them to ever-so-quietly tap the chair into tension. She tried the door handle with a gentle pull. The chair held.

Impact.

Shafts of light pierced the dim exam room. The bullets had torn through the back wall. Officer Laurance gasped and clapped a hand to her head. It was almost as if she'd remembered something in a flash, and had clapped her hand to her forehead in disbelief or exasperation. But then she staggered back, blood from the side of her head spraying onto the line of splintered bullet holes across the exam room door. The gyno scrabbled forward to the door,

"Please, we surrender in the name of Jesus Christ!" She snapped the cross from around her neck and slapped it to one of the bullet door's bullet holes. "I'm not one of them!"

The militia men's laughter rippled through the bullet holes, a ripple that took more than a minute to travel down the hall. How many men were out there? Amanda imagined a militia was maybe ten people. From the laughter, there could have been thirty in the hall.

Didi knelt to press a wad of bunched-up curtain hard against the side of Officer Laurence's head. When she looked it up in the dark with blood in her eyes however, it wasn't to glare at the gyno, but at Amanda.

Oh right, I exist. And Amanda's thought was immediately

141

followed by a bolt of pure, unadulterated rage. How dare Didi remind her she was alive just in time to get shot in the head? The rage built in her stomach, towering, terrifying, and she glared back so forcefully heat filled her cheeks, and her heartbeat thrummed. Christian. *It's not my fucking fault.* The towering fury coursed through her now, and so strongly that it took her a moment to realize Didi's fierce glare had become a grim smile.

"I have, in secret, done Christ's work here. I have saved countless children." Dr. Gilmer said, her lipstick smudging on the bullet hole in the door.

The men met the gyno's mewling with murmurs that she was a liar, no woman of God, a child killer, a working woman who'd abandoned her children at home. Nurse Didi waved her free hand to get Amanda's attention. With one acrylic-nailed finger, she pointed at Amanda's lower half. She formed her hand into an L, winking one eye shut (aiming?). Then, she tipped the top of that 'L' at the door and pulled the trigger. Her full lips pursing into a gentle 'pow.'

She met Amanda's eyes again. What if this was the same as last time? When had she ever been able to control it? She might as well try to shoot ping-pong balls out of her vagina for all the control she'd had over it so far. Nurse Didi must have seen her fear, because she nodded again at Amanda's lower half, emphatic.

Where she once had a gunbarrel, Amanda now had a creature of war crawling out from between her legs — one she had no idea how to use. Amanda's gunbarrel was longer, the metallic coating on her body covering her thighs. Supports had merged with her legs.

Amanda looked back at Didi in panic, but Didi had given up on hand signals.

The nurse lowered her head to Officer Laurence's motionless face and kissed her. Then she lay down alongside the officer, adjusting until she could enfold the officer in her arms completely. They became one dark shape on the barely lit floor.

"But I am a woman of God!"

Dr. Gilmer's head exploded into a mist of blood, the force of the gunfire slinging her viscera to the walls, the dark ceiling light, the cabinets. A thicket of guns bristled through the splintery center of the destroyed exam room door. Then...

Impact.

The militia men's bullets shredded the sheet and skin of Amanda's lower body and legs, metal flashing beneath. *I'm almost back to you.* Surely her consciousness would snuff out soon — but as the bullets hailed into the whole of her, no pain followed. The deafening gunfire stopped all at once. A man made a noise of surprise. The men yelled to each other and reloaded, frantic.

Impact.

The spray of bullets from the militia began again, but this time Amanda raised her head against the impossible force, bending up at the waist. Her naked metal stomach frothed, a fury of boiling chrome, as it swallowed the militia men's bullets. The metal raced down her legs up her midsection, consuming her dangling handcuff. Then, adequately fed, the gun grew.

Like the metal leg of a spider, it stepped out of her womb and rested on the ground, a belt of bullets falling wetly to the floor. Amanda's lower body wrenched, clicking and turning in her gut until she felt very much like she was about to burp. She gave in to the feeling, and pushed.

Amanda returned fire. The force drove her nearly back off of the stirrups but the supports braced against her inner thighs and the floor held Amanda's position. Men screamed, shouting and praying. Her gunfire mowed down the first line of men. The upper half of the door calved away, hitting the floor and the men below it as her line of fire sawed the door in half.

Wave by wave the militia men fell, fed to her by the confines of the hallway, until finally no bullets perforated her metallic body and the men's bodies carpeted the hallway, unmoving. She inhaled, light-headed. *I'm safe.* The guilt that twisted her throat was breathtaking, but whatever part of her body ruled the gun must have felt relaxed. For with the metered ratcheting of metal on metal, the gun barrel and its supports withdrew smoothly into her body. Chrome shimmered in splashes all over her body. If anyone else was coming, Amanda couldn't hear them over the deafening ringing in her ears.

Blood, streaks of guts, the spatter of flesh, and the craggy geometry of bone shards swamped the exam room floor, more leaking in from under the remainder of hallway door. Would any court see what she'd done as self defense?

The floor is lava, her delirious brain supplied. All that remained of the gyno was blood-soaked scrubs, the bloodied chain with its missing cross still looped around her mangled hand. The gore next to the gyno shifted, rippling the pooled blood on the floor to regard her with one dull eye. It was Nurse Didi. She was still curled on Officer Laurence's unmoving chest, covered in the gyno's remains.

She mouthed something.

"What?" Amanda said.

In reply, Nurse Didi pointed at the door then walked her fingers towards it. She mouthed again, and this time Amanda understood: *Leave.*

"Do you need help?" Amanda asked, unable to hear her own voice for the buzzing in her ears. Nurse Didi only curled back into Officer Lawrence's chest, settling into the swamp of flesh and blood.

Amanda's stomach lurched and she heaved sour bile. Her last meal couldn't have been before Christian. The crawl of bugs under her skin, discomfort she could not reach to peel off. The exam room darkness slipped into the darkness of the dumpster, the darkness of Christian's hair, the dark warmth at the back of his head. A flicker of motion drew Amanda's attention back to the lit hallway.

The bodies of the men near the door seemed to be boiling, and the affliction was spreading down the hallway. Amanda removed her feet from the stirrups and, her gorge rising, stepped down into the gore-covered floor. She would run over the men if they began to rise. But it wasn't the dead that sprang from the hallway floor. Moving buds the size of fists breached the many bullet holes of the dead men, fighting their way out of the men's bodies. They were heads.

The bald heads of babies, red and close-eyed in the strobing, broken overhead hall lights, growing up through the wounds. *Are all of these mine?* The baby exiting the headwound of one of the militia men by the door struggled to free their shoulder. Amanda bent to slip the lip of head and skull away and the baby slid out entirely.

Down the hall, the number of babies verged on the hundreds. All covered in the blood, sweat, and refuse of the militia men, the bullet children grew just as the figures at the festival had, quickly reaching toddlerhood, childhood, teenagerhood. They felt their way down the wall, navigating over the bodies of the militia men. Amanda didn't see the bullet people reach the swinging door at the end of the hallway, but when quiet, languageless lows swept the crowd she knew they'd reached an obstacle.

Amanda gently guided the fleshy bodies of the bullet people aside. They parted easily, opening a pungent channel of filth and gunpowder stench that led to the swinging door. She pushed its metal plate firmly, and the bodies spilled out behind her. The Planned Parenthood front door was in view. Soon she would greet the patients and protestors in the lobby as a naked chrome creature. But as she rounded the front desk in between her and the lobby, Amanda's dark amusement ceased.

At first, the waiting room looked like piles upon piles of wet clothes. Every patient in waiting was dead on the floor. She did not look out of respect, only focused on the front door and the press of the bullet people at her back.

It seemed wrong that through the tinted entry door the day was a sunny one. She wasn't a person who could understand death anymore. She'd caused too much, she didn't get to. But seeing dead protestors outside would be too much. She squinted, trying to make out bodies outside. There were large black trucks, but she couldn't see anything else from the brightness. Her ears buzzed. *Will I be arrested for being naked? Does being part chrome count?* Her ears buzzed again. *Oh.* Someone was speaking to her over a megaphone. It was loud enough that she could actually make out the words.

"Come out slowly with your hands above your head."

How can I open the door if my hands are over my head?

Hands up, she walked her belly first into tinted glass of the door. In the moments before she pushed, she made out details in the blinding white light after all — there were men in black standing by the trucks. *More militia men?* The trucks had S.W.A.T written on their sides.

And as she opened the door, the other bullet children pressed behind her, the swat men yelled warnings, panicked amongst each other —

Impact.

The hit buried itself in her chest, calm nothing radiating outwards. It was a neon green-ended dart. *A tranquilizer, smarty pants men.* Amanda's consciousness dimmed, her control of her nervous system fading. It was exactly the opening the gun needed.

Chrome slipped over the rest of Amanda, and the spider leg of the gun and its supports extended from her unconscious body. The SWAT team fired, terrified. But the gun consumed the bullets hungrily, fashioning the new material into limb supports that kicked one of Amanda's legs up and behind her head. Her bones and sinew merged with the corded steel and flashing chrome, releasing Amanda from what remained of her flesh. Her remaining legstick drove deep into the parking lot asphalt, ripping up pavement. Bursting a water pipe. Then, it rooted and stabilized. Her torso spun up in shining triumph, curling along her one kicked-up leg. Finally, her head and neck surrendered, sighing back around the curve of her carbon grey thigh, yielding up to the sun.

Amidst the already-dead bodies of the pro-lifers killed by the gun-rights militia, she rose remade. Amanda the multi-function armament with anti-tank capabilities had been born, and on the Thursday of a long weekend.

∾

"They don't let us practice actual equality in the workplace. It's a double-standard."

The man's voice was cordial and shushed. Amanda the gun awoke with infinite langour. She'd been staring at the sky, a concept it took her a moment to recall. Her control of her body was inaccessible — did she have legs or arms or not? She could not move them when she tried, but she could still sense her surroundings.

She was in a desert, the yolk of an orange sun breaking over its rim. The lush scent of recent rain on creosote and concrete soaked her nostrils. There was also the smell of human sweat. A group of people was near her. The noise of a car's tires on sand and gravel rumbled towards them. Its door opened and shut immediately on arrival.

"Angelina!" said the same man from before, sounds like he bared every tooth in his mouth.

"I know it's a lot of syllables for you, Senator Jefres, but I do go by *Senator Romero*. My team received the wrong time for the test," said a woman, Senator Romero. "Should I draw the obvious conclusion?" It was incredible a voice could sound so breezy yet hate-filled.

Amanda managed to tilt her head enough to see the people behind and beside her. A short woman (Senator Romero?) faced a row of six other people. One wore a suit, presumably Senator Jefres, four were soldiers in fatigues, and there was one blonde woman. She smiled at Senator Romero.

"I'm *so* sorry I know I'm new! But I could swear we usually only add guests with constituents affected by the artillery to these little meets?" the blonde woman tittered.

"You believe this woman wouldn't affect every constituent?" Senator Romero, again.

Senator Jefres laughed, long and easy. "*Ladies*, please. We don't have long and the picketing is already drawing press."

"Shame," said Senator Romero with pleasure. "Now where is she?"

"It's over there." Senator Jefres pointed at Amanda — accidentally meeting her eyes and making an involuntary "*ah.*" The soldiers stood, hands on their guns.

"Amanda?" Senator Romero's high heels slipped on a larger bit of gravel and she immediately reached down to fumble with removing her shoes.

"Ma'am, she's — the gun, it's —" began one of the soldiers, but Senator Jefres shushed him with a chuckle.

"You know that thing ain't moved in days, Lieutenant. Calm yourself."

Senator Romero's face leveled with her own in concern. In the Senator's glasses, she could see the reflection of her own face. Metallic, chrome, placid, sticking out like a strange mask from the flat gunwall of rippling, liquid chrome.

"Is she...alive?" asked Senator Romero. Her eyes traveled over Amanda, her lenses reflecting Amanda's lengthened metal limbs, entwined with the jutting planes of the weapon. The wrench of her torso, one revealed breast. Senator Romero stepped back as if burned.

"Someone cover her with a sheet. Where the hell is the doctor?"

Shuffling steps sounded from behind a tree next to the line of soldiers, an apologetic man in fatigues with a first aid kit.

"Now, now," Senator Jefres patted Senator Romero's shoulder with enough force to push her nearly forward into Amanda. "Wouldn't a mechanic be more appropriate? Look at the chrome!" And he reached forward to slap Amanda on the stomach.

Amanda had thought she'd lost the ability to jump from surprise, but she did, and gunfire rent the still desert air.

Her head traveled to the top of the gun and she could see, hundreds of yards away, a target. From its feet, baby bubbled to adulthood like a fountain just turning on.

"Jesus, something's moving out there," said Senator Romero.

The the most fancily fatigued man handed her a pair of binoculars. Romero took them.

"Finally something God-honoring outta you!" the blonde woman said from beside Senator Romero. The bullet-man at the base of the target had reached adulthood. He stared at his hands in wonder.

"We need to detangle her. Medic —?" But Senator Jefres had no intention of letting Senator Romero finish. He patted — slapped — her shoulder again and the medic paused, uncertain.

"I'm a family man, Angie," said Senator Jefres. "Who am I to take away a mother's god given right to bear arms?"

"You want soldiers for free." Senator Romero lowered the binoculars, shaken.

"Why Ange, such harsh words. Ain't gotta accuse anybody — we're all friends here." He rubbed her shoulder. She ducked his grip into the blonde woman.

"Is that enough of a test, General?" Senator Jefres called over his shoulder to the men in fatigues. The fanciest of the fatigued men shook his head with a laugh. Senator Romero took out her phone and raised it to Amanda, looking green.

"It's against the rules to film here, Ma'am," drawled the General.

"Hon, listen to the general."

"We're both senators with non-California jurisdictions here, *General*. You listen to me too."

The General said nothing.

"Think of it, *Senator Romero*, even if it is soldiers for free, it's better than sending our boys into the fray! Haven't you always wanted women on the front lines? Look how content she is!" Now the blonde woman rubbed Senator Romero's shoulders, and Senator Romero, if possible, turned greener. Amanda felt nothing, and could not move her facial features. The more she tried, she more she found it pointless.

"She's not right," managed Senator Romero.

"Sure, we can fine-tune things! She responds to commands! Er, stomach slaps," the blonde woman said. Senator Jefres laughed heartily at this, and blonde woman glowed under his praise.

"Shut up, Marie," said Senator Romero. "I'm going back and telling the picketers. I don't stand for this."

"*Senator* Marie, right?" the blonde woman, Senator Marie, laughed. Senator Jefres, however, had finished waiting.

"Alright are we gonna test or what? We got the target." He walked up right behind Amanda.

"Sir, you've never shot —" The general stepped forward, but the Senator beamed his blinding threat of a smile at the man.

"I've already done it! Who'd need to know more? Aims itself. I probably don't even have to give her a whack on the belly. Here, honey, go ahead and shoot."

Amanda shot. She was a gun, and it was what guns did. With the shot, her vision dimmed, her ability to move her head slowed.

"Direct hit — on request. An incomparable weapon that generates innocent souls." Senator Jefres bowed his white-haired head in reverence. "Is there any more heroic way for a woman to serve their country?" He spread his arms out and the soldiers applauded, the general nodding.

Senator Marie shifted from foot to foot, her eyes glassy as she clapped. She looked at Senator Romero, who pursed her red lips into a furious line. The two of them held a look, then finally Senator Marie stepped towards Senator Jefres. Maybe she would say something to him after all — but she breezed past to walk to Amanda. She bent her sparkling white teeth to Amanda's ear.

"Hon, do you think you can make it automatic?" She asked.

8

YOU ARE FALLING INTO THE SEA

BRIDGETTE DAY

Every obstacle is only a matter of translation.

(From the joint email signature of Britta Jones & Aino Yeates, 2018–2022)

Aino twisted awake in YMIR's tank of tepid black liquid, wired-up and floating along with the rest of the aftermath garbage of what they'd tried that night.

Like waking bound in clotting blood, like always.

She pitched herself forward as best as she could. The viscous stuff dragged at her mask and wires. Molasses and metal and the inertia of nightmares.

The sick adrenaline churn of resurfacing meant it took a few moments to realize that she was still holding Sawyer's hand.

His already-cold hand.

Aino jerked backward and stumbled down, slipping briefly under the surface. The slopping liquid smelled like metal and would cling to your skin like guilt.

The churn of the tank pulled Sawyer's long body to thump dumbly against her.

She fought her way up to the rim and hauled herself into a sitting position. Her stomach heaved as she clawed off her mask. The electric blue of her eyepiece glittered on the chop and churn of the pool like moonlight. She wrenched it off and flung it aside.

The eyepiece's little glowing logo, a star in a skull, sank beneath the black liquid her legs dangled in.

Getting all the way out would mean it was all over, and that there was no going back.

The first time she had gone into YMIR, she had appeared sitting on a black rock in a cold sea on a moonlit night, her pale feet dangling in the deep. The last place she wanted.

Now, lights banged on all around her — harsh and white and hurting — viciously illuminating the wide warehouse of tanks and consoles. A glass dais lay near the pool, connected to a large console. All this together was YMIR — the Yeates Mind Integration Rendering. And she was Aino Yeates.

She looked up. The high-up windows reflected the white light; there seemed to be no sky at all.

Annoyingly clean-cut analysts and techs rushed all around her on the polished concrete floors, like bubbling water around a rock.

No one stopped to help. No one even looked at her.

Their indifference was an old pain, but unexpectedly sharp now. Hadn't she done what they wanted? What had to be done, to save hundreds of thousands of lives? Surely this was cause to celebrate, even in a subdued way?

Or —

Had it not worked?

Had she ruined it, with her ultimate act of mercy or shame or whatever it had been?

A few techs jostled her as they stepped into the tank. They surfaced Sawyer's body, lifting him like a submerged drain clog.

She blanched.

That had been her only condition for this exercise: that she would never see him again.

"You were supposed to get him out of here before I woke up," Aino spat at the nearest tech, a gangly young man submerged to his waist and pulling the cords free of the corpse. "That was the protocol."

"Don't hold his hand, then," the tech muttered, not looking at her.

"Did the encoding take?"

"You think that's my job to know?"

She bit back what she wanted to say — he should be interested, since Sawyer (or at least his pattern) would be written into his mind, too. A script for — well. She couldn't say yet. Not after how everything had gone south.

The tech and his companions rolled Sawyer over the side of the tank. She heard jerky zipping. They dragged away a black bag.

Which had to mean something more than a tragedy. It had to, had to, had to. It would. It would.

Because Sawyer would never flash that dumb white smile again when he won someone over. Never ask questions till someone gave in. Never pick something interesting off the ground again, even as an adult.

Aino gagged and coughed liquid into the pool.

It didn't help.

She knew tonight would not feel good, but she had hoped it would feel right. At the very least, she never dreamed it would be like this: shaking alone in a pool she designed while everyone bustled electric and uncaring around her.

The fear, the mantra, pulsing again. Sawyer's encoding had to have worked. Otherwise —

Aino finally heaved herself out and pattered barefoot and dripping across the concrete to the nearest terminal. Analysts in badly fitting clothes buzzed around glowing screens, murmuring about signal decay and neural loops.

"Did it work?" she called out. "The encoding." Her voice wasn't even that weak, but only one person even turned their head to shoot her a quick look of disgust. "Please."

"The pulse stalled," someone said. Not to her. "It's not propagating. Send it again."

If the pulse wasn't going, YMIR wasn't updating. Aino pushed her way through to the workstation, still dripping.

"What's wrong?"

The team flinched away from her. Then, one of them — an older woman with long curled hair — pointed at the status monitor, where you could see an approximation of what was inside the machine. "It won't progress. The new archetype isn't propagating to the population. Nothing is updating."

Aino was already cold. But she could have frozen to the spot then as she processed what the woman was saying.

Sawyer was still in there. Still in pain. Still looking at the sky.

YMIR was the touchpoint with the collective unconscious — that shared mythbound memory bank we're all born with. The unconscious sea we all swim in, below the level of awareness.

This whole horrible night was all about encoding a new archetype into every human's brain, in the hopes of stopping the wars that had started spasming through the world. All by writing in a new story, a new script in everyone's heads.

Just last week, Aino had accidentally seen the footage from outside of Lyon before the press buried it — the little boys running from the car after their parents had been shot. How their little bodies had bounced and wobbled as they ran. What had happened to them.

That she could do anything to stop it, with YMIR — she couldn't resist the temptation.

YMIR had always been their shared obsession — hers and her partner Britta's. Aino built the interface, refined the signals, and mapped the stars in neural constellations. Britta gave it its name, its myth, its ambition. Its blood — and, if you believed her, its magic.

But Britta was gone. Had been gone.

YMIR was Aino's now.

Her triumph.

Everyone's salvation.

And all it had cost, was everything she had.

But only if Sawyer had actually been encoded.

"Excuse me," Aino said. Her voice sounded far away, like someone else's. She elbowed her way forward.

She started typing, writing, starting certain processes, and halting others, all in a kind of rhythm. YMIR always worked in waves and tides; they had never understood that.

With a final click, the silver pulses started again.

Sawyer's neural pattern at termination flared on screen — silver, searing, bright — and with the pulses, the constellation of lights spread across the interface, and held with each new wave.

It held. A terrible thrill of finality danced its way from her gut across her skin. Like the first time she realized she couldn't talk to her aunt who had died about how crazy it was that she had died.

Sawyer was encoded now. No longer a man, but a symbol in every human's head. (At least, every human who used her company's products.)

She had made sure of it.

Triumphant cheers rippled through the pool of techs.

Aino smiled without thinking, like a ghoul. Silly to worry; no one looked at her.

Maybe she had saved the world. She would still, it seemed, be left to drown.

Something still was wrong, though, here outside the programs. There was even more of a flurry of activity, and only then was she paid attention to, and taken by her elbow and gently shoved away toward the exit.

She found herself shuffling to the lab's dingy little bathroom, just focusing on putting one foot in front of the other, and to keep breathing. Her body was too heavy, and her skin was too small. She could wash off all this wrong in the shower, scrub so hot and hard the sensory input would carry her, comet-like, over any...what. Grief? Not regret. Never regret.

Vertigo, maybe, at how the world had changed.

Aino's stomach turned again at the thought of the fluffy bathrobe and modest bouquet of roses she had left there. Just for herself, hidden away in a corner in the showers, to celebrate. Which now felt as pathetic and obscene as stashing a birthday cake under the office toilet, in the hopes someone would sing.

Her steps slopped, but they only seemed to echo her heartbeat. Only Sawyer's tears, the slip in his voice as he pleaded.

And here, she had actually driven to the florist that morning. They might not even be the only flowers she got that day, she even let herself dare to think, with a scandalized lurch at the indulgence. Britta would have scoffed, but Britta had always been lucky — even those that hated her couldn't take their eyes off of her.

She swallowed and coughed. There was blood still in her throat, which still hurt badly.

Like someone had had their arm down it, as Britta had put it.

A man, broad-shouldered and dead-eyed, was ushered out of the room ahead of her.

Along with another body bag.

Aino darted her glance around the room — everyone was stealing guilty, furtive looks at her.

And Aino understood —

She was meant to have been killed as well.

And if she hadn't proven herself useful again, just now, by getting YMIR to truly write in new archetypes —

She bumped full-body into a tall man in too-nice cashmere; the feeling of him recoiling felt like peeling off a wet bandage.

He grimaced.

It was sometimes nice to be repulsive. Aino smiled and moved to step around him. Hopefully his sweater was ruined.

He shoved a towel into her arms.

"We have to go," he said. He gestured to the window. A small plane waited outside.

"What? No, I need to—"

"Don't be greedy."

Aino's face burned. They would have taken all she had, had she not proven useful. Surely it wasn't selfish to want to wash the sacrificial blood off her body?

He held out his hand toward the door. "Congratulations, Dr. Yeates," he said, and looked at her.

Until she understood:

She wasn't going to shower. She wasn't going home again.

And she'd never go into YMIR again.

Aino almost did vomit then, as if she actually had swallowed blood.

The cashmere man hustled her out to the small plane, as she tracked black-green footprints across the concrete. She left what looked like a bloody handprint on the cold bar of the exit door.

It made the place look like the stupid horror scene it was.

The air outside was so frigid and black, it felt like breathing water.

Once she had wrung out her hair, the towel was soaked and useless. She let it fall from her hands as she clanged up the narrow staircase to the plane.

Inside, a second towel had been hastily thrown on one of the plush blue seats. Almost like she hadn't been expected.

The unwanted kid at the sleepover party, always.

Except, you know. The spare that they were going to kill.

Aino wrapped the towel tight around her shoulders. It wasn't until the plane lifted that she realized she was shaking.

She turned off her light and leaned her head against the window. The night chill blurred through the glass and cooled her shockingly flushed cheek. Trauma and pain, she knew, crystallized sooner or later into shining points and would not always be sucking at her heart like riptides.

Sooner or later.

Her company minder sat across from her. A man she knew, about her own age, with sad eyes and a quick smile and a tendency to try for conversation. "So," he said. "I heard it went well."

"Did you? Like how? I didn't hear anything."

"Oh. Just that it went well."

The gold flicker of towns rolled under them. Every tumble of seconds took her miles farther from her pool, where she could submerse herself in that connection with others, however forced. Every tumble of seconds took her further from where he existed.

The minder shifted, and cleared his throat. "Hey — I saved these for you."

He held out a crumpled bundle of a dozen roses.

Aino straightened. How kind; how considerate.

How ghoulish.

"What about the bathrobe?" She might as well be greedy.

"Oh." He looked stricken. "Sorry."

Aino reached and took the roses from his hands. She smoothed them in her lap, not minding as the thorns scraped her skin.

He grinned. He was effusive, like champagne spitting bubbles, surrounded by the bitter spirits of every colleague of his that she had ever met. And as always, he mistook her politeness for camaraderie.

The organization he belonged to had originally told Aino and her business partner, Britta, that they were government, which she had believed. They also told her they were CIA, which she did not believe.

Britta hadn't believed any of it, of course.

"So, um. When can I use my DreamWeaver again?" he asked.

Aino took her necklace out of her pocket — a pendant, a single sharp rose thorn cast in bronze — and pressed the point lightly into her lip.

You can use it right now, Britta would have answered him, with a bright and charming smile.

But Britta was long gone. Unless they had caught up to her, as Aino feared.

Britta was beautiful, shining and gold and lush, and so her coldness and venom took people by surprise and gave her an advantage. Where Aino dug into systems to understand people, Britta made people into systems so she could take them apart if she had to.

Aino, slight and dark-haired with those too-big eyes, surprised people just by speaking at all.

Except of course, Sawyer.

He was golden too, but more like sunlight on beach sand than a hard coin. He had been her salvation, back in high school, with his backpack full of books.

Sawyer was gone now, too.

Aino turned over and tasted these thoughts, bitter as broken petals, as she fastened her necklace on. Surely there had been enough cruelty for one night.

"If you're part of any agency that was part of tonight, I'm surprised you'd use a DreamWeaver at all, much less ever again," she said.

"It's fun."

She folded her towel closer around her.

In the worst turn of the night, the man took off his jacket and draped it warm over her shoulders.

"Come on," he said. "You're the expert."

Aino stared at him.

She had been the expert, although the DreamWeaver was always Britta's baby. A plague doctor mask sold as a toy, powered by nothing but your neural matrices and a nine-volt battery. It projected your subconscious onto an internal stage — dreams you could walk through, talk to, touch.

In startlingly real image and sound. Or so the ads went.

People loved it.

Too much, in many cases.

What they didn't know was that every DreamWeaver fed your brain and all its data to YMIR. A little altar, serving up stories.

The plane jerked. Her roses almost slid to the floor. She caught them too late, and they cut her palm.

"Maybe you mean, when will we know," she said, voice soft, "if it worked? If we stopped the war?"

He nodded and swallowed, and she was glad she had shown grace.

"Again. I was hoping you might know."

The minder suddenly had something important to check on his phone.

She rested her head against the window. It was strangely wet with condensation. She tasted salt, too, although that might have been tears falling without permission.

No other windows were so struck.

The sea was still trying to find her, even now.

Sawyer's words he used to calm her — now her words too — came to her:

"You are falling into the sky," she murmured.

She didn't realize she was pressing her thorn necklace too hard into her lip until she tasted blood.

In the cold bloom of stars, Orion glittered. Aino traced the invisible lines between stars with her finger, giving the dead man a rudimentary watery form.

And to think she had dared to bargain to never see him again.

She traced a canoe. Then a hand, reaching out. All the stories those stars had been, hung in our heads like a string of lights.

Until all that was left was a watery smudge, and herself staring back in the black.

A drowned girl hanging in a sea of stars.

Only a few hours before she had woken up next to Sawyer's body, Aino had pretended to sneak him into her lab just as the first stars were coming out.

They stood outside by a side door. She fiddled with a touchpad too nice to belong to the warehouse the lab pretended to be. It's not like they weren't allowed in, she had explained. They just weren't encouraged.

"I don't get it," Sawyer whisper-laughed, pressing himself against the cold steel wall like she had told him to. "Isn't this all yours?"

She scoffed, or tried to. Her voice shook, so it sounded more like an aborted sneeze, and her face flushed warm as the dying light.

"YMIR is mine, sure. But Sawyer, you know I brought lunch to school in a paper bag and had two pairs of shoes total. You think I could fund this myself?"

"At least your parents made you lunch."

That would have been nice, but they hadn't. She had. Aino's parents were always gently confused by her and seemed surprised these days that she was still around. She'd asked them on a whim to the DreamWeaver launch, the culmination of all her work at that point. They couldn't make it because they might need to babysit one of her erstwhile brother's kids.

She didn't ask after that.

"That was nice of them," she lied.

"Should I be kneeling, if there are cameras? What does hugging the wall do?"

Aino froze as the fingerprint scanner beeped, and the door swung open.

Everyone knew they were there. Hugging the wall was nothing but theater, so Sawyer felt like he was getting access to something rare.

So he'd cooperate.

While he could.

"It makes me more relaxed," she said, which was the truth.

"Then I'll do it all day," he winked, and followed her in.

The allegedly CIA people in brandless, expensive clothes had sworn it could only be Sawyer for tonight. Good to remember, as he kept hugging the wall and humming the James Bond theme to make her smile.

The warehouse was prepared for them. She prayed Sawyer wouldn't notice.

The raised metal pool in the center was filled, and the liquid lapped gently at the edges, jostling the wires that hung down like dejected tentacles. All the lights were off. Only the stars leaked through the high slats, a wet white bleed in the dark.

Aino stood by the main console, already dressed, along with Sawyer, in the loose black immersion clothes you needed for YMIR. The screen tanned her taut face an electric blue.

Sawyer spun through the place like a tourist in a shrine. He scribbled in his blue leather notebook as he went, making little sounds of excitement as he found things. Aino knew he wasn't aware that he did that. His face shone.

He thought this would be his big break.

To be fair, it would be.

Everyone in the world would know him soon.

Sawyer sounded just as excited when he called months ago. Jolly and warm, and so happy to speak to her, like no time had passed at all. She smiled automatically, as always when they spoke. Like the room had ballooned with color and light.

Then, he launched into his pitch.

An exclusive on the new DreamWeaver. She could do it for him, couldn't she? It would mean so much.

Aino kept the smile in her voice, stitching it over her collapsing heart.

He hadn't dug up her number to reconnect. Just to breathe life into his stagnant career.

She had told him no.

Then the organization had told her — it could only be him. If she gave him up, untold numbers of people would live.

So, Aino called Sawyer back and offered him one better than DreamWeaver. One the plebeians didn't know about.

YMIR.

And she would wonder for the rest of her life what it would be like to have an old friend just want to see her.

She stole glances as he marveled at her work, at the machine that felt like an extension of her own body. It had always been a dream, to be seen clearly. That's not what he wanted from this, though.

Tonight would kill him, if they kept going. To encode a mind as an archetype, required dissolution. Which was to say — to make a myth required death.

But if all he wanted was to turn her into a story, let him try. She could show him what that meant.

She could turn him into a story too.

And save more people than herself as she did.

Sawyer leaned over the tank. "Could we go to the Ocean, instead of the Forest?"

"The Forest is my specialty."

"Why's that?"

"There are rules.

"You've never been fond of those."

"I'm fond of whatever you can hold on to, to keep from drowning. OK. One last thing."

She typed into the console, confirming the program and participants. Then, she opened the drawer — only to find it empty. Her jaw tightened.

Second drawer. Third. All empty.

"Something wrong?"

"No. Yes. I can't find the last thing we need." Were they sabotaging her? Just incompetent?

Worse — was there something happening here she wasn't seeing?

"What thing? I'll help look."

"We could just go home. I could get in huge trouble for this, you know." She left the last part hanging in the air.

"No," he said, too quickly. He didn't care. "Please. We're talking Pulitzers and no more cold pitches again, here."

"All right," she said after a moment. "I'm looking for a hypodermic needle. We need some of your blood."

"Mine?"

"We already have mine. They're small, the needles. In little plastic wrappers. We don't need much."

He swallowed, and started looking, with just as much luck. Any drawer just held sanitation equipment, spare keyboards, and outdated consent forms.

Aino was glad he didn't ask more about the blood. There was a scientific justification — something about generational DNA memory. And then there was Britta's eldritch blood magic she'd dug up and used. Or claimed she had. Aino never got far asking for the exact details; Britta would get flustered and redirect. But Britta's weird little glyphs somehow made Aino's programs work beyond their wildest dreams. Maybe that was better than an explanation.

The last drawer slammed on Aino's finger, and she cursed. Still nothing.

Fear like bile bubbled up. Were they just testing her?

"We'll get this," he said. He rubbed her shoulder, like he always did.

Aino nursed her finger, and watched him search. Watched him scribble in his little notebook, like they were two kid detective best friends solving the mystery of the week. They had used to be such close friends.

Even if he only saw her as a story now — was this a good trade?

His life, for countless others?

Part of her wanted him to pass the test. To ask why she was shaking and sad. To remember who she was, not what she could offer.

Sawyer looked at her like a revelation, and her heart leapt.

"While we look," he said, "tell me more about YMIR. Like a DreamWeaver, but with archetypes?"

She clenched her teeth.

Britta would have made the explanation sound sexy and compelling. Aino just fell into the same trap she always did:

She made the mistake of answering.

Aino launched into a small lecture — Jungian scaffolds, symbolic memory, neural constellations, phylogenetic substrata. She said engram a lot.

A lot. She couldn't stop.

Sawyer scribbled a note or two. Once, he even remembered to nod.

And just like that, she was back in middle school. Too bright and too much, a compact acid-eyed girl who had only distilled herself into a more feverish intensity as her peers all soared into their futures, clicking her tongue when searching for a word, hoping Sawyer would see her as a peer and not an object of pity.

Or see her at all.

She hissed in frustration. "Let me just show you."

At the dais, she pressed her hand to the glass plate like a machete coming down in the rainforest brush. A shimmer and a whir, and then a holographic galaxy bloomed above them, a billion little constellations containing a whole soul.

"A brain," he whispered.

"Your brain."

He laughed and waved his hand through the projection, catching starlight on his skin.

She smiled.

"Memory's not storage," she said. "It's constellations. Patterns of neurons that flare to life. One star lit triggers another. Sunscreen, maybe, sand, the sound of waves —"

She touched a point of light, and it lit up a chain like flash paper filigree.

The rush of waves and far cries of seagulls. A man shimmered into view on the display — golden and handsome, like Sawyer — swimming out to sea. They watched him lose his breath in the green surf, his head going under for the last time.

Sawyer's father.

And the last time Sawyer had ever been looked after.

Aino cursed and tried another cluster. She had been aiming for a different memory of the sea, with both her and Sawyer in it.

The same thing came up. His father, golden, drowning.

Sawyer had told her over dinner he didn't like DreamWeavers. "You always end up pulled back to the same places," he'd said. "The same people."

This must have been what he meant. At least he had someone who wanted to reach for him — but she supposed that made it worse.

Grief made you perfect for YMIR, because grief pulled you halfway into another unknown world already.

Just like being too clever. Or whatever was wrong with Aino, that came with its own grief. Of always feeling underwater and watching the world from far away — a world you could never reach, and you'd never be part of.

Britta, with her sweeping tangled pains, had navigated YMIR brilliantly at first, but had soon burned out.

Aino, with her billion little pinpricks, took longer. But, in the end, she was better.

She could fight currents Britta couldn't.

Sawyer stared at the image, stricken.

"I didn't know you had that."

He should have. He signed the DreamWeaver data waiver like everyone else.

"I didn't mean to," she said, quickly. "Here." She tapped another cluster — one that was echoed and fed from data from a billion other people.

A copse of trees appeared, with faint footfalls on a hidden path.

"A forest," he said. "I don't recognize the place, though. Germany?"

"No. The Forest. Most constellations are our own," she tumbled on. "But some — many, actually — are shared."

"Shared."

"Patterns passed down and inherited."

"Like...from my father?"

"Bigger than that."

"All my ancestors?"

This wasn't working.

"It's the collective unconscious," she blurted. "YMIR. It's our interface with the collective unconscious. All of humanity; all of us who have ever lived."

He sat down awkwardly on a dead console.

Aino grinned. It was wonderful to be a wonder, to create wonders for others.

"It's where all the stories come from. Not the ones we write — the ones that write us. Places like the Forest and Ocean. People like the Mother and the Magician. The Wolf and the Dragon. All hung in our head like stars and shared like we share the sky."

She leaned in. "We can go there, Sawyer. We can see it."

We can change it, she thought.

Sawyer's eyes lit like a neuron cluster firing, and he smiled like she was forgiven. He stood and waved his hand through the holograph forest. This time, leaves danced across his skin. "And we're going to the Forest."

"If we can find the needles. It's best for beginners, The Forest. Like I said, it has rules. You already know them: stay on the path. Be kind. Don't look back. The Ocean's trickier."

To say the least. The Ocean was traitorous; it shifted and shone like mercury.

"Path of needles, path of pins," he murmured, hand drifting through the lights, where his mind connected to others.

They stood in the glow of the neuron stars. He looked like some kind of god, bathed in unnatural light.

She always had admired Sawyer.

His words and warmth radiated outward, versus how she inserted herself into unknowing skulls. Any qualities she had, tunneled inward.

It was cruel, wanting to make him a beacon. To string him into a story.

But he had wanted to do the same to her, after all.

And no one had asked Orion either.

"Are you wearing makeup?" he asked.

Aino stared at him.

Sawyer used an improvised blade for the blood.

With fists and a safety manual, he cracked open the cheap plastic eye pencil sharpener that he had found in her little red makeup bag. The blade was barely wider than a paperclip, and caked in pigment and wax. He wiped it nominally clean on his shirt.

Aino winced as he hacked at this forearm. The cut was wide and messy and shallow; all he did was bite his lip. He even had to squeeze to get the blood to trickle in the slender glass receptacle Aino held to the wound.

"I wanted this to be easy for you," she said, miserable.

Which was true. It was why she had worn makeup, like she never did. She wanted a layer between them, especially a normal one. Something people did every day.

"It's fine. Whatever it takes." He handed the blade back to her.

She grimaced at the ugly thing.

"Throw it away."

Aino plugged the vial into the control dais, wiping the blood that stained her fingers on her pants.

Then, she pressed in the final sequence. The perimeter of the pool lit up in a sterile white halo that only made the liquid seem darker.

A chill seized her.

It was time.

Aino fitted his gear quickly, trying to keep momentum.

She only paused before the black and brutalist mask.

The masks were necessary, as were the breathing harnesses and wires and the dark. YMIR interfaced directly with their brains.

And, as she told him: on some level, there was no separation of consciousness and matter.

Which was why (she didn't tell him) encoding meant dissolution.

He had a sweet face, Sawyer, with turned-down eyes. He had been her friend when no one else would. She was about to cover that up forever.

Aino had been so happy to see him again. Sawyer, who glowed golden and attracted others like honey. Who did normal things, like have a salary and go to the gym, and had probably been a groomsman in a wedding. Someone who knew how to be loved.

"I can do it," he said, and lifted the mask up.

She only tightened the straps once he had them fastened.

Only.

Her own headset was different. Heavier, with one eyepiece large and glowing electric blue.

Aino stepped into the pool, grimacing at the warm oily texture. She turned to face him once she was in the middle, submerged up to her chest. Her suspension wires turned with her.

She looked frightening, she knew. A drowning marionette, in a dark rippling pool.

But he followed her in. She helped him adjust the breathing mask, showed him how to dip his face in first. How to trust the water. How to float.

Her voice echoed through the concrete chamber, flickering around them like light off seawater.

"Close your eyes," she said. She held him in the crook of her arm, like a Pietà. "Lean back."

He panicked and flailed as she tried to put him under.

"It's all right," she admonished, even though it wasn't.

He laughed and tried to speak, but his mask muffled his voice. Instead, he reached out to tap the hollow where her collarbones met, and then pointed up.

She laughed, softly.

He remembered.

∾

They had been in the south of France a decade ago, on the study abroad where they had grown close. The one that she had funded with loans.

All the students had stayed a few nights in a town by the sea, where by day they had examined the old film equipment and shooting locations the town was known for. Nights were for the beach, with its rocky outcropping holding them like an outstretched hand as they downed cheap wine and swam under the stars.

One night, Sawyer and a few others decided to swim out to the far rocks. As the others debated drunkenly how to avoid the waves, Sawyer saw Aino sitting alone in the sand. She had been chewing on her sharp necklace, studiously ignoring them, but throwing them hungry glances whenever she thought they weren't looking.

He called out and invited her to join them.

She hesitated when she heard their plan and pointed out that sharks often hunted near nightfall.

Sawyer had just smiled, warm as always. Asked again.

She said yes.

Once in the deep icy water, she panicked. She thrashed and gasped and scrambled onto a black rock, curling her knees into her chest to not let any part of any limb dangle into the deep.

The others laughed and splashed on.

Sawyer swam over.

He sat next to her on the rock and listened to her strange fear of deep water, and of other people, and how they seemed to be the same thing sometimes.

"My father drowned," he said, simply. "I get it."

She had apologized and apologized.

But Sawyer had just shrugged. He had only told her that to let her know he understood. They both shivered in the cool night air, on the slippery rock that dropped off into endless black water.

"It surprises me, then, that you love the sea," she said. It had been his idea to swim out.

"I love the beach, anyway. I like finding what the tide brings. Me and my dad used to take walks and find treasures."

He looked at her. "It surprises me you don't love the ocean. You have that little shark tooth necklace you always wear."

"It's a rose thorn," she murmured. "Everyone thinks it's a shark tooth, but it's a rose thorn."

"Oh." He paused. "Well, either way, I love it."

The rock felt warmer.

"You're the only one who knows what it really is."

"But not the only one who noticed. Does it matter what you call it?"

The moon shone on the choppy sea, and the stars were out. His usually warm face was chill and silver.

"Of course it matters," she said. "Look at Orion." She pointed to the constellation. "To us, he is a hunter. Fleeing his scorpion nemesis on the other side of the sky. But the same set of stars, to another set of people, is Maui's hook and canoe. To another set, a woman's hand, reaching for something she shouldn't have taken."

"What makes them different?"

"Where you look from, I guess," she said. "What you need them to be."

Sawyer jumped into the black water.

Aino tensed. She would have to make it back on her own.

"Are you scared of the sky?" he called.

"No? Nothing lives there."

"That's not true. You just told me otherwise. Come on in. I'll show you a trick."

Against all her better judgment, she slipped into the water beside him.

He had leaned her back, so his warm hand was at her back, and she was staring at the stars in the sky. Little crystallized points, carrying stories they would never know anything about.

And then he had said something.

Now, in the black pool, she echoed him.

"You are falling into the sky," she murmured. An incantation and a lullaby.

He relaxed into the dark, as she had, back then.

And he went under for the first and last time.

At least there was nothing to fear, where he was going.

She lay beside him after she put on her breather, letting the warm black pool over her.

Something fumbled at her, hit her wrist.

A hand, searching.

She took it.

He laced his long fingers in hers.

For just a hissing machine breath, it felt like belonging. Maybe for both of them.

Aino reached up to her eyepiece.

It took an extra click to activate, which was strange.

YMIR turned on, and she fell back.

Aino had always loved this part.

The brief weightless moments between activation and full immersion when you hung in the dark. Before the system resolved meaning, and memory and foresight had any shape.

Where there were no expectations and no failures.

Just floating in your own skull. Waiting to be born.

Aino could still feel her body, in a distant sense. The way the memories of summer nights from childhood teased and ached.

She hoped Sawyer wasn't frightened. She hoped he found joy in it, too.

Britta had named YMIR after a god in Norse mythology whose death created the world. His flesh became the earth. His blood, the sea.

His skull, became the whole sky.

Britta always liked that part. The idea they were all in someone's head.

Aino never liked that story. She didn't like the thought of being taken apart to become something new. Something useful. It seemed too close to the real world.

Not long after the study abroad, she and Sawyer had crossed paths in another faraway town. They had grabbed dinner and sat outside.

Aino had looked at the stars while she spoke of her work, and he had smiled fondly.

"You get that same look," he'd said. "That one you used to have at the beach. When you were watching everyone else."

She remembered being embarrassed.

But he wasn't wrong. It was the same feeling. Sadness and hunger and a longing to understand others.

The way Sawyer did so effortlessly. To be part of the shining sea of humanity.

"It's not a bad look," he had said, and meant it. "It means you're going places, I think. I get kind of jealous, to be honest."

Sawyer could never break away from his tethers to others, including those who had drowned, who pulled him even now downward.

He was fascinated by Aino's cold and distant world, he had told her; he was still fascinated. If Sawyer was always looking to the sea, then maybe she was always looking to the sky, longing.

And that was a pull, too.

Aino turned it over in her head. He wouldn't be jealous, if he knew how she understood people by taking them apart. Even YMIR han't been the secret key she hoped. She could see the stories now, sure, all the stars across all the skies. Just not anything she was part of.

The first time she had gone into YMIR, she had materialized on a black rock in the sea, off the shore, her pale feet in the cold deep water with only darkness beneath her.

"You always get pulled back," Sawyer had said.

She swam the freezing hundred yards to the Beach alone, praying she encountered nothing, even knowing it was pretend. And then, sand clinging to her wet feet, she had fled to the Forest.

Where the fairytales were from, and where there were rules.

And here they were now, fingertips entangled in the dark. Waiting to fall. Waiting to rise.

We frame our traumas and delights, put them up in electric neural lights, for all of us — when had she told him that?

We trace the star maps and follow them, and by these we are joined. We all have the same stars, even if we can't see them all from where we stand.

And it is here we are all at home.

Or so she had to believe.

For Sawyer's sake.

That, in some way, she was sending him home.

~

It only ever hurt a little, going into the Forest.

Just like lying to a friend.

It wasn't the forest itself. Just the moment of transition — that lurch as you slammed back into your mind like gravity.

Aino usually landed neatly on her feet. This time, she stumbled forward like a sleep-twitch.

She caught herself on the wet prickles of dead leaves, palms pressing into cold loam that smelled like rain and rot and new life all at once. The path beneath her was narrow and faint, twisting through the ancient woods like a half-remembered song. Sinuous dark trees, impossibly tall, curled around her like closing hands.

The light — what little made it through the canopy — was how it always was. A strange luminous bruise of blue from the time of twilight where light seemed like water.

Sawyer hit the ground beside her with a graceless thump, groaning into the earth.

"It takes a little practice," Aino said, offering her hand.

He took it. "Or maybe you just showed up first and are pretending."

She smiled. So did he.

They were both in their own black immersion clothes, with no hint of wires or masks. The system excelled at disregarding what was irrelevant. Mostly. Her left eye never lost the faint electric glow of her eyepiece.

Sawyer brushed off twigs and dirt and leaves — real, as far as his nervous system knew, you could feel their rough and dusty crumbles and hear their crisp whispers — and looked around in awe.

Aino couldn't help but grin and join him.

They were in a forest.

The Forest.

The one from every story, where you only found yourself by getting lost.

Neither of them had grown up with trees like this. They were both from a city in a dry scrubby rolling land, devoid of tall trees or silence or darkness.

But this place lived in their bones anyway. It lived in everyone's.

You could taste the strangely rich air here, like breathing only oxygen, carrying the Forest with it in the cold clear water of gurgling streams and the dirt aerated by ancient roots. Fireflies twisted in looping patterns and birdsong fluttered in the air.

For a moment, Aino could forget what she was here to do, and just believe in fairytales again.

But the chill crawled back up her spine pretty quick, as she realized:

Her handlers hadn't told her what to do next.

"It will be clear," the cashmere man had told her.

But so far, nothing was clear here but the air. And where the edges of the path ended.

Maybe it was just incompetence. If it had just been the missing needles, she'd chalk it up to that.

Or maybe something darker ran under this day.

Sawyer kicked the leaves. They flew out and floated up, like gravity had reversed, gilded in the last rays of the sun.

He laughed, like a child.

A silver shimmer pulsed across the clearing — almost imperceptible, unless you knew what you were looking for.

When the pulse reached the leaves, the scene was reset. The leaves were right back where they started.

"Stay on the path," she said.

He glanced sideways, then tossed a stick in the air.

The shimmer came again, and the stick was back by Sawyer's foot.

"Data update," she explained. "It works as a reset loop. Data comes in from brains, but it doesn't go out. We can't affect anything."

At least, not without an astronomical cost.

Sawyer looked up and around. His eyes were narrow and assessing. The reporter in him, surfacing like a shark. "You made all this?"

"Translated it. Built a frame for it, maybe. A pit for it to pool in."

He turned back to the trees. "It's beautiful."

"That has nothing to do with me."

She said it too sharply, and he smiled with easy grace.

"I doubt that. I think you found a way to where you always talked about — place behind our eyes, where matter and consciousness meet. That place beyond all we know, where all the truths are found. And I know I've always wanted to get there. Ever since..."

He shrugged, and stepped forward. "Why did you let me in?"

She didn't answer right away.

"Because we're friends," she finally said, which was true.

It was one of the main reasons he'd been chosen, even.

She had thought it would be the softest answer, but it still stung with awful surprise. A scorpion in your shoe.

He grinned, like she had said "because I missed you."

"Well, lucky me. Because this story is going to change everything. For both of us. And all because we took the same film class in college. Get ready to shine, Aino!"

It was so easy to get carried away in the flood of his joy.

She almost said: Let's just go home.

Then, he winked at her.

"But," he said. "I'll need more for my story than just a pretty place with your pretty face," he added.

Aino's smile seeped away from her electric eye first.

There it was. The twist, the hidden want, she never wanted to see.

"Sawyer's a hunter," Britta had told her, once. "That's why he's a reporter. He finds something rare and gorgeous, and runs it to ground. That's why he was always circling you."

Britta said a lot of things. Unfortunately, she was often right.

Sawyer wanted more. As if all this wasn't miraculous enough for him. As if she wasn't enough.

Aino looked down the path. Left usually meant you'd find the Crone, and she kept the Wolf away.

She looked to the right.

Maybe they were both calling each other's bluff.

"Let's go right," she said, at the same time as he did.

"Jonx," he said. A texting mistake turned into an old private joke.

"Jonx," she said back, softly.

But intimacy wasn't friendship, she had to remember. Even if he was her friend — there would be no more little children running to their death, if she could help it.

And maybe once they were moving, what she was supposed to do would become clear.

They set off to the right, silent as they walked.

Aino dug her fingernails into her palms, looking for any kind of sign in the still trees for what was going to happen.

The Forest still looked perfect. It always would, no matter what horrors happened here.

Sawyer glanced up at the branches. "So, we're still in the tank."

"Mmm."

"And this is all built from DreamWeaver user data?"

"No," she said flatly.

"Yes it is, Aino."

She sighed. She hated when people tried to reduce her treasure.

"YMIR draws from shared neural architecture, for sure. But this —" she gestured to the path, the trees, the world around them "— is very much a 'whole is greater than the sum of its parts' situation. Especially for the archetypal entities. Like Magician, Mother, Beggar, Wolf, Witch—"

"Father?"

"Oh. You don't want to meet him in the Forest."

He made a noncommittal sound, and pointed to a flickering point of light in the woods. "Will we see any of them?"

"No one's figured out how to predict that. Not even me, and the Forest has rules."

"Like, stay on the path."

"Right. Feed the hungry. Don't give your name." She paused. "The Wolf doesn't always look like a wolf."

He stopped, and turned towards her.

"You don't sound like an academic. You sound like you've lived here."

178

"I suppose I have."

"Does it feel..." He gestured to the Forest around them, the fireflies and the will-o-wisps and birdsong and magic streams, and the silver shimmer, "more real than real life?"

His blue eyes were bright. Not skeptical. Just curious.

Whatever she gave him now would stay here. Just like he would.

"I think it can be more honest. Easier. It knows it's a story, and that can make it true."

"And you think this makes it okay? Taking people's data, and turning their minds into myth?"

Her face burned. "The collective unconscious exists whether people like it or not. Or can see it or not. Archetypes aren't invented. They're just what's left after a thousand retellings. Like constellations — traced with a shaky finger until the stars finally hold still. And anyway," she added. "Everyone who uses the DreamWeaver signs the waiver."

He raised an eyebrow.

"Page four."

Sawyer laughed. "What if they feel like they were violated? That two entitled young women turned the deepest parts of themselves into a product."

Aino's stomach knotted. "We didn't take anything. We just translated what was there."

Sawyer stopped walking.

"Do you really believe that?"

She stopped too.

"Why do you want to go to the Ocean, Sawyer? Instead of the Forest."

He blinked. "What?"

"Is it because you hope to see your father there?"

Now who felt small and pathetic.

His mouth opened — stunned.

Did Britta always feel this nasty, after a jab? Probably not.

Sawyer reached out to grab a pine branch as he steadied himself.

Fair is fair, she could see him tell himself as he recalibrated, before he turned back to her.

"Oh, I always see my father there, Aino."

She stayed quiet.

"But I never can reach him," he added, gently. Almost an afterthought.

Of course he couldn't, she didn't say.

If you cared about truth, dreams never offered absolution. Just life unfinished, as you found it here.

Britta had found the same thing with her dead husband.

They stood in the hush of the simulated dusk. It was growing darker. The air had turned violet wet and worried, like a first snow approaching.

The path ahead looked more narrow.

"Wait," Sawyer cried out. "What's that?"

Before she could answer, he stepped off the path.

Just took off, like the rules meant nothing. Just one more step toward something gleaming in the dark.

As if the Forest didn't always give you exactly what you earned, in the end.

"Sawyer! Don't!"

She floundered after him, pushing away branches that scratched and whipped at her until she stumbled into a clearing she had never seen before.

It was just a little break in the trees — like surfacing from a dream, for a moment, until you're pulled right back under again. Roses grew everywhere, dark and luminous in the emerging starlight.

Something wasn't right. The usual YMIR reset pulse came faster, with a green tinge. Like something had excited its heart.

Above them was the sky. More sky than Aino had ever seen in the Forest, every time put together. She felt she was standing before a great chasm in the earth that had opened up into nothing but stars.

She touched her chest, where her thorn necklace would have lain, had she worn it. But all you could bring into YMIR was yourself.

Here she was, in her own head, under the stars, in Ymir's head, under the stars, dreaming all of it in a skull under the stars — the recursion hit hard, and vertigo swelled.

She swayed.

Aino reached out for a tree branch but found Sawyer's arm instead.

He patted her hand, so pleased. Like he had coaxed her back out onto that black rock in the sea once more.

Something ripped, and Sawyer yelped and jumped back.

A silver axe clattered into the moss between them.

They stared at it.

Sawyer picked it up. "Um...I think this just came out of my pocket. Is this usual?"

Aino blinked. Then she laughed. "Oh my god. That dumb sharpener blade. You put it back in your pocket, didn't you?"

"I panicked."

She leaned over the axe. "YMIR must have scanned it, and turned it into something it found more...fitting." She smiled, wide and wan, and curtsied. "The good woodcutter of the Forest!"

"Aino," he murmured. "Your teeth."

Her fingertips went to her mouth.

Her teeth had all gone sharp.

The Forest was changing them. Or maybe it was revealing what they were becoming all along.

But she wasn't supposed to be part of that at all.

"Let's go back to the path," she said, through her hand over her mouth. "Now. I mean it. Now."

But Sawyer just turned to the roses. "One second. Before things get reset."

He lifted the axe, and reverently sliced a scarlet rose off a bush. The stem fought him, shredding like something between silk and tendon.

"Thank you," Sawyer said. "For bringing me here. I always knew I could count on you."

He held out the rose. "Now quick, take it. Before it gets reset."

"No!" she cried, and lunged for the flower. Too quick — thorns bit her hand. She tried to place it back in the bush.

The silver shimmer passed through them, and this time, Aino felt it like the beat of a drum.

The rose did not come back together, or join its sisters in the bush. It stayed gone. Cut. And blood bloomed a red sister rose for it across her palm, pattering to the brush below.

Sawyer stared at the rose.

"Oh," he said. "You are writing data, aren't you. If I'm understanding what is happening right."

There wasn't a script for this. No interview talking points. She had been left out to hang. To make this cut as brutal as possible.

"You're changing everyone's minds," he said. "All of them, that use the DreamWeaver. On a level they'll never know."

Aino raised her hand, sucking the blood from it like a sullen child.

Sawyer didn't understand all of it.

He never would.

"What does that do? If you rewrite a rose in people's heads?" he asked. "Or — no, it wouldn't just be that, would it?"

"I was surprised too, when I figured it out."

"Aino."

Would he really make her say it? Would they?

Everything was becoming too messy.

She brought the rose to her face and inhaled.

"It's sweet," she marveled. "The sweetest I've ever been given. The only one I've ever been given. Thank you."

Sawyer reached for her. She jerked away.

Her mouth left blood streaks on his arm that turned her stomach. In her mouth, her teeth were sharp, and the taste lingered, bitter and blooming metallic. There were tears in her eyes she didn't care to acknowledge.

She had to end this. It was all going wrong.

"Why did you bring me here, Aino?" His grip tightened on the axe.

He was catching on.

Her bloody hand hovered near her electric eye, ready to get herself out. She sucked down the blood in her mouth.

"It's your time to shine, Sawyer," she repeated, and then couldn't stop a giggle at how stupid and cruel it sounded, even if it was true. "You'll get what you want. You'll help people. Be remembered. Famous, even. As the honorable woodcutter, maybe? I'm not sure. A risk that backfires. That's what you're supposed to be encoded as."

"What does that mean?" His voice cracked. He was much taller than Aino; he loomed. "What does encoding entail?"

She spat a petal that had somehow gotten into her mouth, a crumpled red glob.

His fear was already haunting her. Why weren't they doing something, her handlers? Why weren't they saving her from this?

"Encoding means dissolving your neural matrix into YMIR, at a very specific point," she finally said, hiding behind honesty.

But Sawyer wasn't stupid.

"Dissolving? The pattern? You don't mean..."

"There is no consciousness without matter," she said, as she had said before, and what she was saying finally sank in, and he understood.

He would not survive this.

Archetypes were rich. They were patterns and stories that persisted throughout all humanity. You couldn't just write a program to make one that stuck.

(They had tried. Aino, most of all.)

The only thing as rich in meaning and potential, was a person.

The trick was:

You couldn't just copy a person over.

You had to burn them in.

In encoding — scanning the raw material and writing it in — the person was destroyed.

Like melting the wax from a mold with fire. Like casting a sigil by reducing to ash.

The pattern, the story, it lived on in all people.

The archetype survived; the person did not. Or so the theory went.

Sawyer would be the proof.

"It'll save millions," she said. "It'll keep us from the war."

He stepped back. "Please, Aino. Please. You can't. I have a family."

"So does everyone," she lied.

She didn't have one anymore.

He laughed in disbelief. "So, you won't stop."

"I can't," she said.

The starlight reflected on his wet cheeks. He slammed his axe into a nearby tree. It didn't heal.

"This was the only place you were ever home, isn't it," he said, and how calmly he said it made it slip sharp between her ribs. "In your head. And now in others' heads. But you can't do this. People have to invite you into their heads and hearts. I invited you, Aino. I was the only one who did."

She bit her lip until it bled.

He didn't look, as he pulled the axe out. "Or are you just happy now that you can force people to pay attention to you."

The jabs weren't unfair. Aino backed onto the path. "For what it's worth, you were my friend," she said. "My only one left."

He raised his axe with a cry. To cut her in two, like the wood-cutter cuts open the wolf in the story.

She stood.

He couldn't hurt her here, but he didn't know that.

Then he lowered his arm, with the same cry.

"You were mine," he said, instead.

"This is the only way to stop what is coming," she said miserably.

"Is that what they told you?" he almost hissed. "Whoever is behind this? If they'll take me, they'll take you too."

He jabbed a finger into her chest. Where her thorn would have rested.

"You're part of their plan too," he said. "I'm certain. Will you be dissolved too?"

"What?"

"How could you not be? Why did you have to take me, otherwise? Why did we, the two of us, matter?"

Her eyes flared.

Of course. Not a risk. A ritual. Not a messenger, but a match.

She was the other half of the fire that would burn them both in.

So much fell into place. Why it had to be him, especially after Britta had fled. It wasn't about him at all, really — it was the both of them.

Or what either of them became in this act. What she'd become by doing it. What he would become by having it done to her.

What they'd be, together.

They had lied to her.

It wasn't about risk at all. Not really.

But then — if they lied about this, what else were they lying about?

What if this whole thing wouldn't help anyone but them?

Good God, what would she have done for them?

What had she done already?

Her hands shook.

Sawyer placed his axe in them.

"Remember me, at least," he said.

What monster was she becoming, trying to do right in a way only she could?

"You're right," she whispered. "I'm so sorry. Let's go home. Let's get you a real story."

His shoulders collapsed, and he hugged her. Without his support, she might have fallen.

185

She adjusted the controls on eyepiece to include him in the exit, and pressed the button at her temple to take them home.

She started fading — a pleasant, numbing sparkle of a feeling.

But Sawyer started screaming.

He fell to his knees and his body arched backwards. Light erupted from his outline, branding him into her eyes.

He was dying. He was being burned in.

Mind is matter is soul is consciousness. That's why you had to dissolve someone, for it to work. That's why you had to kill them.

And they had rigged the exit protocol so that if she tried to save him, to take him out too —

She'd be the one to set off his encoding. His death.

Maybe they had always known she would have second thoughts, and try to save him.

She clicked every button she could, blindly, frantically.

Nothing would let her stop what was happening.

Aino cried out. She flew down to him, to hold him. It was all she could do, was be with him at the end, as he burned away.

He gripped her wrists, pleading as best he could.

Dying.

Becoming a myth.

She could barely feel him, she was fading so fast. But held on with all her might, cradling him like she was holding him up in water.

Like he had once held her up in water.

"Shh," she sobbed, and pressed her forehead to his for a moment. "Shh. Look up. Look up at the stars."

His eyes fluttered open, and he obeyed. Some of his pain seemed to still. The stars above him were sharp and glittering, in a velvet sea past all the tangled branches.

"You are falling into the sky," she said into his ear.

Sawyer smiled, and closed his eyes. He relaxed into her arms.

By the time she disappeared, he was already gone —

Dissolved into a thousand points of scattered light.

I t had been so easy to say yes.

The first so-called government rep came to the rented offices Aino and Britta rented off a scrubby little feeder highway. The building was limestone, but so was everything there. They were way overdue for a move — too much success in too little time — but they both liked how hidden it felt.

Felt, until he showed up.

He was a middle-aged man, dark-haired and disarmingly handsome.

"Too handsome to actually be government," Britta muttered, just outside the glass walls of their only meeting room. "He's wearing cologne that costs at least five hundred."

"You can't know his cologne just from letting him in, and also that makes no sense you can't be too handsome for something," Aino said.

He politely gave no sign he heard them, or the examples Britta gave to disprove Aino. All he did was invite them to a meeting at his organization's offices.

"Who says organization," Britta said.

"Government," Aino answered, and Britta blew a raspberry.

The proposition took place in a squat brick building solidly from the 1980s. Outside, the smell of cedars and the harsh buzz of cicadas and sunlight. Inside, there was a certain unsettling gloss, as if it had been recently renovated to look exactly the same.

Waiting for them was a woman their mothers' age, but dressed like a Cold War secretary: pumps, pearls, nylons.

She flattered them first: Britta, the born artist and self-trained linguist, and Aino, the born engineer and self-trained architect. Both of them neuroscientists.

"How so much, at such a young age?" she asked.

"We're maladaptive," Britta smiled. "Like you must be, to be here in this circumstance."

The woman laughed. That was the right way to deal with Britta.

"We've been keeping a close eye on your progress for some time. And with the unrest in Europe and now Southeast Asia — well." She slid a manila folder across the table. "We have an opportunity to prevent what's in this folder."

Aino opened the folder. Full-color photographs of atrocity. Wounded families. Rubble. Dead children.

She pushed it back, reflexively.

"You just printed those out at the office printer?" Britta sneered.

"We don't want this coming here," the woman said.

"I'm sure they didn't either," Aino said.

"Exactly," the woman said. "We want to stop it."

The agent leaned toward Aino. "We believe your tech might let us encode...a directive, into the collective unconscious. Something stabilizing. Something merciful. If we do this right, we could save —"

"I don't think we've told anyone about that," Aino said, startled at her own interruption. "About the collective unconscious."

"No," said Britta, eyes locked on the agent. "We haven't."

"A close eye," the woman said again, gently. "If you could do it..." She pushed back the folder, spilling out the pictures. She opened the folder again — this time to a proposal, typed and footnoted, beside the bodies.

"We can't." Britta started stacking the photos, like a dealer folding a bad hand. She snapped away the one Aino had been staring at, of a little child newly orphaned.

"We can," Aino said, already far away in the future, mapping it. She held up her hand when Britta protested. "Not yet, of course. But we are ourselves only so much data. Any obstacle we face, is only an issue of translation."

"What a miracle that would be," the woman said. "You'd be beloved the world over. A few hundred years ago, they'd have named a constellation after you."

"If it went right," Britta said, her eyes on Aino.

Aino looked at the folder, then out the window at the wide white sky.

~

Britta and Aino met again that night in their old university library. Britta's idea; she now thought their entire office was bugged.

Aino arrived first. Their favorite study room was just how she remembered, with its beat-up pine table, bleeding dry-erase stains, and beautiful view of campus.

There was a single worn book wedged in a corner: The Blue Fairy Book. One of their old source texts for the DreamWeaver, when they were mapping and translating archetypes. Wild, it hadn't been put away.

Aino was flipping through it when Britta burst in.

"I think we should say yes," Aino said quickly.

Britta sat down and laughed. "Oh, it's not a choice, Aino. It's an order."

"That's ridiculous. And not legal, I think."

"Well, I think this isn't the government. It's something worse."

Aino rolled her eyes. "You can't just force people."

Her friend's mouth twisted. "Really?"

Britta pulled the book toward her. It was open to an illustration of a girl walking through a thick forest, from the story Diamonds and Toads. The tale of two sisters — one kind and giving, the other selfish and cruel. By the end, the unkind one was cursed to spit out serpents and toads when she spoke. The kind one, diamonds and roses.

She tapped the page. "This isn't the Forest, Aino. There aren't rules. People do whatever they want out here. Whatever they can."

"So, we have to say yes? Then we agree."

"No. We have to run, is what I'm saying."

Aino looked at her friend. The dark circles under her eyes. The strange gold pendant hanging around her neck — the one she claimed was magic, and that now held her husband's ashes.

"You need sleep."

Britta's mouth curled. "Yeah, yeah — crazy Britta and her dead husband and her dead god."

Aino took a slow breath. Ever since Britta's husband had died last year, Britta had become more erratic. Beautiful, dark-haired, good with a pitch, her husband had been their press and funding guy.

His death was sudden. One of those stupid tragedies, where he just got sick and accidentally tipped over into a coffin. And Britta had never really come back from it. Just buried herself in her Dream-Weaver, until she'd claimed she had met someone. A god, that could bring her husband back.

"I think we can help people," Aino said.

Britta opened her mouth, then closed it. She rubbed her hand over her face. "I may not know exactly who those people are, Aino. But I know what they are. People like that will take everything from you."

She jabbed the picture of the sister in the fairy tale. In the Forest.

"This girl, the "kind" girl, she becomes beloved and revered in the story. But that's not what happens in real life. In real life, you drop roses and diamonds from your throat, soon they won't wait for you to speak."

Britta closed the book.

"Soon, they'll just cram their arms down your throat. And pull everything they want out, bleeding."

Aino flushed. She knew why Britta thought that way; she came from a family of wolves that ate her up when she was small.

But surviving that upbringing had made her selfish and hostile.

And Aino knew fairytales too. Her namesake was from a fairy tale.

"What if the roses are human lives," she said. The pictures haunted her. Less important of course, was that this was the kind of thing that won the Nobel.

"What if they tell you it's lives, but it's just money," Britta snapped back.

"Then we'll be richer and can help that way."

Britta scoffed. She was losing.

Aino looked down at the picture of the girl and her roses. Britta didn't understand — people would always want to bask in your glory and use it to their advantage. That didn't make them evil, necessarily. Just disappointing.

Anyway, she wasn't saying yes to them. She was saying yes to the numbers; it was just good math.

"We should just see if we can," Aino urged.

Britta didn't look at her. "If you can. I'm just the translator," she said, after a pause.

Aino sighed at the bitterness in her friend's voice. Britta had clearly decided Aino wasn't going to listen, which was unfair.

Britta wasn't stupid. She was probably right to be wary. Even afraid.

But the dark truth was: Britta's pain and ambition and grief weren't the fuel she thought. They were blinders.

Aino was smarter than that. Kinder, too. She could save people, if she wanted. She could give wonder, safety, possibility to the whole wide world — not just chew it all up chasing down some selfish impossible goal like resurrecting a dead love.

Besides, who could make her give what she didn't want to? She'd destroy YMIR before she let that happen.

Whatever came from her, diamonds or treasure or revolutionary tech, was hers alone.

Alone, like always.

Aino's name meant Only One. And the story of the fairytale Aino, was of the girl that drowned. And so Aino had always had to hope that you could escape your own story.

She looked out the window.

Outside, the stars were like diamonds, waiting to be plucked like roses.

The price to buy her way in. The price to ransom a whole world.

Or maybe just the price to rescue one child, weeping in a photograph.

And it wasn't so much they were asking, after all.

Just translation. Just alchemy. Turning words here into something more precious than diamonds.

And those stars could be hers, like how they belonged to everyone else.

And maybe if she gave enough, they'd let her join them.

On some level, Aino knew what would happen to her, even then.

Translation, as Britta always said, was the business of being carried from one place to another. Into another state of being entirely.

"Right," Aino said, far away and flying once more. "If I can."

As it turned out, they could reach down your throat and rip your very heart out.

Britta had been right. Even Sawyer had been on to something. But it had been more than a year since she had seen either of them.

There was no one left to tell.

Aino got up from her desk and started packing up.

It didn't take long; they didn't let her take much to "work" these days. Lip balm, water bottle, wallet, hand lotion. It was still shocking they let her keep her original computer — a little out of date now, with a peeling sticker of a star inside a skull. The logo — or sigil, as Britta called it — of their old company.

She traced it absently with her finger.

Soon, it would be gone, too.

Even with the little they had her do, the days they called her in felt endless, working under low fluorescents and high surveillance, and only in the rooms adjacent to YMIR. Of course, she didn't need to be close to see how they were prying apart the world, a hundred thousand brains at a time.

Every visit, they assigned her less and less.

She helped them make their little changes, their suggestions, aesthetic updates, emotional feedback loops, and the like.

Mostly, she did maintenance: restarting the update pulse whenever they clogged the works.

And, just like every day, she searched for a way back into YMIR — a security gap, a backdoor, a sympathetic soul, anything.

She always came up dry.

And so she always came back the next time they asked. There were more effective ways than violence to make someone comply.

Aino had learned little about that night in the tank. Only the encoding had worked how they wanted.

She hoped it was a lie. Life outside of YMIR was getting worse and worse.

The wars had stopped, yes. That math added up.

But another darkness had taken their place.

And that equation — whatever it was — seemed to hemorrhage.

Her minder next to her jolted a little in his chair when she stood. A new one, since the plane. This one was compact and officious, and long past pretending he was working on YMIR too.

"Remember, the party this evening," he said.

She slowly uncapped and recapped her lip balm. "Oh. Yeah, sorry. I'm gonna miss it."

"I can't call a car for you until after." Even his small frown was overbearing.

She jammed the tube into her little clear bag. This place did so love a little rote humiliation.

"I'll walk," she said airily.

She left with her cheeks flushed. A ghost exiting her own haunting.

"I wouldn't," he called after her.

She opened the door out, and nearly choked on all the sound and indignation.

A crowd had gathered outside the fence. Not the usual loose handful of crazies and the curious. A throng. Chanting and singing God knew what.

Nobody but employees were allowed past the fences. But their voices and signs made it through just fine.

Aino had already stepped outside before she could think better of it. The sight of her was chum to sharks. The unseasonal heat slammed into her along with the fury of the shouts.

She squinted against the sun, trying to make out what they wanted.

Silly of her — it could only be one thing.

A law was going through today, canceling all the nation's monopoly laws. It was the reason for the awful party tonight. The organization started lobbying for the removal soon after they black-mailed Aino into signing the company over to them.

She walked closer to the protestors, smiling.

In another timeline, she might have stood with them.

Though maybe not this particular group. These ones had a repu-tation for quite literally burning cities down to get what they wanted.

The Wolfcutters, they were called.

Some held banners and poster boards. Others held plastic toy axes.

Some of them even wore painted plastic masks that looked like something from a children's cautionary tale.

The sight was so strange, so childlike and grotesque at once, that Aino almost smiled.

Then, she recognized the face.

Sawyer.

Her breath caught. She hadn't spoken his name in months, hadn't let herself. But she knew, with that sudden internal chill, exactly what this was.

At least a dozen of them were wearing his face.

Not exactly. But close enough: an echo, stylized. A folk-hero mask filtered through riot aesthetics.

Maybe this is why they lied to her, and told her the encoding worked. Because it had. Just not in a way they wanted — in a way that would hurt them.

Aino walked closer to the fence, not caring about the security shadowing her. She smiled, letting their chants and taunts and fence-rattling fall on her like welcome rain.

A small plastic axe hit her shoulder. She bent to pick it up.

Something was scrawled in permanent marker on the handle:

If you want it, you must need it.

Her heart sank.

She began to really see the signs they held.

TAKE OFF THE SAFETIES

LET US DREAM

IF YOU WANT IT, YOU MUST NEED IT

The words floated past her at first like fallen leaves. She blinked, trying to puzzle them into any kind of meaning.

What did any of this have to do with monopolies?

Then the chant broke through:

Take the shackles off of me!

Let us all be free to dream!

And it clicked.

This wasn't about corporate law. This was about the Dream-Weavers.

They wanted the organization to remove the safeties from the DreamWeavers.

All of the safeties.

The filters that kept out torture. Genocide. What some people wanted with children.

And they were doing it all while wearing Sawyer's face.

She staggered back a step. What had she done?

Her knees buckled. She knelt in the gravel and concrete at the base of the fence.

This wasn't even about power, really.

This was about permission.

It was about the monopolies, in a way. That was one protection pulled down. But it didn't upset them — it just wasn't enough.

These people raged at the very idea of being told no.

And they had somehow made Sawyer their patron saint.

No, not Sawyer. Whatever he had been twisted into.

She looked up at a poster board, hand-drawn in black and red. A cartoon woodcutter—grinning, triumphant—stood over a pile of severed wolves, and a woman pierced by roses.

The caption read:

IF YOU WANT IT, YOU MUST NEED IT

Fine sentiment, if it's a child in need.

Less fine if it were any kind of bully, or abuser, or anyone else mistaking their desires for entitlements.

Axes everywhere. Signs with that warped face. The little plastic axes at their sides. All crying to kill.

She pushed past the guard to go right up to the fence and lace her fingers through the lattice. Maybe she was wrong. She had been wrong about so many things lately.

Near her, a man with a sweat-damp torn paper mask shouted the loudest. His eyes were glassy; he had already been looking at too many things he shouldn't have for far too long.

"Why are you the Wolfcutters?" she asked.

He told her.

They called themselves the Wolfcutters like they were cutting down the wolves — not seeing they were the wolves themselves, cutting down all that kept them safe.

In their minds, they were heroes.

In humanity's mind, they were wolves.

He smiled at his righteousness through her friend's torn face.

~

Aino didn't go home. There was no home to go back to, now. Wherever she could flee, what was in all their heads would already be there.

She ran back inside the warehouse, and had to wait in the hallway to catch her breath. Hugging the walls like she was back with Sawyer, pretending the cameras couldn't see her.

Cold light hummed and spilled over the scuffed tiles, a harmonic with her panic.

There was only one thing to do. Like always, lately, it was the last thing she wanted.

Up to now, Aino had avoided learning too much about what she'd done. She figured it would only hurt till she could get back into YMIR and fix things. So, she'd dodged the news, skipped every comm she could, and flinched away from any movie or media he might flicker through.

Like chewing around a rotten tooth.

Now, though, she had to bite down hard.

She had to find out exactly what she had done. Only then, could she fix it.

She returned to her station, breezing past the security checkpoints like she had only stepped out for a little smoke. Her minder hunched at his console, composing an email that probably subject-lined something like "I told her not to, very strongly, and yet."

"Still having trouble finding Sawyer?"

He closed his draft. "Who?"

She kept her smile bright. "The Woodcutter. Like, y'all can't find him in YMIR, right? Other than his encoding."

That got his attention. He swiveled all the way around. "We asked for your help months ago."

"That was before I saw the protestors," she said. "All Woodcutter iconography. Did you know?"

He shrugged. "Just because I know something doesn't mean it matters."

Aino bit her tongue. "Words to live by," was all she said. "I'd love to see the research. It might help me find him."

"Why? You know what? Never mind. Sure. You got a few hours." He turned and forwarded something. "There. Check your inbox. That'll be the 501st time I sent it."

"And 502 thank you's shall be yours. I won't even copy-paste."

"It really doesn't matter anymore."

She ignored the bait, and sat down and started reading.

There were hundreds of entries of how Sawyer popped up in the material world: incident logs, synaptic readouts, simulation reviews, ads, academic articles, meme sets, sentiment trackers, news clips, secondary characters in films.

The Woodcutter: the kind man in the woods. He was everywhere.

Especially in the new packaged Dreams her organization sold like aesthetic poppers, so people would never have to touch their own tacky aching subconscious.

A resonance archetype, they called him. It. A new pattern.

The axe seemed to be at the center. Sharp and self-effacing and always present; power, turned on itself.

In the old fairy tale, the axe was used to cut someone out of the belly of the beast. To find truth. In this version? It never swung. It was given up.

This woodcutter, he gave up himself to a kind of wolf, the Eater of Roses, and this put a new spin on the story. He didn't cut. He gave up.

All because Sawyer couldn't hurt her.

That's why it had to be the both of them, in the original encoding.

Aino felt sick. All she had wanted was to help. All she had wanted was to belong. And maybe to get a little credit for what she created. Surely these appetites were not monstrous.

Even if she had left an echo in YMIR without dying. At least, not physically.

But in this framing, anything, any power that was not the wolf's, was monstrous.

Certain phrases kept cropping up; variations on a theme. Don't ask what it costs. You should be happy to keep them warm. And of course:

If you want it, you must need it.

Aino stared at that line a long time — the phrase from the protest signs, flickering on her screen.

It seemed good on the surface, as did the others. Charitable and kind.

What she'd seen inside this building and out was anything but.

The problem, of course, if you only saw a sliver of a sentiment. Not the whole pattern or archetype. Even the monstrous could be palatable.

Aino felt cold. The protestors hadn't fought to help. They had fought for the rights — not even rights, but wants — of the wolf.

That's all any of this was.

Britta had been right. She always was, about people. She had certainly seen that Aino would fail her too.

Aino covered her mouth with her hand. But she kept reading. Something was eluding her.

Sawyer had been encoded into the collective unconscious as an archetype, a kind of pattern, sure. Regular archetypes were powerful, and popped up everywhere in the real world. But they were more about describing the world, than totally rewriting it.

The Woodcutter was too everywhere. And too powerful.

You could chalk it up to zeitgeist, but there was a more cold and sinister undercurrent to it.

He wasn't just an archetype. He definitely wasn't a cautionary tale like they promised.

No, he seemed to be a blueprint. A pattern of action.

A man who didn't fight back. Who let the wolf do as it pleased.

Who gave his boundaries, his blood, his name, to the people who needed it more. He would never say no.

The generous Woodcutter, who made a living off the land and brought you fuel and who somehow never left a mark. Who gave up his axe, his boundaries, his life, his name. A symbol of surrender and self-abnegation disguised as nobility.

How was this possible?

Also in the folder were neural maps and feedback looks. This was DreamWeaver stuff, and strange stuff at that — it shouldn't be here.

Whatever it was, it was only activated for the lower models. For those who couldn't pay enough to opt out of them.

It seemed almost as if —

She was still reading, hands numb, when someone tapped her shoulder.

"Party's started," her minder said. "You'll want to be there."

The cake bar had been set up inside the empty YMIR tank. Convenience or a joke, either was equally repulsive.

Aino stayed back, until one of her "friends" pulled her in. She almost tripped on the rim. She was handed a plastic glass of moderately-priced red wine, and was surprised enough to say thank you. There was a fingerprint of frosting on it.

The speech began, from the manager that she still thought of as the cashmere man.

He listed the company's wins. The new DreamWeaver model was shipping soon, one that didn't need Aino at all. YMIR's final update was live. The monopoly laws had been repealed.

"This means no one can touch our Dreams," he said, "or undercut our Woodcutter."

Sawyer. He wasn't the Woodcutter. He was Sawyer.

He raised his glass for a toast. "We'll keep giving our clients exactly what they want. What they need."

She kept her empty cup clenched at her side.

"Come here," he said, and gestured for Aino to come up. Horrified, she complied. His grip was firm on her thin shoulders. "And of course, we must recognize Aino. None of this would have been possible without her."

He handed her a small box, hand-tied with blue ribbon.

"The axe that stopped a war," he said. "For our hero."

She unwrapped it with thick fingers and, finally, teeth.

Inside was a tiny silver object: the sharpener's blade; the one Sawyer had used.

Aino stared at it. It still had dried blood on it.

"You've been such a help. It's a pity we won't need you back after the new DreamWeaver release."

So they were firing her, too.

"Thank you," she finally said again, so he would let go of her, and she could reel back against the rim.

Someone pressed another full wine cup into her hand, so she could join the cashmere man's next toast.

"To Aino," he said, "And the pattern she encoded. And to everyone who helped it along, with the neurotransmitter boosts."

Aino looked sharply at him.

So that's why Sawyer was everywhere.

"If you want it," he said, smiling, raising his glass, "you must need it!"

They all echoed it back. The new corporate slogan. The new catechism of the unconscious.

She drank, and they all drank red wine where Sawyer had died, and where Aino realized finally what she had done.

The neural maps she had been confused by were dopamine-trigger instructions. Further encoding ecstasy when they saw the Woodcutter archetype, wiring together all those pathways.

People got a rush of moral self-righteousness by agreeing. By surrendering.

By yielding.

That's why he was stronger than an archetype. He was a pattern of action, that they had twisted by emphasizing the wrong parts.

They had paired Sawyer's face with a behavioral loop so potent it made people give themselves away—and feel good about it. It made the eradication of boundaries holy.

Both sides of the idea, that no one should ever say no to you.

Of course, the dopamine loops were only in the non-elite models. It was really:

No one vulnerable should ever say no.

Her stomach turned.

The cashmere man had told her the truth. He had told her true things, anyway.

The wars ended, mostly. That part had worked.

But only because something worse had taken its place — a kind of spiritual rot.

And now she understood what she saw in the news.

Boundaries fell. People stopped protecting themselves. Just a little at first, then more. The vulnerable given to the strong, because after all, if you want it, you must need it.

You deserve it.

There was no need for war because no one stopped bullies from taking whatever they wanted.

And everyone forgot how to say no.

People clamored, in fact, for you not to be able to say no.

This was what she had helped encode.

Not safety. Not peace. Not caution or gentleness or collective care.

Not charity.

Compliance.

She had written obedience into the walls of the world.

She had made a Christ of the consumed. Not the risen or the redeemer, but the one on the cross, forever. The golden boy with open hands, pinned in place for everyone's convenience.

One that never once asked for it all to stop.

One who got nothing in return except eaten.

But sacrifice wasn't sacrifice if you didn't get anything back, including the good of someone else. She hadn't sacrificed Sawyer.

She had just fed him to the Wolves that ran out here in this world. And in doing so, helped feed the whole world to them.

The wine in her throat turned to acid.

Aino wandered the edges of the room, smiling automatically, until she made it to the back of the tank. She refilled her glass and drank, and refilled it again. They hadn't even really cleared out the tank. Shoved to to the side, were coiled wires and obsolete ports and, at the very bottom, her old Runner headset. Electric blue and dormant.

The eyepiece still gleamed like a faraway star.

Kneeling, she slipped the little blade from her pocket. After only a little sawing, she cut the cable and freed it.

The wine in her cup was still dark and red.

Aino dropped the headset inside her cup, and let it sink into the dark liquid.

They'd let her take the wineglass with her home, in the car they would eventually call for her.

It was, after all, her last day at work.

Aino slammed the door behind her and flicked on the watery kitchen light. It sputtered, like always, and she killed it again. She crossed the apartment in five strides and upended her purse on the chipped bar counter — in this place, the surface served as altar, grave, dining table, desk.

The black Dream eggs skittered in all directions. She caught them with a practiced arm.

This wasn't her first vending-machine-dream-rodeo, as the saying went. Although it would be the last.

Her eyepiece hadn't been enough to help her get back into YMIR. She needed something that dealt with its stories and patterns, to wend a way back. She needed Dreams.

After this week, nothing her stupid shadow agency (company,

org, whatever) released would run on her DreamWeaver. The new models were as sterile and locked down as most of the Dreams. There'd be no more cracks she could slip through, to undo what she had done. These little eggs held her last hope.

She lined up the metal cartridges like a firing squad, with their stupid names in lurid shrink-wrap packaging. Yes Mr. President. Pastoral Drift. Girl's Night 17.

Outside, rain blurred the world like she was underwater already. The false streetlamp's oily orange light was all she would work by.

This corporate apartment was new, and a far cry from the luxe little hideaway she'd bought when Britta moved into her sprawling mansion. But she hadn't been brave enough to sleep there in a year. The press painted her as someone profiting off the minds of others, some sort of selfish monstrous cross of a vampire and lotus eater that also (somehow?) wasn't sexy at all. She'd become a target.

This place was one of the new apartment complex/corporate colonies built to keep workers close and dependent. Desperate, most of all. Sometimes the shoddy little faux-homey corporate touches like fake woodgrain on the floor and false windows turned her stomach.

But at least here, she was invisible again. And it was better than what lay outside.

Out there, the wolves she had freed tore through everyone's skulls.

After the party, after she realized what they had done with Sawyer, it felt like she walked through the world with peeled skin, open and raw. She could escape nothing. Every sadness and horror she encountered flayed her further.

Like how you could sell people now, if someone agreed to it.

She had walked the whole city that evening, trying to pick up every piece of the new batch. You got them for a dollar, these price-less pieces of tech. And in return, you got what the company felt you deserved.

She'd passed two little boys on the way home with dark-rung eyes, staring at a display for a Christmas dream.

"Maybe this year," the smaller one said. "We'll be good enough this year."

The older one just looked at him. The man who dragged them away, barked like he owned them. And maybe he did.

How she had failed them.

Her hand shook. She picked up a cartridge and cracked it with a kitchen knife. It hissed and uncurled, the evil little thing, like a black scorpion.

She and Britta had built the DreamWeaver to map your mind, and maybe even show your soul. These pre-made Dreams, filtered and scrubbed of anything fertile, were a way to forget you had either.

But they were still dreams. They still could hold a pattern that could crack her way back to YMIR. Back to the scene of the crime against all humanity.

She leaned back, and clipped the scorpion to her ear. It pierced her temple; a sting she was used to. She had, after all, traded much worse for less.

The strange Dream smell filled her nostrils — rose and ozone. The company hated it, but couldn't get rid of it. Only Aino knew what and whose signature it was. She was the only one left who did.

She breathed in deep.

And once more, like always, Aino let herself fall.

The first dream was shallow. Action-sci-fi nonsense made of repurposed neon and old robot rules with no archetypal resonance. A scrawled cartoon that would starve anyone who tried to live on it, and gave her nothing.

Aino reached for the next. And the next

Fantasy tavern runner. Frontier ghost romance where the happy ending was erasing yourself. Cowgirl werewolf wedding. Fairy court drama where the rejected lover coughed up rose petals.

Each cartridge clattered off her head when she woke. Each Dream punctured a little deeper.

This wasn't just wasted time, now. This wasn't just lost hope.

This was the world now, doled out in little metal eggs, bleached clean of any memory or meaning.

The last one on the table caught her breath: a descent beneath the ocean, light falling away—until it bloomed again from below, into anglerfish with real lanterns, in an ocean of stars.

She pried open the cartridge with a knife and plugged in her eyepiece. Her pulse pounded in her bleeding temple as she examined the code.

Just trash data; a lazy echo of what had been in someone's head.

Still nothing.

She swept all the cracked and emptied shells off the counter. They clattered to the floor, hollow husks of what might have been.

None of them had anything true. So none could take her back.

Aino only had one last hope: the little egg that had taken all week to hunt down, at a cost that watered even her eyes.

She fumbled it out of her coat pocket.

Cabin Companion, the label said, under the bright RECALL sticker. Every so often, a Dream would mutate into something interesting, and it would have to be recalled. It had been smashed, as was protocol.

But this one's program was still intact.

It uncurled best it could, with a hiss. She repaired it with tweezers and solder, trying to focus on fine and finicky work and not why she had saved it for last —

Because this one truly held all her hope.

She clipped it to her ear, and fell again.

A cabin, rustic, in the fairytale forest. Familiar and warm. She reached for the silver gleaming doorknob.

The world went dark around her as she opened the door.

And from the dark inside, out burst Aino.

Or what they'd made of her.

If Britta had stayed she might have spat serpents.

But Aino now, was Eater of Roses.

Stringy black hair. Tattered white dress. A bloody, bloody too-wide mouth, an open wound with too many teeth.

The counterpart to Sawyer. The monstrous dark inversion of the girl who spat diamonds and roses.

An archetype of appetite and entitlement, who would steal roses (or anything beautiful) just to chew through and devour them, and keep anyone else from enjoying them.

The worst kind of woman — one who did not know her place in the world.

Who had no place in the world.

Who Aino had always feared she was, when she wanted anything at all.

The creature screamed and lunged, knocking Aino over. She screeched, blood pouring into Aino's mouth.

Aino thrashed under the weight. Her own scream tangled in its hair, at her fear and fury of how she had been written over, what she had been written into.

She tore the Dream free, gasping.

Fingers shaking, she cracked it open. It was an archetype — her archetype, even. Maybe...

But the Dream didn't hold a complete description of the archetype; just a sliver. Just enough to frighten. Not enough to resonate Aino a way in. A crude drawing of a door, and just as useful.

She looked around at the massacre of broken shells on the counter. All her dreams and failures, bingeable. And now, on her walls too.

The Eater of Roses was everywhere now—movies, music, pop-up ads. Another archetype smoothed into fashion. As if she'd always been there.

All around her, Eater of Roses in any permutation she could purchase lined the walls and shelves. Another past, rewritten. A punishment and a tomb.

She rested her hands on the desk. All around her, Eater of Roses stared and laughed. This version of her, at least, had won.

Aino's mouth tasted like metal. That had been it.

She would fade away into nothing, not even allowed to explore the land she'd discovered.

Well. Not quite

Even after she was gone, after she had watched the world degenerate into slop and misery —

She would always be Eater of Roses.

The doorbell rang.

Aino startled. The cracked cartridge slipped from her hand and shattered on the floor.

She was supposed to be invisible here.

Behind the flimsy door stood a courier — soaked, underdressed, and blinking like he'd stepped into someone else's dream.

"Dr. Yeates?" he asked, peering past her into the strange, cramped apartment crowded with Eater of Roses merchandise.

She started to close the door.

Then she saw the bag in his hand.

Her breath caught. "Oh," she said. "I hired you."

"I hope so."

They stood looking at each other.

He took a breath. "I thought I should come in person."

The man stepped inside slowly and set the crumpled, bloodied bag on her counter. Gently, as if it might be wounded.

Aino opened it. Inside was Britta's DreamWeaver — dented, scorched, streaked with dried blood.

She went still.

Then she pushed the back across the counter, like it might bite her.

"They found her. In Norway. Hiking accident, it looks like. I'm sorry. We only found this." He hesitated. "There's something inside for you."

She nodded. He left without another word.

Alone, she opened the bag again — carefully, without letting her fingers touch the blood. Inside, wrapped around the bent wiring, was a scrap of parchment. Britta's terrible scrawl ran wild across it.

For a long moment, Aino didn't read. She just let her hand rest on the paper.

It felt warm.

Like Britta was reaching back.

From whatever void waited for girls like them. The ones who asked to much, and ventured too far into the dark to get it.

The last time she had seen Britta was in the dark. She'd woken up screaming in her bedroom.

Britta was at the foot of her bed, gently tickling her foot.

"What are you doing?!" Aino gasped, kicking.

"I thought it would be less scary if I did it this way!"

"You were so so wrong!"

Undeterred, Britta dragged her chair from the foot of the bed to the head and sat down again.

"You're leaving," Aino said. She already knew it, miserably, deep in her gut.

"Don't tell them."

"I told them no, though. I said not to. About you."

Britta sighed.

It was useless to plead. Aino knew that.

Britta wasn't only fleeing dissolution in a dream machine. She was chasing her lost god she swore she met in YMIR, to try to bring back her dear dead husband with his deep dark eyes.

"They will find someone you will say yes to," Britta said, slow and tired. "Someone who maybe doesn't know what's coming. Someone the calculus of millions of lives will come out to sacrificing. Someone you cared for that could have been kinder to you, maybe."

Aino sat up straighter and clutched her blankets closer. "No worries there. I don't have anyone anymore." She gave a laugh as bitter as bile. "Speaking of — Sawyer, you remember him. He called today."

Britta's eyes narrowed. She had never liked Sawyer.

"I was excited. But all he wanted was a scoop for his stupid career," Aino blurted out, and looked to her friend for some soothing outrage.

"People are starting to notice what you are doing," was all Britta said, carefully.

Aino frowned. She didn't like to think of it.

At first it was just little things, small changes made to existing archetypes. The Ruler tweaked to have the hairstyle of the current US president. Change the Lover to a rock star who paid enough.

Cosmetic, temporary things, that you could brute force for long enough to be useful, until they dissolved in the waves of the collective.

Stupid stuff, that they swore helped keep the wolves at bay.

But then Paris had fallen, and then London, and Shanghai.

And, well. Desperate times, as they said.

"Come with me," Britta begged. "They don't know what they have, with YMIR. They will ruin it. But you and me, we can still do our work. I'm bringing my own DreamWeaver."

Britta's DreamWeaver was strange, enhanced by some kind of magic. Aino's mind tended to slip around the logistics if she thought about it too much.

"No," said Aino. "I'm going to stay. And help."

"Like hell you are."

"Not just use it for myself."

"Oh, like me?" Britta laughed. "Fine. I'll be the mean one, like always. I'll live. You can be the kind one, and have your throat torn out by thorns and diamonds."

"I'll be the one who saves people," Aino said, softly. "Who does the right thing."

Britta sneered at her.

"Yes, you always think and do the Right things, don't you?" Britta drawled. "What's recommended in the upmarket press. You never had to learn that what's Right capital R doesn't have anything to do with what is safe or true. Just what serves the most powerful people at the time."

"Yes, yes, you learned it all the hard way; I have no idea, etc."

"That's right. You never had enough people around you to learn it. Just me. And I'm mean, but not mean enough to drive the message home.

"There was Sawyer too." The words fell flat and humiliating between them.

Aino lay back down and turned away. "I'm tired. Please turn the light off when you leave."

Britta stood.

"I know you figured out how to do it — make a new archetype. All it takes is a life, right? A human life. One mind, one neural matrix — dissolved. And then you have a new sign in neon in the heads of every human. Below all their defenses."

Aino said nothing. Her outrage burned hot in the room between them. Britta should have been proud of her. But Britta had always been a little jealous of Aino's superior skills.

"Good luck finding him," Aino said, and didn't know whether she meant the god or the husband.

"You'll think it was a choice, Aino. Later, you'll know it never was."

Britta opened the door. Paused.

"Don't tell them about Sawyer."

The bedroom door closed. All that lingered was hurt, and the smell of rose and ozone.

Britta's signature, already a ghost.

Now, in the too-quiet apartment that smelled of burnt electronics and blood, Aino unfolded the note:

No one ever saw you for what you were, did they. Not even me. We all had the wrong story. I hope you'll someday want more than what scraps others are willing to throw you. I'll miss you.

Aino wept.

But not for long.

Because when she looked up, at all her horrible posters and the burned cartridges and little statuettes, she understood.

Britta was right.

Eater of Roses was only a facet of the archetype.

She — Aino — was the rest of it. And she could heal.

With Britta's DreamWeaver — broken, sure, but she of all people could fix it — she could connect back to YMIR. To the collective unconscious. And release Sawyer, somehow.

At least make the whole archetype known. The whole star-story.

She couldn't undo what had happened, but she could fix what came next.

Any obstacle, as they had always said to each other, is only a matter of translation. Of being carried from one state to another.

She was Aino Yeates and all the stars in YMIR's skull were hers.

Maybe she was the girl who ate roses.

But she was also the girl who made them bloom at all.

I t took about a month to build her own YMIR, back in her house where she'd have the space and privacy. Aino had chosen her house to work from. It had the space, and the silence, and she had worked hard for it. If it was bugged, what she was doing must seem too pathetic and unhinged to stop. But she rather thought the company was done with her.

She patched and threaded together Britta's DreamWeaver, her stolen eyepiece, the recalled Cabin Companion Dream, and a second-hand float tank purchases after a humiliating cryptocurrency struggle.

Her creation was monstrously strange and ugly, and she loved it.

She called it MIMIR. Short for MY YMIR, the name Britta had

originally wanted for the DreamWeaver. Another Norse mythology pun the marketing team said no one would get but her.

Now, it was just Aino's joke — or legacy, maybe. Either way, her way back in.

Aino knelt on cold bathroom tile before the tank. Cables snaked across the floor, tangling with spilled salt, cracked cartridges, and the bitter sting of solder and gas flame. Her skin smelled like metal and seawater.

She hadn't slept.

Soon she'd do nothing else.

Britta's DreamWeaver glowed faintly at the head of the pod, its wires spreading out like roots cracking through concrete. Maybe her Weaver had actually been enhanced with the ancient magic Britta claimed. it was how they got YMIR running, after all. Aino had never been able to reverse-engineer its capabilities. No one else had, either.

But she could still use it.

Aino took the recalled scorpion dream and her old YMIR eyepiece and routed them through Britta's...well, glyph work, was the only word that felt right. Like all semioticians, Britta had been more vibes than protocol. But Aino could work with the weave.

When it all connected, the glyphs flickered and glowed, once. Aino wasn't sure if it was a trick of the rippling light, or her friend signaling approval.

Or, one last warning.

She turned MIMIR on, and the whole thing lit up, the glyphs and cables both glowing gold and ice-sheet blue.

She exhaled. With this, she could get back into YMIR.

Just once. Just long enough, she prayed, to finish it.

She wasn't sure what she would do when she got there. Was the best tack to erase him? How? If she tried to burn him out, would she hurt all of humanity? Was it possible to defeat a dream, especially one shaped like a person you used to love?

Like before, all she could hope was that the path would become clear. That she could, in some sense, heal what had been to Sawyer and to them all — carving down Sawyer's kindness and fear down to a function. Tortured his expansive soul into the small cruel shape they had a use for.

How small it all was. How lacking in vision.

She turned off the bathroom lights to admire all her cold glittering work reflecting in her little personal sea — and to make the final adjustments to the program that felt like they were best done in the dark.

The sun shone so beautifully when she had finished, and she could not make herself go inside MIMIR immediately.

Instead, she walked through the redwoods above her house, where the fog and moss billowed through the trees like smoke. On her favorite bench on a high hill, she sat alone and ate a raspberry sandwich, washed down with mint tea from a thermos.

Just as she had when she was young, eating lunch alone on a scrubby playground on blistered blacktop, a thousand miles away.

If there had been a door back, she might have gone through, and might have seen once more how the sun would arc across the pavement as she sat on the lone rise, and the grackles would scream, and the kids would move and circle in patterns beneath her in a dance they didn't understand, and she would only ever learn from a distance.

Yes, she might open that door without another thought.

Aino had been happy, it had to be said, even alone. In her head, in her own world, there were always such wonders.

And maybe she had spent her life being pushed away.

But from up here, she could see everything.

The faraway ocean, even. And the tea and jam were so good, blooming hot and red on her tongue.

When the first stars came out, she went back inside to her pod.

She clasped the rose thorn necklace at her throat. The thorn lying in the hollow like always, like it had always been part of her.

Aino stepped into the warm saltwater.

She wouldn't have much time till they found her. But when they did, if they tried to force her back — YMIR would burn like a fairytale forest set alight.

Only the truth would remain, and the collective unconscious would be returned to its rightful owners:

Those that lived and dreamed. The tide of all humanity.

She closed the pod, and lay back. And in the dark, she floated.

She felt, like a ghost, someone lacing fingers through hers. The touch wasn't frightening, just gone too soon.

Aino closed her eyes in the black.

These tanks could cause those kinds of hallucinations.

She raised her hand and turned on MIMIR.

And she went under for the last time.

Aino landed at the very edge of the Forest, exactly like she wanted.

Her heart sank. The Forest had changed since she had last been in. The trees were sparse anyway at the edges, but there were even fewer here than she remembered. Any trees that remained jittered and flickered, their edges glitching and uncertain like the beams of a dam, straining. The silver pulse, once rhythmic and cleansing like breath, was now a jerky splash of static. Each wave hit like a blast of sand.

Those hapless ravenous monsters.

Even the brush underfoot felt brittle. She'd have even less time than she thought.

They'd been searching for him in the woods, YMIR's meddlers. But they never understood the importance of truth, so they never found him.

Even in YMIR — maybe, especially in YMIR —

Who you are always comes out.

And Sawyer never belonged to the Forest.

Aino ran.

She followed the brightest star through the gaps in the canopy, the brambles snagging her skin and clothes. Her breath caught when she finally saw the cabin.

It leaned right at the edge of the tree line, where the Meadow began, half-swallowed by a riot of rosebushes.

Her heart beat the same acid static as the silver pulse.

Not because of what might be inside, but that she might write it wrong again.

Aino took a breath on the doorstep. Even the air tasted electric, here at the end. She reached out and creaked open the door —

— just as Sawyer barreled out.

He slammed her down, and raised his axe as he stood over her. His eyes were blank, and his face was wrong.

"Eater of Roses," he spat. "Come for to kill."

She raised her hands to shield herself, and saw her clothes were the tattered black dress again, stained and torn. Her mouth tasted like metal, and her teeth were sharp once more.

Here, in this place, she was Eater of Roses.

To the whole of existence and for the whole of eternity, an archetype of appetite and selfishness.

If she died this way — what would that encode?

There was no time for tricks. Just truth.

"Sawyer," she cried out. "Sawyer. That's who you are."

He froze. His eyes didn't seem to register her at all.

What she said wasn't true.

What stood before her wasn't Sawyer, the one who had held her hand in the tank, or made her raspberry sandwiches before finals, or dared her to fly. This was the fossil of him. The form of life, with none of its marrow left. Just stone, with no bone left at all.

Who he was, though, was her only hope.

She kept her hands raised, and her eyes on his.

"We swam into the sea," she whispered. "You told me I was falling into the sky."

Something in his eyes flickered.

216

"I said it back to you," she said.

The blade trembled. He breathed.

Aino tried not to move.

Whatever happened next could define the lives of future generations.

Of the children Aino would never have. Sawyer either.

He stepped back, confused.

"Aino?"

"Yes," she lied.

He helped her up and smiled, a dumb echo of the searing light his smile used to be. He looked down at the rosebushes.

And, gently, he raised the axe.

Once more, he sliced a single rose, and held it out to her.

"If you want it," he said, "you must need it."

Her hand closed around the stem. She squeezed it tight, and the blood welled hot and bright like the tears in her eyes.

It was too late.

Sawyer wasn't there. Only the Woodcutter.

"But," he added, almost like himself again. He reached out to touch the petals. "I think this one was always yours."

Aino looked up sharply. And then down at the rose.

There was one of Britta's little golden glyphs on it.

A star in a skull.

The sign for YMIR.

"You were never the Woodcutter," she murmured, smelling the rose. "But they never saw that."

He knit his brow, like she was speaking nonsense. She stroked the golden glyph. Britta's color was gold; Aino always preferred the silver of starlight.

"They had the wrong story," she went on. Just like Britta had told her. "You were always the boy that found beautiful things. That hunted down the exceptional."

"The miraculous." He pushed the rose closer to her. "I think you should take this with you."

"I think you're right."

Aino looked down at the rose.

They thought a story could only be cast from ash. That to encode something powerful, you had to destroy.

That meaning required sacrifice. That only patterns deserved to survive, and that whole souls could be swallowed.

But maybe that was just the old way.

The rose in her hand was alive. Sharp, fragile, whole.

And it was hers.

Yes—everything here belonged to everyone. But this was hers to taste, because she was the one who gave it form.

It was, after all, her YMIR.

Her rose, here at the center of all things.

Her miracle.

Maybe she couldn't undo what had been done.

But she could make sure they couldn't do anything else.

What they called monstrous, was only really having a mouth at all.   These beautiful things were hers. They were meant for her, and she was meant for them.

She opened her mouth and put the rose in.

And ate it.

The petals folded over her tongue, bitter and fragrant and holy. Thorns pierced her gums and cheeks, and blood trailed in spit down her chin.

The rose sung in her as she swallowed.

And for the first time, it didn't feel like loss.

It felt like transcription.

Not destruction.

Translation.

Being carried, as if flying, from one state to another.

It was the best thing she ever tasted.

What she saw, swallowing the rose, almost made her choke:

That YMIR was only a lens. It would only show one facet of one thing at a time. And the real story, was so much bigger, so much more radiant, and could never be comprehended by their fragile skulls here and now.

And maybe you couldn't become anything.

But you could become something more.

A pulse went out from her, a silver tsunami, that left some leaves burning in their wake.

What they never figured either, was that YMIR was alive in its own way. And the rose Sawyer had found for her, was all of Aino's work.

Only then did she know exactly what to do.

Because maybe she couldn't undo what had been done. But, she could put it in proper context.

"Thank you," she said, wiping blood off her chin. "I have something for you too."

She unclasped her rose-thorn necklace, pooled it in her palm, and held it out to him.

His eyes flared in surprise that she was giving him something.

"A rose thorn," he said.

"No," she said. "Remember? A shark's tooth."

And she slunk it into his hand.

When she pulled away, the thorn had changed. Instead of little and brass, it was long and ivory, bound to the chain by its rough foot.

A small white shark's tooth, gleaming.

"You were right all along," she said.

He dropped his axe.

She took the tooth back, reached her arms around him, and fastened his necklace around his neck. Sawyer's eyes stayed wide. The world held its breath.

And then —

The door opened.

The world split and spun around them, dissolving and reforming.

When it resolved, they were on white sand. The sea stretched out before them. The moon and stars glittered down on the glinting black water.

A shark's tooth didn't belong in the Forest, after all.

It belonged here, on the beach.

Where Sawyer always had.

The wind here was bracing and salty, and the shush and slur of the dark waves pulsed almost in time with YMIR's jittering static. The cliffs curved into an outcropping of familiar jagged rocks.

Aino turned to Sawyer to speak —

But Sawyer wasn't steady anymore. His form wavered, like a candle guttering in a coming storm.

He wasn't supposed to be here.

Or at least that's what she thought, until she saw the figure in the sea.

It was a man, swimming far from the rocks. His arms clawed against the waves, silently. His head sank lower with each swell.

Sawyer's father.

He had died trying to save his son. They had loved beachcombing together, finding sea glass and forgotten treasure, to be treasured again.

Curious that he was here now. The Drowned Man, like the Hanged Man. What would his impact be?

Pain stabbed through Aino like a cold needle, and she gasped.

They had found her. Whoever was watching YMIR had triggered the pullback protocol — the one she'd poisoned herself, with a code that would destroy YMIR as it encoded her into it.

And with her devouring the rose, they'd never be able to rebuild it, either. All its magic returned to the void with her.

Her last pattern would be encoded, and live forever in the collective unconscious. And all it would cost was her life. The original was destroyed, but the pattern lived forever.

They'd never eat up anyone else again.

There was no more time to wonder. Only time to make things right.

"Sawyer," she said, but there was nothing to say.

Aino leaned forward and kissed his cheek. A smear of red stayed behind — crushed petals and a little blood.

Her own signature.

"Why?" he asked.

So I can leave my mark. So you'll remember I was here, and you were loved. Because our paths crossed. Because I was here, too.

And I am sorry.

"Because we never see until it's too late," she said, finally.

"That's what the sky is for," he said.

The cold spread to her chest. Her breath shortened.

Aino looked to the sea.

"Someone always ends up in the water," Britta had told her, once. Maybe Aino had always known it would be her.

Aino stepped into the surf. It was cool, and welcomed her.

She kept walking, bracing against the waves, until she reached the edge where she had always been afraid — where her feet would leave the sand.

She leapt up from the seafloor, and swam out. Past the point of return.

When she reached the man struggling in the sea, she touched his shoulder.

"This is my place," she murmured, best she could while treading cold black water.

The sea answered.

With a great silver pulse —

Aino took his place.

She was the one in the water now. The one watching from the waves, as Sawyer and his father stood on the beach together, side by side.

Sawyer was small again, now. Twelve, maybe. His father looked like Sawyer had, when he died. When they both died.

Now, they were laughing. Collecting shells. Not the Woodcutter and the Drowned Man, anymore:

The Beachcombers, now.

They had always been meant to find each other again. A closed circuit. A loop made whole.

They had saved each other.

And maybe all archetypes were like constellations. The same stars could hold a hundred different stories, if you knew how to recognize them.

She had told him that, once. In another life.

She had forgotten, till now.

Aino lay back and let herself drift.

The waves rocked her gently, and salt stung her skin. Above her, the stars winked.

The cold spread through her, then past her, until it met the warmth at her core.

A final silver shockwave rippled out from the center of her chest.

And the water began to glow.

She could feel them — all the dreamers. The sea was raw dream-stuff, coursing with grief and joy and wonder. More than any archetype could carry. More than any system could contain.

That's why they'd never mapped the ocean.

It wasn't empty.

It was everyone.

And I was never, never alone.

She laughed, softly, floating.

We all came from the sea, didn't we?

And now she was going home. Back to the place from where we're all born.

The cold reached her skull like piercing light, and her thoughts began to smear. It was hard to keep track of where her body ended, and even harder to care.

She was rising now. Not swimming, but lifting. Flying, above her body now, which had dissolved into tide and rose petals.

Aino floated higher and higher. All of her felt cool and shining, like Sawyer had been. Like a star. A constellation.

But the sky was very very cold and black, and fright seized through her like frost.

Then she saw them.

Sawyer and his father, walking the shore. Gathering treasures. Talking softly and laughing. The child and the man. The living and the dead.

Whole.

Aino's heart burst open like a flower in deep water.

And the question — What will I become? What will I be encoded as?

It drifted away.

It didn't matter.

She would be herself; the rose in the equation all along.

Joy exploded through her like a cloudburst, just before everything became light and tide.

Here in the wide sea, the wide sky, the white skull, she was known and welcome. Not as a role or as a ruin, but as herself.

Even as what was left of her was hard to see, now, so far below.

And if she found herself frightened, in these her last moments, she could say to herself, and hear Sawyer's voice, and Britta's too. They were never gone. Never dissolved. Just somewhere she couldn't see—until now. Still part of the tide she was joining. And not just them — a warm chorus of innumerable voices joined from just beyond her reach, saying to her, soothing her, celebrating with her —

Inviting her:

You are falling into the sea.

~

Britta sat on a beach in the south of France, the sand cool beneath a floral blanket. She was unwrapping, with some difficulty, a stubborn little crumple of plastic wrap.

She was something other than alive now. Just like Aino.

223

Although you wouldn't know it unless you looked closely.

A man — something that wore a man's shape — sat next to her. He watched her dubiously with golden eyes.

"Do you need —"

"Nope."

The rose thorn necklace that had been Aino's poured into Britta's hands like ink. She had used the same "courier" service Aino had used for her DreamWeaver, which Aino would have found funny.

"An heirloom?" the man guessed. "An arrow?"

"A story," Britta said. "A fairy tale."

Aino always had liked her husband. She would have hated this guy. Britta smiled. Aino would have called him a snake.

The wind rose, warm and billowing, and Britta stood. Her long cover-up whipped around her knees. "Look," she said.

White petals were washing up on the shore, tracing each wave.

Roses.

Impossibly, joyfully. Roses.

Since YMIR's collapse, all the untrue things encoded in it were washing away as if with the tide.

But not Aino.

In fact, Britta had seen all kinds of Aino since then.

Eater of Roses, yes.

Attar of Roses, too.

Adder of Roses, Adder of Rose, A Dame of Roses.

A soul rising into the heavens. Healer, witch, wounded, witness. The one that rose above to see the beauty. All different facets. All the stories the stars could hold.

No one could agree what she was, in her original.

It made Britta miss her all the more sharply.

Because only Britta would ever know what it had cost, to finally become part of the story.

They had both found what they were looking for. Britta her ghost and her god. Aino and her sea of stars.

Neither had looked how they expected. Both had cost them their lives.

Britta walked into the sea up to her waist, letting the chill lick at her ribs. Then she looked to the stars, where her friend stayed, for now.

In linguistic translation, a little was always lost on the journey. The end result was always smaller than the start. You only could choose what facet to focus on, when you translated something.

Whatever this was, was the opposite of that.

Orion and Scorpio seemed always to chase each other from the heavens. But they are always sharing the same sky.

Our sky. Our starlit skull of a past god. Our own starlit skulls.

The same thing. The same, like we are.

The tide was going out, and the waves pulled at Britta.

Petals from nowhere — from everywhere — danced in the surf.

And if they weren't together here, they would be someday.

Even stars are carried by tides we cannot see from where we stand. Until, one day, we join them in turn.

She stood there, until the tide was all the way out.

ABOUT THE AUTHORS

ELLY CALL

Elly Call is a speculative horror writer and narrative designer. She's worked on Lord of the Rings: Return to Moria amongst other games and is currently working on a traditional novel inspired by the Bloodborne universe. You can respectfully and with great admiration follow her on Instagram at @calllelly or on Bluesky at @allcapscall.bsky.social. For best results, you can even follow her on both.

KATHRYN DANETTE

Kathryn Danette is a writer of mystery and psychological thrillers. She currently lives in Istanbul, where she teaches English and sustains many interesting local cats.

Her first novel "Half a Mile Out and a Quarter Down" is a historical mystery about a string of killings following a mining boom in Denver, Colorado. It is scheduled for release in 2025.

BRIDGETTE DAY

Bridgette Day was so impressed by "Signs & Symbols" by Nabokov that she moved to Denmark to pick up a cognitive semiotics degree on purpose and a husband by accident. They live in Utah now with their two children.

Her next project is Heartlines, a Nordic-inspired fantasy about fate and entanglement — featuring Britta, from *You are Falling into the Sea*.

Find her at bridgetteday.com.

MARLENA DUTCH

Marlena Dutch is a writer of speculative fiction, primarily horror. She has lived in two haunted places and has had a number of supernatural experiences. Once a city dweller, she now lives in the rural countryside of Texas.

"The Bridge at Drowning Man Creek" is part of the Hound Hollow universe. The series, comprised of short stories and novels, focuses on a group of vampire hunters, werewolf hunters, and paranormal investigators. To read more, keep an eye on Marlena's social media for updates. Find @marlenadutch on Instagram and Bluesky.

G.M. GRAY

G.M. Gray is the author and illustrator of the queer-normative, adventure space romp light novel series, Triple Strike. A sharp reader may wonder if "Last Flight of the Glamr" is part of this universe, and indeed that reader would be right. And exceedingly good-looking. The other short stories by G.M. in this collection are part of larger stories as well, because G.M. is incapable of writing one-off shorts — much to their chagrin.

Follow G.M. on Instagram with @gmgraywriting, on Bluesky with @gmgray, or join their Discord using this QR code.

THE CROSSROADS ORACLE

Before you go, here's a parting gift:

The Crossroads Oracle.

Each card of the Crossroads Oracle deck holds a relic from the stories here, for when you find yourselves at crossways.

Draw a card, and let it light your way.

If you'd like a printable deck with reading instructions, send along your email at bridgetteday.com or by using this QR code:

THE BLUEBIRD'S FEATHER

The memory of summer that glows bright and pristine even through the long winter.

**STORY:
FOREST EYES**

THE TOOTHLESS KEY

Promises of freedom whispered to you through a prison's crumbling walls.

**STORY:
THREE ALGORITHMS**

THE SEXTANT

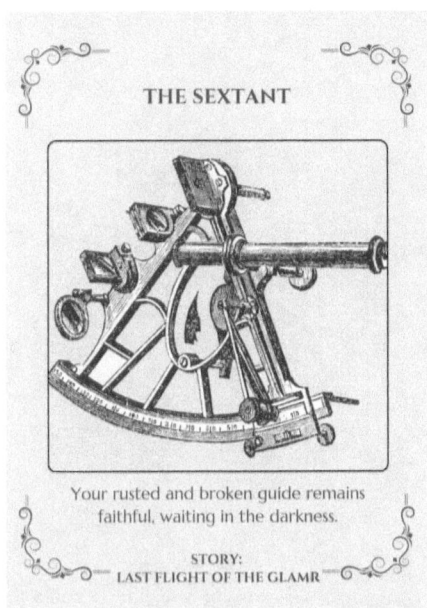

Your rusted and broken guide remains
faithful, waiting in the darkness.

STORY:
LAST FLIGHT OF THE GLAMR

THE EATER OF ROSES

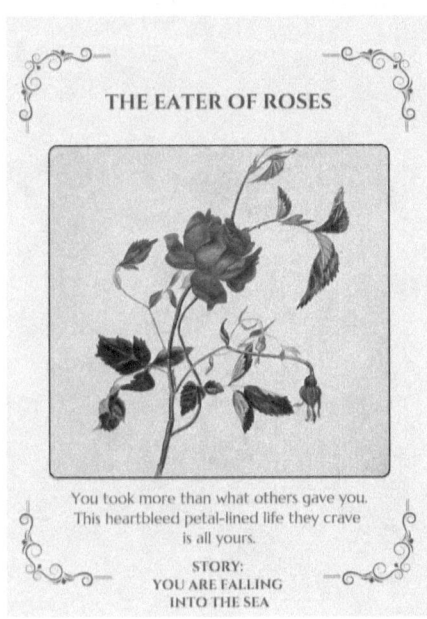

You took more than what others gave you.
This heartbleed petal-lined life they crave
is all yours.

STORY:
YOU ARE FALLING
INTO THE SEA

THE SKULL AND THE SEA OF STARS

It's cold out in the icy vast black.
From here, you can see salvation.

STORY:
YOU ARE FALLING
INTO THE SEA

THE WOODCUTTER'S AXE

What serves you, changes.

STORY:
YOU ARE FALLING
INTO THE SEA

THE HEIRLOOM

jacket

It's always belonged to someone.
A weight like this must always be carried.

STORY:
MEMORABILIA MORI

THE CHARM

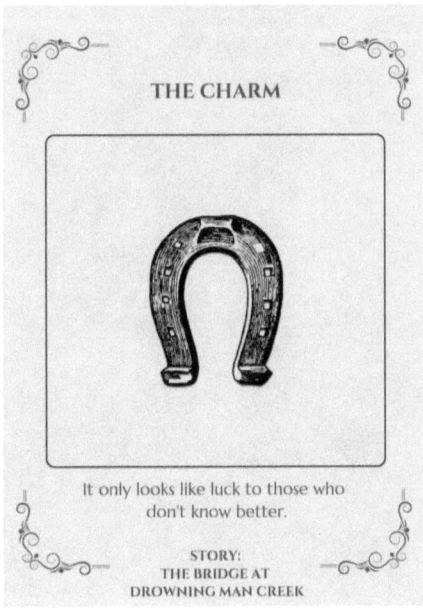

It only looks like luck to those who
don't know better.

STORY:
THE BRIDGE AT
DROWNING MAN CREEK

THE TRIGGER

This blazing power was born with you, and there are those who will kill for it.

**STORY:
THE BLOODY SHOW**

THE COULOIR

Your way was carved for you eons ago. The one who comes through is not who started the journey.

**STORY:
THE THIRD MAN**

THE CROSSROADS

Every story splits here
and no map will help you now.
Look close enough, and your path is lit.

**BOOK:
CAMPFIRE AT THE
CROSSROADS**

THE FACE IN THE FLAME

Firelight flickers and lights wild
a fellow wanderer's face.
The truth they speak is yours; you are home.

**BOOK:
CAMPFIRE AT THE
CROSSROADS**

www.ingramcontent.com/pod-product-compliance
Lightning Source LLC
Chambersburg PA
CBHW022031120726
47899CB00007BA/2171